SHOOT TO THRILL

"[A] fast-paced thriller . . . Powerful chemistry."

—*Publishers Weekly*

"A wonderful, suspense-filled, nonstop action thriller. The chemistry between Kick and Rainie is explosive."

—*Fallen Angel Reviews*

"Sexy, suspenseful, and so gritty you'll taste the desert sand. A thrill ride from start to finish!"

—Rebecca York, *USA Today* bestselling author of the 43 Light Street series

"A provocative, sexy thriller that will get your adrenaline pumping on all levels."

—Tamar Myers, award-winning author of *The Girl Who Married an Eagle*

"Intense pacing . . . powerful characters . . . searing emotions and explosive sexual tension! Once I started reading *Shoot to Thrill*, I couldn't stop!"

—Debra Webb, bestselling author of the Faces of Evil series

Berkley Sensation titles by Nina Bruhns

SHOOT TO THRILL
IF LOOKS COULD CHILL
A KISS TO KILL
RED HEAT
WHITE HOT
BLUE FOREVER

PRAISE FOR THE NOVELS OF NINA BRUHNS

Winner of the National Readers Choice Award and three-time overall winner of the Daphne du Maurier Award for Excellence in Mystery/Suspense

WHITE HOT

"Such a fast-paced, exciting book that you cannot stop turning the pages . . . Nina Bruhns has a winner with *White Hot.*"

—*Fresh Fiction*

"Unbelievably steamy. Each page turned was a moment lost in time for me. I could not get enough of the dark and smoldering hero, Clint . . . *White Hot* is simply amazing and I cannot wait to read the next novel Ms. Bruhns produces."

—*Romance Junkies*

"Ms. Bruhns is one of the top romantic-suspense authors out there. If smoking-hot sex wrapped up in a well-written, supersexy, Navy SEAL romance is what you want, this one is IT! Don't miss it!" —*Night Owl Reviews* (top pick, 5 stars)

RED HEAT

"Bruhns starts off her new series with sizzling suspense. Her characters are sexy and provocative, but that's not all—they continue to grow on many levels with a story that takes you through page-turning action and suspense. The sexual tension is palpable and when Bruhns's latest couple gets together, sparks fly." —*RT Book Reviews*

"A great cast of characters and the heated sexual tension between the hero and heroine keep this romantic suspense story moving . . . A perfect blend of romance and suspense."

—*Fresh Fiction*

continued . . .

"The action is fast paced and *Red Heat* is full of deception, secrets, and intrigue . . . will keep you guessing until the very last pages."

—*Smexy Books*

A KISS TO KILL

"A thrill ride of fast action and hot sex in the steamy Louisiana bayous, Nina Bruhns's latest delivers it all!"

—CJ Lyons, *New York Times* bestselling author of the Angels of Mercy novels

"Rich with dialogue and filled with tight suspense, Bruhn's latest holds true to the excellence readers have come to expect from this author."

—*RT Book Reviews*

"Greg and Gina are one of the hottest couples I've read lately . . . There's not one thing I didn't like about this book."

—*The Good, The Bad and The Unread*

IF LOOKS COULD CHILL

"This is a fast-paced action adventure with a steamy romance . . . A keeper."

—*Night Owl Reviews*

"Anything but chilly—the sexual action is as hot and steamy as the action in the field . . . If you like a thrill a minute, you will enjoy *If Looks Could Chill*. The gripping tale is well written and filled with intrigue and passion."

—*Romance Reviews Today*

"Suspense just got a whole lot hotter with Nina Bruhns's dynamite romantic thriller. A hero to die for and a heroine to cheer for . . . An awesome, sexy story."

—Allison Brennan, *New York Times* bestselling author of the Lucy Kincaid series

BLUE FOREVER

NINA BRUHNS

BERKLEY SENSATION, NEW YORK

THE BERKLEY PUBLISHING GROUP
Published by the Penguin Group
Penguin Group (USA)
375 Hudson Street, New York, New York 10014, USA

USA | Canada | UK | Ireland | Australia | New Zealand | India | South Africa | China

Penguin Books Ltd., Registered Offices: 80 Strand, London WC2R 0RL, England
For more information about the Penguin Group, visit penguin.com.

BLUE FOREVER

A Berkley Sensation Book / published by arrangement with the author

Berkley Sensation Books are published by The Berkley Publishing Group.
BERKLEY SENSATION® is a registered trademark of Penguin Group (USA).
The "B" design is a trademark of Penguin Group (USA).
For information, address: The Berkley Publishing Group,
a division of Penguin Group (USA),
375 Hudson Street, New York, New York 10014.

ISBN: 978-0-425-25094-5

PUBLISHING HISTORY
Berkley Sensation mass-market edition / September 2013

PRINTED IN THE UNITED STATES OF AMERICA

10 9 8 7 6 5 4 3 2 1

Cover art by Kris Keller.
Cover design by Annette Fiore Defex.
Interior text design by Laura K. Corless.

1

**A REMOTE MOUNTAIN VILLAGE,
HAINAN ISLAND, CHINA
MAY**

It *would* be a woman.

Hell. Could his day get any worse?

U.S. Marine Corps Intelligence operator Major Kiptyn Llowell swallowed a growl of irritation as he regarded the trim figure descending from a white SUV sporting a familiar international hotel logo on its door. In a situation like this, Kip would much rather deal with a man. You could talk to a man. Reason logically with a man. No muss, no fuss. Women were just so damn . . . emotional. And unreasonable. Not to mention highly unpredictable.

This mission had already skidded so far outside the realm of predictable, Kip did not need a single other wild card spinning him off in yet another direction.

What he needed was to get his head examined.

Send me, he'd told Colonel Jackson when a navy rep had come looking for a Marine Special Operations Intelligence Battalion operator they could borrow for a quick solo mission. Kip and his MSOIB team had been on a jungle recon exercise in the Philippines, relatively close by. The navy needed someone immediately. Naturally, he'd volunteered.

Because when had he *ever* thought things through before acting? Never. Hell, no. Flirting with disaster was his specialty. Living on the edge was the thing that had taken him so fast and so far in his career. It was also what had driven him so fast and so far from home, family, and the life he'd once expected to lead.

"Practical" and "predictable"? Not in his vocabulary. Which was one reason he loved his job. The Corps kept him grounded and provided a semblance of structure in his life, while his work in intelligence gave free rein to his wild side.

He eased his weight off his bad leg and shifted his rucksack into a less conspicuous position under his grungy, oversized, cotton peasant jacket. The pack held his camera and what remained of his equipment, the rest damaged from a bad landing when he parachuted onto the island night before last.

Jetting out a breath, he surveyed the woman getting out of the SUV as she dusted off her clothes with quick, efficient movements. Well, at least there was little doubt as to her nationality. She had the look of a typical U.S. government geek. Sensible gray suit skirt hitting sensibly at the knee, paired with a sensible white blouse. Practical leather shoulder bag. Practical flats. Chestnut hair in a practical ponytail. Jesus, even her height was sensibly practical—not too tall, not too short.

State Department foreign service officer, maybe? He could usually spot an FSO a mile away, thanks to his blessedly short stint as an embassy guard. He shuddered inwardly.

Whatever. Ms. Sensible was his ticket out of this goatfuck of a day. Assuming he could talk his way into that

SUV when it left this flyspeck of a Chinese village in the back of beyond.

Not that he'd give her any choice in the matter. Women might be emotional and unreliable, but, notwithstanding his penchant for doing the opposite of what was expected—and despite what his father thought—Kip sure as hell was *not* emotional or unreliable.

The last time he'd acted from emotion was when he'd stormed out of his father's house eighteen years ago and joined the Marine Corps. Since then, not once had Kiptyn Llowell III delivered anything less than what was asked of him . . . one way or another. He'd never failed to complete a mission.

He had no intention of starting now.

Even though his cover was blown, his leg hurting like hell, and his equipment useless, he had every intention of seeing this mission through.

He'd do whatever it took to get to the rendezvous point at the appointed time tomorrow to pick up a replacement camera and the other things the guys in his unit were delivering. Which meant getting himself a ride down the mountain from Ms. Practical.

No problem. She didn't look that tough. A wink and a smile and she'd be putty in his hands. Women loved to be needed.

He wandered over and leaned against the rough trunk of a tamarind tree near the SUV, resting his leg and watching the woman from under the obscuring shadow of his billed cap. She was discussing something with the Chinese driver as her traveling companion climbed from the vehicle. The other woman was an aging hippie type wearing loose, colorful clothing, and gesturing expansively with her hands when Ms. Sensible joined her. The pair turned and walked toward the nearby open-air market, chatting amiably.

Kip surmised Ms. Sensible must be there in some official capacity—a trade liaison, a translator, maybe a cultural advisor to the other woman, who was clearly the party interested in the marketplace offerings. This village specialized in the highly sought-after traditional textiles and weavings of Hainan Island's native Li people. No doubt the artsy-fartsy woman was a gallery buyer or some such thing. Which would explain why they'd made the arduous drive to this remote mountain village rather than parking themselves on one of the many idyllic beaches that rimmed this tropical South Seas island paradise.

Still, the two Americans were the one bright spot in this fucked-up day. If the SUV hadn't shown up, he might have had to do something a lot more dangerous to get down to the coast. Small favors.

The women disappeared among the tall, primitive stalls festooned with a fluttering rainbow of handwoven textiles. Despite the village being so out of the way, in addition to his two targets there was a decent crowd of people browsing the marketplace. All Asian.

Kip didn't dare approach a single one. His Chinese language skills sucked. And the last thing he wanted was to be ratted out to the security police by some overeager Chinese national who'd seen his photo on the morning news. The photo had been accompanied by a dire warning splashed across it in big red characters:

Beware! American spy!

At least that's what he figured it had said.

He bristled. He was *not* a spy.

Okay, fine. At the moment, technically, he was.

His mission was to do a sneak-and-peek at Yulin Naval Submarine Base down on the coast near Sanya, where the Chinese were about to deep-water test a newly designed, ultra-long-distance autonomous unmanned underwater vehicle that was as small as a torpedo and cheap to build. If the tests were successful, the new Chinese AUV would be mass-produced and let loose on the coastlines of America to spy on military and shipping installations with impunity.

Unless the navy could design countermeasures to stop them.

Which was where Kip came in.

A prototype AUV was being delivered to Yulin day after tomorrow from a factory on the mainland, and the U.S. Navy wanted photos of it. Detailed photos.

Photos, Kip could do.

A childhood hobby he'd honed to an art over the years, photography was his *other* specialty. What the best Force Recon sniper could do with a rifle, Kip could do with a camera lens.

But for that he needed a lens that wasn't cracked to bits.

Which brought him back to Ms. Practical.

He smiled.

Her, he could also do.

Adjusting his peasant jacket, he scanned the marketplace for her practical brown ponytail and limped after her.

He decided to separate his target from her companion and talk to her on her own. Ms. Artsy-fartsy might be one of those conscientious objector types who opposed espionage on principle. But if it was as he suspected, and Ms. Sensible was attached to the U.S. consulate in any kind of official capacity, she'd have an obligation to help a citizen in need of aid. Especially when he told her it was a matter of U.S. national security. Which it was. Aside from the whole threat of being tortured and hanged as a spy thing. Which he'd just as soon skip.

Doing his best to shrink his six-foot-three frame down to blend in with the shorter tourists around him—the newscast would surely have mentioned his height—he slowly picked his way toward his target until he was standing a few yards away from her at the end of a large stall. Her friend had quickly become absorbed in examining the textiles on display, and the stall's owner was smiling and chattering nonstop in Chinese as she spread out more and more weavings for them to look at.

Ms. Practical was translating. Good. Language skills could come in handy.

He waited patiently, hanging back until the proprietress hurried off to fetch the ubiquitous offering of tea, over which they would start price negotiations.

He stepped in close. Ms. Practical glanced up at him, startled, and started to say something in Chinese.

He cut her off in a low voice. "I'm American. I need your help."

She did a double take, her gaze darting up to his in surprise. Her eyes were large and blue. And startlingly pretty.

Hello. He did his own double take.

Suddenly her blues widened in recognition. "You! Oh, my— You're that—" She swallowed the offending word and glanced around furtively before turning back to him. "Major Llowell, I presume?" she whispered.

It was his turn to be mildly surprised. "How did you know?"

Her brows flickered. Those cornflower blues tracked down his body, then up again. "You really think that outfit is a disguise?"

He stared back at her in chagrin. Of all the— "It's what was available," he said a shade defensively. "Got a better idea?"

Her gaze glided across the breadth of his chest, lingering for a brief moment on his pecs. "Nope." She turned aside and cleared her throat.

For a second his jaw slackened. Wait. Was she *cruising* him?

An unexpected rush of physical awareness flooded through his body. He took another look at her. A thorough look. And his earlier opinion of all practical and sensible resolved into something quite different.

Yeah, she was wearing the typical drab uniform of a federal bureaucrat, but the skirt actually hugged her shapely hips nicely, and her white blouse was soft and clung to a really outstanding set of—

"What do you want?" she asked, jerking him out of his reassessment.

"Pearl buttons," he blurted.

She blinked. "What?"

He slammed his eyes shut for an instant, then opened them and smiled. "Sorry. What were you asking?"

"You said you needed help?"

Right. Damn. *Get a grip, Llowell.* He forced his focus back where it belonged. "I'd like a ride," he said.

She shot him a frown.

"Down to Sanya, on the coast," he clarified with an inner wince. Had his voice betrayed his inappropriate thoughts?

Christ.

"You do realize," she said quietly, "there are at least three military checkpoints between here and Sanya?"

He shrugged. "Yeah." They could be dealt with.

She didn't look particularly happy, but she didn't tell him to take a hike, either. She indicated his rucksack. "Anything in there I should know about?"

"No."

Which was true. Just a dented camera and useless telephoto lens. And a few other assorted odds and ends she shouldn't know about. For her own good. In case he was caught.

She nodded, and he had the distinct feeling he wasn't fooling her for a nanosecond.

Of course, the only really incriminating thing—the photos he'd been sent to take—were not in his possession yet.

The Chinese would have nothing to hold him on but suspicion.

The real danger would come later.

Provided he made the rendezvous tomorrow.

"So. Can I get a ride?" He plastered on his most winsome smile.

She pushed out a breath, and shot him a sardonic look. "What the hay," she said at length. "I've always wanted to see the inside of a Chinese prison."

2

The astonished expression on the man's face almost made Deputy Director DeAnne Lovejoy of the U.S. State Department smile. He looked so charmingly taken aback she nearly forgot that the last U.S. Marine she'd smiled at had merely stared icily back at her and told her she was a damn useless female.

But that was ancient history.

"I—I'm sure that's not—" he almost stammered.

She waved him off. "Kidding." Apparently Major Llowell had never encountered a State Department official with a sense of humor. Granted, there weren't a lot of them. And she wasn't completely joking. Espionage was a serious offense. Especially in China.

But what was she supposed to say? "No, forget it, you can't have a ride?" Hardly. As a foreign service officer, her job was to protect American citizens abroad. At any cost. Yes, even of her freedom.

Besides, her boss, the deputy assistant secretary, would kill her if she let anything happen to this particular citizen. The hotlines from Guangzhou to Foggy Bottom and the Pentagon had been burning up since dawn with speculation as to the alleged spy's health and whereabouts. And here he'd walked right into her hands, healthy as a lion and asking for help. She could already smell the promotion.

"DeAnne! Look at these fabulous—Oh!" Chrissie Tanner faltered at the sight of the tall, broad man standing so close to her.

Oops. DeAnne took a step away from him. "Chrissie, this is Mr. Llow . . . enstein. He's here, um . . ."

"On business," the major supplied smoothly, extending his large hand. Which was attached to a muscular arm. Which in turn led to that impressive body. "My rental car conked out and Mrs. . . . uh . . ."

That *very* impressive body. From a purely objective feminine perspective.

He raised an expectant brow at her.

What?

She lurched out of her lustful thoughts. "Oh. Lovejoy. *Miss* Lovejoy." Okay, maybe not completely out. "DeAnne," she said, determinedly businesslike.

He inclined his head politely. "DeAnne offered me a ride down the mountain."

"Oh?" Chrissie appeared flummoxed for a moment.

Lord, that imposing body was a problem. It was far too noticeable. And not in a good way.

Okay, maybe also in a good way.

Chrissie tipped her head way back to look up at him. She brightened. "So you're here for the weaving, Mr. Lowenstein?"

Uh-oh. DeAnne interrupted before the major could say anything. "I'm pretty sure my cell phone won't work up here," she said breezily, "but I thought I saw one of those call-for-assistance buttons in the SUV. Maybe they can get hold of the rental company."

"Do those things actually work in China?" he asked skeptically.

"I guess we'll find out," she said. "Will you be all right on your own for a few minutes?" she asked Chrissie.

"Oh. Sure," Chrissie said, and good-naturedly indicated the market stall's owner returning with a tray of refreshments. "I'll just drink tea, nod, and smile a lot."

DeAnne chuckled. "Sounds like a plan." She gestured toward the SUV. "Shall we, sir?"

As they started walking, she noticed he was limping a little. She decided she'd rather not know what had caused it.

"Please," he said when they were out of earshot. "Call me Kip. You really have a cell phone?"

"Yes, but it really isn't going to work. No bars this far from civilization."

"And the assistance button?"

"Sorry, there's no button." At his raised brow, she said, "You stick out like Gulliver in Lilliput. We need to get you tucked out of sight."

Thankfully, he didn't argue.

They passed a vendor selling rolls of fried rice, lamb, and vegetables wrapped in pak choi leaves. It smelled delicious, and she could see him eyeing the food. She checked her watch. Nearly noon. On impulse, she stopped and ordered a half-dozen rolls from the vendor, then glanced at that large, delectable body again, and changed the order to a dozen, with a cup of coconut milk to wash them down. She paid and grabbed the food.

"When was the last time you ate?" she asked as they hurried on toward the SUV. The television "Most Wanted" broadcasts detailing his "horrible treachery" had started cycling yesterday afternoon. He must have been in hiding since then.

"This morning," he said, as he accepted the newspaper cone of fried rolls from her. "There are fruit trees everywhere. But these smell great." He put a hand on her arm. "Slow down. Here. We'll share."

She winced. *His leg.* "Sorry. I didn't mean to—" But the words died in her throat as he plucked a roll from the paper, pursed his lips, and blew on it. *Oh, man.* Those lips were— The guy was—

Omigod. *Feeding her.*

She felt herself flush hotly as he put the cooled-off roll to her parted lips and waited for her to take a bite.

This was crazy. Major Llowell was a fugitive. A *spy.* And was no doubt being hunted by every cop, security agent, and PLA—People's Liberation Army—soldier on Hainan Island. His life was in danger. Heck, *her* life was in danger just being with him.

And the man was *flirting* with her?

Ho-boy.

She took a bite.

He smiled a slow, sexy smile, and her heart did a high dive off the cliff of serious attraction.

And landed on the painful shoals of reality.

No, no, *no.*

She was *not* attracted to him. He may have a disarming smile, but she knew too well the thoughtless betrayal that could lie behind that captivating façade. No *way* was she making the same mistake as her mother. Not even opening that door.

"Major Llowell," she managed after chewing and swallowing. And refusing to look at his sensually curved mouth. "You don't seem to be taking me—your situation very seriously."

"Hey, you're the one who stopped for lunch."

She glared at him. "And this is the thanks I get."

He waggled his brows. "I'd be happy to thank you properly." He popped another veggie roll in his mouth.

She didn't know whether to grit her teeth or smack him. She definitely didn't want to think about any other possibilities. *Not happening.* "The only thanks I need," she said primly, "is you staying completely out of sight until we can figure—"

He let out a curse.

She frowned. "There's really no need for—*Oof!*"

All at once she found herself jerked to a halt against a set of hard masculine ribs. "Shit," he muttered.

"Honestly, Major Ll—" she began. But that's when she saw what had prompted his curses.

A trio of green army Jeeps overflowing with PLA soldiers was barreling up the mountain track toward the village—heading straight for them. "Oh, lord," she squeaked, her voice going up two octaves as her pulse took off.

Major Llowell grabbed her by the arms and pushed her toward the vehicle. "Scream," he ordered. "Like I'm kidnapping you." He opened the driver's side door, shoved her in, and vaulted in after her.

After a befuddled hesitation, she screamed. Not terribly convincingly. More like baffled.

What on earth was he—

He hustled her over to the passenger side. "Buckle up."

Good grief. He really *was* kidnapping her! She screamed again, more convincingly this time.

"Wait!" She looked around wildly. "What about the driver?" He was nowhere to be seen. "We'll get in trouble if we take the car without him."

The major flashed her an incredulous look. "You're kidding again, right?"

Not really. But too late now. The SUV's engine roared to life.

By this time the three Jeeps had reached the outskirts of the village. The soldiers were shouting and waving their machine guns. They must have spotted the major.

The SUV ground into gear and lurched forward. The driver's door slammed shut with a bang like a rifle shot. She nearly jumped out of her skin.

"What about Chrissie?" she croaked, grappling for her seat belt.

"Forget Chrissie," Major Llowell gritted out, throwing the vehicle into a rooster tail and heading in the opposite direction. He jerked his chin at the advancing Jeeps. "You've got more important things to worry about."

Her seat belt snapped home.

Just as the soldiers started shooting wildly.

At them.

3

"Get down!"

DeAnne felt Major Llowell's powerful hand shove her shoulders and head down to her knees, out of the line of fire.

"Stay there," he commanded.

She wasn't about to argue. Machine gun fire sprayed the air. All around them bullets whizzed by, plinking into the thankfully solid metal of the SUV. She laced her hands over her head in a protective gesture. A useless one, she knew.

"They can't shoot at me!" she cried indignantly. "I'm an American citizen!"

The SUV took a sharp turn, whacking her into the door.

"In other words, a foreigner. Who's giving aid and comfort to a spy," he returned between clamped teeth, whipping the wheel back around with white-knuckled hands.

A bullet slammed into the door inches from her ear. She squeezed her eyes shut, trying desperately not to panic.

What was needed here was calm and logic. "What are we going to do?"

"Drive like hell," he shouted above the grinding of the gears as they banked up a steep, rocky slope. "And hope we can outrun them."

"Three jeeps? And a dozen armed soldiers?"

"I've been in worse jams." His voice was as strained as the engine. The SUV shot over a rise and jolted a hard landing with an explosive crash.

Her eyes flew open. But it was just the steel on steel of the chassis, not a grenade. "I haven't," she croaked past her heart thundering in her throat. Working for the State Department could be dangerous sometimes, but she had managed to elude life-threatening situations. Until now.

The *rat-a-tat-tat* of machine gun fire continued to split the air behind them, but the *plonk* of bullets had mercifully ceased. Had he really outrun them?

She turned her head and glanced up at Major Llowell through the crook of her elbow. Her fingers still had a death grip on her scalp. She was trembling from the roots of her hair clear to her toes. But the major didn't look terrified. He didn't even look scared. Just grimly focused.

The cords of his neck stood out as he gripped the steering wheel, his eyes darting this way and that, sweeping the terrain for possible escape routes and checking the rearview mirror for danger. The sleeves of his peasant jacket had ridden up, and she could see the ropes of muscle in his forearms ripple as he shifted gears and wrestled the SUV onto a path up the mountainside barely wide enough for an ox team.

Irrationally, she felt the knots in her stomach unclench . . . just a tiny bit.

She knew from bitter experience that the one thing—okay yeah, the *only* thing—a U.S. Marine was really good at was being a Marine. Her whole life she'd resented that fact, but at the moment she admitted to being grudgingly grateful. If anyone could get them out of this alive, it was a Marine.

The irony did not escape her.

She suddenly wondered what, exactly, a *U.S. Marine* was doing on an island in China, accused of being a spy. Espionage was generally CIA's turf.

"Are you on a covert mission?" she blurted out, figuring it had to be something like that. The major had spec ops written all over him.

"Just a tourist shooting pictures," he answered blithely, as if it were the most natural thing in the world.

Not that she believed his answer for a moment. This man was no tourist.

He hit the brakes, gunned the SUV into neutral, and threw it into four-wheel drive. In the lull, she listened intently. The gunfire had stopped. She risked lifting her head to take a quick peek behind them.

"Have we lost them?" she asked hopefully.

"Hell, no. They're just saving ammo." He cut her a frown. "I told you to stay down."

He let out the clutch with a wince of pain on his face, and the SUV jumped forward, jerking back and forth over the rocky path as it climbed the steep mountain at a bone-rattling speed.

"I'll duck back down when they start shooting again," she promised, gripping the armrest.

"Speaking of which, I don't suppose you have a pistol in that purse?" he asked, indicating the shoulder bag lying next to his rucksack on the floor.

"What? No."

"I've got an M9 on me," he informed her.

That put a whole new spin on shooting pictures . . .

She grimaced. "I don't like guns."

He made a deprecating noise. "But you can handle one,

right? They make you learn to shoot as part of your Foreign Service training."

She stared over at him. "How do you know I'm Foreign Service?" She hadn't told him. She was sure of it. Not that it was any big secret, but . . .

He raked his gaze over her clothes, brows hiked in amusement. "Really?"

Her lips compressed and she was about to retort when a tire hit a rut and he swiveled his attention back to the road.

His hands tightened on the wheel. "We need to start shooting back. But I'm a little busy here. You'll have to do it."

She shook her head, still miffed by his unspoken slight. "I told you, I don't like guns." Guns belonged to her father's world. His world. A world of dress blues and camouflage. A world she wanted no part of.

Llowell's dubious eyes pierced her. "Are you serious right now?"

She lifted her chin. "I'm a diplomat. Words are my weapon of choice."

"Tell that to the guys with the machine guns," he muttered.

She jetted out a breath. The man was—

Logic. Calm. The man was right. Under these circumstances, acting on her distaste was irrational. "Fine," she conceded, and reached for his rucksack.

"That's not where it is."

She grabbed onto the dashboard as they hit another rut. "Then where?"

"My shoulder holster. Under my shirt."

For a second she just stared. Then his eyes met hers and she could swear he grinned. She looked down at his peasant jacket. It was just baggy enough that the bulge of the holster didn't show. "Surely, you can reach it—"

The SUV jolted over a jumble of rocks. His muscles

labored to hang on to the steering wheel. "What's the matter? You afraid to touch me?" The corner of his mouth twitched up.

"Don't be ridiculous." She reached out toward him, but her hand faltered inches from his torso. "So, am I just supposed to, um . . . ?"

"Put your hand up my shirt? Yeah. That's the idea."

She felt her cheeks go hot. Okay. Not a problem.

She went determinedly for the hem of the boxy handwoven garment. She grasped it delicately with two fingers and pulled it away from his body. With her other hand she reached up under the fabric, gingerly groping the empty space for the holster. And found nothing but air and skin. *Ho-boy.* She delved higher. The vehicle rocked violently and she gasped. Her splayed fingers landed solidly on his bare torso.

The expanse of masculine chest was rock hard and hot to the touch, dusted with a smattering of coarse, curly hair. *Sweet mercy.*

She jerked her hand away. The SUV rocked violently back and forth, throwing her off balance. Both her hands collided with warm skin. She sucked in a breath. But didn't take them away. This hesitancy was ridiculous. It was just a man-chest. No big deal.

Moving with the motion of the car, she slid her hands up his torso searching for the holster. Her fingers found a flat male nipple and skittered over it. It pebbled beneath her touch.

His chest expanded with a spasm and he cleared his throat. "The, uh, gun is on the other side."

The *far* side. Naturally. Her cheeks grew even hotter. "Oh."

She hesitated, licked her lips, then shifted her seat belt so she could lean in and run her hand across the broad geography of his chest. Perversely, the SUV chose just that moment to jerk back and forth over a patch of cobbles, and her hand zigzagged across his pecs like a puppet on strings.

She gasped in embarrassment and tried to pull away, but with an *oof*, she found herself flung flat against his chest, his shirt up and her arms bracketed around him.

Mortified, she lifted her gaze to his face. His jaw was tight, his nostrils flared, his blue eyes dark as indigo. Her fingers grasped leather. *Finally.*

"Got it," she croaked.

He grunted. And glanced down at her. Their noses bumped. Their mouths were millimeters apart. The car jostled again and their lips touched.

She turned her head aside, heat blasting through her as she groped madly for the gun, wrapped her fingers around the hilt, and slid it up out of its holster.

Ho-freaking-boy. The symbolism of *that* was just a little too vivid.

She sat up quickly, throwing herself back onto her own seat. The seat belt snapped tight across her chest.

She stared straight ahead through the windshield, gripping the gun in her shaking fingers, face burning. "I'm sorry," she said hoarsely. "I didn't mean to—"

The roar of an engine suddenly revved behind them. She spun around to look as one of the PLA jeeps leapt over a rise into view, gaining speed. The Chinese soldiers in it raised their weapons, aiming at them.

Her pulse went into hyperspace. "Oh my God! They're—"

"Shoot!" he commanded as he put pedal to metal.

"What? *Me?* No! I can't—"

The machine guns opened fire. A hail of bullets pinged into the SUV. The back window exploded in fireworks of crystalline cubes. DeAnne strangled a scream and ducked, her heart racing.

"Shoot! *Now, goddamn it!* Aim for the tires if you're squeamish! Anything! Just shoot back, for Chrissakes!"

She peered around the seat. *The jeep was gaining on them.* She swallowed heavily. Then raised the gun with both her hands, squeezed her eyes shut, and started pulling the trigger.

4

"Incoming helo. Clear the decks."

The announcement boomed over the topside PA system of the USS *Something-or-other*. STORM Corps operator Darcy Zimmerman couldn't quite remember the name of the navy ship they were on. Just that they were out at sea, somewhere off the southern coast of China.

Standing well to the side, she watched the helo approach.

Darcy's head and her legs were feeling wobbly, but whether from the rocking and rolling of the deck or from sheer exhaustion, she wasn't quite sure. The hastily assembled team had been traveling nonstop for nearly twenty-four hours straight, and hadn't gotten a wink of sleep since pulling this assignment day before yesterday.

The others were lined up raggedly beside her, a handful of the best operators in STORM—though you'd never know to look at them. Zane, Jaeger, and Quinn all matched her for dark circles, wrinkled fatigues, and hair sticking up in every direction.

The helo reached the ship and circled once directly overhead, whipping up a froth of wind and sea spray. A man was sitting casually on the edge of the open bay of the bird, one leg dangling out the door.

Their boss. The legendary Commander Kurt Bridger, head of the Strategic Technical Operations and Rescue Missions Corporation—known throughout the world as STORM Corps.

As they landed, Bridger was shouting back and forth with a grinning navy guy in headphones who stood leaning just as nonchalantly against the other side of the open bay. The second the bird sat down, Bridger jumped off, turned to catch a small duffel, and hunch-ran over to them. He didn't pause, just straightened and shouted, "With me, people," over the noise of the rotors and kept going.

She, Zane, Jaeger, and Quinn all turned and trotted after him. The team was unusually small—STORM almost always sent out teams of six—and unusually experienced. The job should be an interesting one. Interesting was always good in Darcy's book. Even if the transpo could be hell.

"Is this everyone, sir?" she asked when Bridger slowed.

His gaze sliced over them. "I understand the client's bringing in a couple of their own people," he said.

The client being the U.S. Navy, she surmised, based on where they were.

The four teammates exchanged looks. *Hell.* No one liked working with outsiders.

"I don't want to hear it," the commander cut off any protests. Not that anyone would dare protest. Well. Except maybe Quinn.

Just then, a white-clad officer hurried up, a captain

according to his insignia. "Commander Bridger? I'm Bill Jenson, ONI. Welcome aboard."

Office of Naval Intelligence. One of STORM's steady customers.

STORM Corps was a nongovernmental spec ops outfit that hired out to private companies and individuals, mainly to recover and defend hostages and other assets. But they were often used to carry out sensitive or controversial covert ops in locations and situations where official government agencies couldn't or wouldn't go.

She wondered if they were there to break some poor schmuck out of a Chinese prison. Good luck with that.

"This your team?" Jenson asked Bridger, with a glance at Darcy that carried a shade of disapproval.

No doubt one of those old-school asshole chauvinists who didn't like women in his navy. Or in private military companies, either, it seemed.

Yeah, screw you, too, buddy.

She felt Quinn's hand settle lightly on her back, and her anger evaporated into an inner smile. He knew her so well.

"The best in the business," Bridger replied, and she knew he meant it. One of the many reasons she would never work for anyone but STORM Corps.

Jenson led them into the ship, through a maze of passageways and ladders, and opened the door to a small stateroom with four berths. "Sorry, I wasn't expecting a woman," he said, glancing at her uncertainly.

"I'm fine," she said, and tossed her duffel onto a top bunk. This was not the first time they'd all shared accommodations, and it wouldn't be the last.

The others claimed berths, as well, no one batting an eye.

Commander Bridger tossed his gear in a corner. He wouldn't be staying. He never did. "Let's get right to it," he told Jenson.

With a nod, they were led up a couple of decks to a

compact conference room. He went to the intercom and told whoever answered, "Send them in," then turned to Bridger. "Have a seat. The others will be here shortly."

They all remained standing. They refused his offer of coffee, too, though she knew they were all dying for a cup—or five. But that would come later, when they were alone and hashing through the best way to accomplish the job, whatever it was.

There was a knock on the door.

"Enter," Jenson called.

The door swung open and to Darcy's surprise, a woman walked in. Almost as tall as Darcy, she had pretty red hair and was wearing a classy black Dior suit and elegant pumps.

Whoa. She felt the men beside her stir.

Suddenly, she felt underdressed in her travel-stained fatigues and tank top. The woman was frikkin' gorgeous.

And there was something else . . .

Hmmm.

"Come in, come in," Captain Jenson said, gesturing to two men entering the room behind her. "Join us."

The first guy was tall and lean, with Native American features. His shoulder-length black hair was pulled back in a ponytail. He was in jeans—faded with holes in them—but his black T-shirt stretched very nicely over a broad set of shoulders.

Damn. *He* was gorgeous, too.

The second man stepped into the room and the entire team froze in place. He was in uniform. Navy. Big and muscular. He looked like a classic movie star who'd just stepped off the set.

Of *Hunt for Red October.*

My God. That was a *Russian* uniform!

For a moment they all stared in astonishment.

"What the hell," Quinn muttered next to her.

Who *were* these people? Surely, *they* weren't on the team . . . ?

Captain Jenson attempted to herd everyone toward the table, but no one moved an inch, so he gave up. "All right. Then let me introduce everyone," he said, mildly flustered. "Commander Kurt Bridger, this is *Kapitan* Nikolai Romanov of the Russian Navy." He pronounced the rank with a terrible accent, like "cap-pee-tan." "Kapitan Romanov is currently a guest senior lecturer at the U.S. Naval Submarine School in Connecticut."

Bridger said something to him in Russian. The man smiled broadly and said something back. They both chuckled.

Jenson, clearly surprised, rushed to complete the introduction. "Commander Bridger is chief in command of STORM Corps, the outfit running the operation you'll be helping out on, *kapitan*."

Hel-lo. The *Russian* was helping them? The team glanced quickly at Bridger. From his expression, this was news to him, too.

Jenson moved on. "And this is Lieutenant Commander Clint Walker of—"

"Just Clint," Walker interrupted, holding out his hand to shake theirs, one by one, "currently of the ship *Samantha Joy*. I'm a civilian now, happily retired from the navy, and sailing the world with my new wife."

Which explained the ratty jeans. But not why he was here.

Darcy turned her head aside and murmured softly to Quinn, "We need to get everything we can on these guys." She knew the whole team was glued to every word being spoken.

"Mm-hmm."

Darcy was the Internet whiz for the team—among other things. She glanced at Rand Jaeger, their communications specialist, Predator pilot, and sensory operator—filched four years ago from the Air Force 17th Squadron, though he was originally from South Africa—and all-around enigma. She met his gaze, and saw he was reading her mind, as usual.

"And last but not least, this is Mrs. Julie Romanov," Jenson began, but again was interrupted.

"Oh! Not quite yet," the beautiful redhead said, sending a smile to the big Russian. "We can't get married until Nikolai has his green card in hand. So ridiculous."

"They'll think it's a marriage of convenience," Romanov explained in a sexy accent, his eyes twinkling as he winked at his fiancée. Judging by the adoring looks they were giving each other, nothing could be further from the truth.

Awww. Darcy's heart gave a warm squeeze.

Then she caught herself. Jeez, she must be getting sentimental in her old age.

Quinn, too. He moved closer and let his hand brush hers, giving her even more warm and fuzzies. Because arrogant, irreverent, and handsome-as-the-day-was-long Bobby Lee Quinn was *her* fiancé. Over two years, now.

No, they weren't waiting on a green card, but they did have issues to work out.

Still.

But they would.

Eventually.

She was sure of it.

"Anyway," the pretty fiancée said, preempting Captain Obnoxious and extending her hand to Darcy first, then to the others, "I'm Julie Severin. I'm with—"

"CIA," Darcy supplied, and smiled at Ms. Severin's surprise. As former CIA herself, Darcy had caught the indefinable vibe almost right away. There was a certain, unmistakable aura about a true denizen of Langley.

"Yes, well, um." The woman's expression turned wry. "I guess you really are as good as they say you are."

Darcy shrugged modestly. "I have my days."

Quinn snorted under his breath.

He'd pay for that later.

"I'm obviously at a disadvantage," Clint Walker said as he shook her hand. "You are . . . ?"

Bridger answered for her. "This is Darcy Zimmerman, comp spec and home base six."

Oka-ay. Not a good sign. The commander was devolving to grunt-speak in a room full of squids. He must be irritated about something.

Darcy cleared her throat. "Computer specialist and in charge of mission base operations," she translated.

Quinn stepped forward. "I'm STORM Commander Bobby Lee Quinn, alpha six of mission sortie operations." He gestured to the others. "Alex Zane, dive and desert spec, and Rand Jaeger, communications and Predator pilot."

Polite greetings were exchanged all around.

But Bobby Lee was not known for either his patience or his tact. He folded his arms over his chest and said in that Tupelo honey drawl of his, "So. Why exactly are *y'all* here?"

There was a brief, assessing silence.

Then the corner of Clint Walker's lip curved up. He leaned back on his heels and regarded them. "We're just here to lend a hand," he said pleasantly.

"To do what?" Darcy asked, unable to stop herself. She was dying to know what the mission was.

"Oh, didn't they tell you?" Walker asked with mild amusement. "Why, we're here to steal ourselves a top-secret Chinese AUV."

5

The trio of Chinese jeeps was gaining on them.

Kip's mind spun and his body hummed as he sent the SUV careening around the final curve of the rough ox trail, just before hitting the main road.

Whoa! Way too fast.

The SUV tipped onto two wheels before smacking down again. *Almost there.* Just a few more yards and they'd be back on the well-traveled path to civilization. *Or away from it*, he reminded himself as he jammed the accelerator to the floor. Depending on which direction he chose at the last second.

DeAnne was still firing blindly through the shot-out back window. The clip had to be nearly empty by now, but all she'd managed to hit were trees and rocks. If the situation wasn't so damn serious, he'd be laughing. *Was she cute, or what?* It reminded him a little of that old movie where Frank Sinatra played a pilot who ran out of ammo and went down shooting at the enemy with a fizzy seltzer bottle.

Kip forced the grin from his face. This was no time for levity. The situation could get really ugly. If those jeeps caught up with them—

From behind, he suddenly heard a loud pop and a high-pitched whistle that sounded like a geyser erupting.

Relief hurtled through him. *Yes!* “Good girl,” he shouted with a whoop. “Kill shot!”

“What?” Her eyes sprang open in dismay. “*Kill?* No! I—”

“Radiator,” he clarified. A split second later came the sound of screeching metal and breaking glass, followed by a deafening *crrrash!* “And then there were none,” he drawled and hit the steering wheel with his palm. “Bam!”

She jumped.

He flashed her a huge smile. “Remind me to kiss you later, when we get where we’re going!”

Her eyes went even wider.

The SUV flew off the ox path and onto the main road. He skidded into the turn, then braked to a halt to yank the old-school gears out of four-wheel drive. As he did, he glanced at DeAnne.

She was still holding the Beretta M9 in a death grip.

He swiftly eased it from her rigid fingers, digging in his rucksack for a fresh clip. In two seconds he’d switched the clips and stuck the Beretta into his waistband.

She watched him with round eyes. “By the way, um, where *are* we going?”

A million conflicting emotions were reflected in those expressive eyes. She looked . . . lost. And . . . expectant? And beautiful as all hell.

Adrenaline surged through his veins, along with a burning need to wrap her in his arms and protect her from the very thing he was getting her into. Every cell in his body was alive with that need.

And with a sudden, fierce desire to taste her.

Later? *Fuck that.*

He grabbed her, pulled her to him, and kissed her. Hard.

A noise of surprise gurgled up her throat, but it melted into a reluctant mewl of pleasure as his tongue plied her lips and slipped into her mouth. His own moan joined hers at the feel of her soft curves pillowed against his chest. The tips of her breasts swirled to stiff points beneath the smooth silk of her blouse.

He was instantly, throbbingly hard.

And completely insane.

Jesus.

Hel-*lo? Earth to Major Kip! Bad guys? Remember?*

He broke the kiss abruptly, and set her away. With a curse, he jammed the stick into gear, and took off down the mountain.

And did a giant mental backpedal. Or tried to, anyway.

Holy crap. What the *hell* had just happened? He was not some wet-behind-the-ears recruit on a weekend pass from Pendleton.

He risked a glance at her. She was staring at him, her kiss-moistened lips parted, as though hypnotized. Then suddenly, her mouth snapped shut and she turned frontward, gripping the edge of her seat even though the road was now paved and jostle free.

They drove in tense silence for several minutes.

"I, um, actually meant that question," she said. "You realize there's a checkpoint coming up soon. We're sure to be stopped."

"Yeah," he said. "Which is why we're not going that far."

"Okay."

He knew she was waiting for him to elaborate, but the truth was, he hadn't formulated a plan yet. "I need to contact my team and change the rendezvous point. We'll take it from there."

She looked doubtful. "Your team?"

Whoops. "You do actually have a cell phone, right?"

"Yes." She straightened and glanced down, seeming to reorient herself, then plucked her bag from the floor. "I'll check for bars." She withdrew a smartphone and punched buttons. Then shook her head. "Sorry. Nothing."

He hadn't really expected any. They were driving high above a narrow valley surrounded by even taller mountains. "We'll have to get up to higher ground."

She pointed in the direction they were driving. "Going the wrong way for that, Major."

"Call me Kip," he reminded her. "I think we've whipped right on past formalities, don't you?"

The color rose in her cheeks as she cleared her throat. "Yeah. Well. I assume someone in your profession is familiar with the endorphin rush that comes with fear."

It took him a second to wade through to her meaning. "Is that what you think made me kiss you?" he asked wryly. "The heat of battle?"

"No," she said primly. "I assume my outfit made me irresistible."

He almost choked, and shot her a glance. She was doing it again. Saying something completely unsexy—goading, even . . . but in a way that made him squirm with awareness. *Anti-flirting?*

He said, "Just like Kate Hepburn."

The tiniest muscle in her lips quirked. "Good save," she conceded.

He tore his attention from her lips to watch the road. He seemed to recall from his pre-mission map studies that there was a steep cliff right around—

There. He swung onto the narrow shoulder and brought the SUV to a gravel-flying halt.

"Hey! What are you doing?" she squeaked.

"Time to bail," he said, yanked on the brake, and turned to her. "What kind of supplies are in the vehicle?"

Taken aback, she hesitated, then tossed a glance toward the back seat. "Nothing much. A first aid kit. A cooler with water. Chrissie's and my overnight bags. Some fabrics she picked up earlier. I saw an extra petrol can. I . . . I'm not sure what else the driver has in back. Tools, maybe? Why? What do you mean, bail?"

"I mean ditch the car. Even as we speak, descriptions of this SUV are being flashed across every TV screen, and sent to every law enforcement outpost in China. They'll be coming for me in full force. I do not intend to be caught." He leaned across her legs, snapped open the glove box, and started riffling through it.

"But how will we get back down to the coast? To Sanya?"

"We don't. Well. *I* don't." Giving up on the glove box, he pointed at the terrain above them. "I'm going that way. Into the mountains." He straightened away from her. Mostly. "But as you said, we're close to the government checkpoint. Just walk down there and turn yourself in. Say you escaped your raving lunatic kidnapper. You should be okay."

"Should be?"

He wasn't going to lie. "You're obviously familiar with this country. Nothing here is ever certain. Especially when it concerns Westerners."

She considered that somberly. "I was just kidding about the Chinese prison thing, you know."

He reached out and tucked a loose lock of hair behind her ear. "Yeah. I'm really sorry about dragging you into this mess. I'd never have—" Frustration stabbed at him and he shook his head. "I have no idea how they located me so fast."

Unconsciously, she started to touch his leg, then thought better of it and curled her fingers away. "Don't worry, Major," she said. "I'll get you out of this."

Her expression was so damn sincere he had to smile. Ironic, considering he'd just been saying the same thing in his head about her. "Hey. Don't forget, *I'm* the Marine. I do the rescuing around here."

He'd expected her to smile back, maybe take one of her unflirty little jabs at him, but instead her eyes went cool and she turned away. "No. I won't forget."

Oka-ay.

She opened her door and climbed out, yanked open the rear door and started going through the things that were scattered on the back seat and floor. He did the same, glancing up at her every few seconds, but she wasn't meeting his eyes. Was it something he said?

Not that it mattered. In a few minutes they'd part ways and they'd never see each other again.

Which felt surprisingly disappointing.

Damn if he didn't like the woman and her dry sense of humor. And her very kissable lips. Which he'd hardly gotten to taste.

Even more disappointing.

But he'd get over it. Such was his life—never in one spot long enough to enjoy all the benefits. Not that he'd ever go beyond the physical with her, even if he had the opportunity.

Kip didn't do relationships. Not serious ones.

Getting serious meant falling in love.

Falling in love meant getting married.

And marriage was not an option for him.

Definitely not now.

Possibly not ever.

There were lots more lips in the world to kiss. Tomorrow he wouldn't even remember how amazing that kiss with her was.

He grabbed his rucksack from the front and loaded the water bottles into it from the cooler, along with a bag of chocolate and a few chilled apples.

"Here," she said, and handed him a plastic box with a red cross on the lid, which he stuck in the rucksack, too. She went to the back of the SUV and lifted the hatch to study the contents. "Hammer and screwdriver?" she asked.

"Nah," he said.

"Ax?" She lifted a small folding hatchet for him to see.

"That could come in handy."

She tossed it his way and kept scrounging for a moment. "That seems to be it. Except for these." She shook a small, orange waterproof container and he recognized the rattle of wooden matches.

"Definitely," he said, reaching for them over the seat and looking at them consideringly. "All right. Got everything you need out of the vehicle?"

"Hang on."

He pulled out a long piece of Chrissie's fabric bits that he'd already selected, unscrewed the lid of the petrol can and stuffed part of the cloth inside. Meanwhile, DeAnne fetched a fabric shoulder bag off the rear seat, emptied the entire contents of her sensible leather purse into it, along with a few other things, then pulled the strap over her head and settled the bag against her hip. Grabbing a jacket from the seat, she said, "Okay. I'm ready," and stood looking at him expectantly.

He nodded, slammed the doors shut, and reached in through the window to release the parking break. "Stand back. It's showtime."

He strode to the shattered back window, lit a match, aimed and tossed it into the vehicle, and gave the SUV a solid push when he saw where the match had landed. The SUV started rolling toward the edge of the cliff.

DeAnne's jaw dropped in astonishment and she jumped back. "What on earth are you doing?"

He gave it another two-handed shove so it gained momentum. "Killing myself."

She looked from him to the SUV as it sailed over the cliff. It was a long way down to the canyon floor below. They both stepped to the edge and watched its elegant dive. It hit the boulders below with a resounding crunch of metal on rock. Then all went silent again.

She swallowed hard as they stared. "They won't find a body," she ventured. "Or blood. They'll think you survived and are okay."

Seconds later, the canyon echoed with a loud *ka-boom*. The SUV exploded into a huge fireball of flame.

"Well," she said in a strangled voice, "no, probably not now."

Quirking a smile, he swiped up his rucksack from the ground and slid on the straps. "You can tell them you witnessed the whole thing. I slowed to take the curve and you jumped out of the SUV to get away. I grabbed for you, lost control of the vehicle, and it went over the cliff." He gave the burning fireball a little wave. "So long, Major Llowell."

"It could work," she said.

"They'll believe you. You're a diplomat."

She wadded up the puffy jacket and stuffed it into her fabric bag, making it poof out like a pillow. "There's just one problem."

He tilted his head at her mildly stubborn expression. "What's that?" he asked.

"I can't do it."

He frowned. "Why not? Surely, you can tell a small lie to save my life?"

She turned, looking somewhat offended. "Of course I could."

He should have felt relief at that. He didn't. "Then what's the problem?" he asked.

She peered at him as though he were dense in the head. "Because I'm going with you."

6

He actually laughed.

DeAnne wanted to kick the obnoxious man in the shin. Instead she lifted her chin. “Is there something funny I’m not aware of?”

He stared at her for a second. His smile faltered. “You’re serious.”

Why was it that men never took her seriously? It was maddening. She wasn’t even a blonde!

“Do I look like I’m joking?” She tried to keep the annoyance from her voice but failed.

He sobered quickly. “No. But the idea is ludicrous. You can’t come with me. It’s much too dangerous.”

“And being arrested and thrown into a Chinese prison isn’t?”

He shifted his rucksack a little and walked onto the road, limping slightly. “That isn’t going to happen.”

She followed after him. “Really? I could have sworn you just said—”

"Even if that did happen," he cut her off, "*which it won't*—do the words 'diplomatic immunity' ring a bell?" He stopped to peer down the road for a moment in the direction of the checkpoint. Apparently satisfied, he did an about-face.

She stepped into his path before he could start walking away from her. "That won't help when they put me in front of a firing squad for aiding and abetting a traitorous spy."

No, she didn't actually believe they would go that far. But he obviously had a skewed idea about how diplomacy worked.

He looked at her impatiently. "Why the hell would you want to come with me, anyway? I'll be moving nonstop, hiding from the entire population of China. It'll be exhausting during the day, cold at night, and—"

"You see? Right there"—she emphasized her point with a finger poke to his chest—"that's exactly why you need me to come with you."

He blinked down at her, and she could practically see his mind fastening on the cold night part.

She gave him a withering look. "What I *mean* is, your natural response to this situation is to run and hide. To sneak away without being caught."

His eyes narrowed. "I prefer the term 'covert,' or 'off-grid.'"

She held up her hands. "No insult intended."

"Fine." He started to limp around her. "But your point is . . . ?"

"There are other ways to handle this. Better ways."

He shook his head and kept walking. "You're talking about using your words again, aren't you?"

She hurried after him. "Is there a problem with that?"

"Yeah. Words don't work."

"Spoken like a true Marine," she muttered. Using words

had never been big on her father's agenda, either. Maybe if he'd tried it once in a while instead of—

Llowell spun around and scowled down at her, his hands fisted on his hips. "You've got something against the Marines, lady?"

Telling him the truth was not going to advance her cause. "I have nothing against you personally, Major Llowell—"

"For Chrissakes, it's *Kip*," he ground out.

She held up her hands. "Okay, okay. *Kip*. I'm just saying maybe we can solve this without you having to run . . . go *off-grid*, and maybe get yourself killed in the process. Those guys chasing us were not shooting over our heads."

"You noticed, huh?"

"Let me call my boss at the State Department. Get him to set up a dialogue with the Chinese government about letting you out."

He moved in closer and laid his hands on her shoulders. "Listen, DeAnne. I appreciate the thought. I really do. But I'm a fucking *spy*. The Chinese know that, somehow. There's no way in hell they'll willingly let me off this island. Not while I'm still breathing." She must have flinched because his expression softened. "I'll be okay. I promise. This is my job. It's what I do."

"I've no doubt you're good at what you do. But so am I. Give me a chance," she said earnestly. "It's *my* job to protect American citizens in trouble abroad. What have you got to lose? I'm not asking you to turn yourself in. Just one phone call."

He hesitated. "Even if I thought it was a good idea—*which I don't*—there's no cell reception here."

She smiled, triumphant. "But there will be further up the mountain, where you're headed anyway. Let me come. Just far enough to make the phone call."

His fingers tightened on her shoulders, leashed strength radiating through them. "And when the State Department says, sorry, their hands are tied, have a nice day, you promise you won't interfere anymore? You'll go back to your embassy and leave me to do what I have to do? Right?"

She nodded. "Right."

But State wouldn't say that. Her boss would see to it. Because a quiet, successful rescue of an American spy right from under Chinese noses could be used as a trump card in the intricate game of diplomacy with China, which often shifted on the merest suggestion of superiority, or losing face. Let alone the actual fact.

Probably best not to tell Major—er, *Kip*—that the government would be using him as a pawn. It shouldn't matter, though, as long as he received the help he needed and got off the island in one piece.

"This is such a bad idea on so many levels," he muttered, and glanced down at her clothes, looking even more pained. "How do you expect to hike through the jungle in a damn business suit?"

"I'll manage," she said, easing out from his grasp. Thank goodness she'd worn her walking shoes today. "What about your leg?"

He scowled. "What about it?"

Touchy. "Nothing at all. We should get going. So. What's the plan?" She took off up the road at a brisk pace.

She could feel his eyes on her back. After a brief moment of hesitation, his boot-steps crunched up unevenly behind her.

"No plan. Just get up the mountain and don't get caught. But we need to be off this road, ASAP."

"Agreed." They definitely did not want to be seen by anyone, and this was the main thoroughfare over the mountains. The problem was the steep incline going up from the shoulder of the pavement. Only a mountain goat could climb that.

He moved up beside her and matched his pace to hers. "There should be a dirt track that branches off pretty soon."

That was the second time he'd known what was coming up ahead. "You have a GPS hidden in that backpack or something?"

"Nope. The enemy could locate my position by tracking it. I do everything old-school."

Good grief. He must have memorized the map.

Sure enough, about a mile later, a narrow, deeply rutted path veered off into the mountains, following a small, tumbling stream up into the thick forest. They took it, and were soon immersed in the cool, damp dimness under the jungle canopy. The path was only wide enough for one, so Kip took point and she fell in behind him. The track wasn't goat-steep, but steep enough to require all her breath and prevent them from chatting.

Which was just as well. She had enough to do to keep from tripping over her own feet.

Not because of the uneven path, but because her gaze kept fastening on Kip's very attractive posterior. Even under the rough cotton homespun of his peasant pants, she could see the impressive muscles of his thighs and backside flex and bunch as his legs worked. It was tough to keep from drooling. The man was in amazing shape.

DeAnne's male colleagues at the embassy ran to analysts and intellectuals, more at home behind their desks or in a tuxedo than pumping iron at the gym or hiking through the wilderness. The Marine guards were always fit and toned, of course, but they tended to be young, fresh-faced kids right out of school who were too cocky and full of themselves to be attractive. In her opinion, anyway. But the major was a grown man in every respect of the word. The whole package—mature, handsome, strong, and capable. And obviously intelligent.

If he weren't so completely and utterly wrong for her, she'd be crushing on him big-time. Good grief. She hadn't had these kinds of butterflies since high school. What was wrong with her? She was smarter than this. She knew better.

Boy howdy, did she ever.

The man was nothing but pure unadulterated trouble.

T.R.O.U.B.L.E.

But oh, man.

Major Kiptyn Llowell was nothing less than pure walking temptation.

And DeAnne had the sinking feeling she was getting dumber by the minute.

7

Darcy and Jaeger had set up their laptops in the wardroom where everyone had finally gathered for a hot meal. They desperately needed some shut-eye, but the whole team was too wound up to sleep. The Russian, Romanov, and his fiancée, Julie, were having afternoon tea with the ship's captain, but Clint Walker had joined them—after making a phone call to his wife.

"She worries," he'd said with a little smile. He seemed like a good guy.

They'd all been arguing over the best way to steal a thousand-pound, ten-foot-long, torpedo-like object from a highly secure army transport or an even more secure navy base without the Chinese noticing.

But Darcy had overheard a couple of the ship's officers talking excitedly at the coffee urn about some alleged American spy who had the Chinese authorities' knickers all in a twist over on Hainan Island. Which just happened to be where the team was supposed to be stealing that AUV sometime in the next few days.

Now, there was an interesting coincidence.

Except Darcy didn't believe in coincidences.

So between interjecting her opinions on the various outlandish operational proposals being tossed around, she was scouring the Internet for information about this supposed American spy.

Turned out the Chinese somehow knew the guy's name, and had gotten hold of his passport photo, and they were plastering it all over the Chinese media in hopes a conscientious citizen would spot him and turn him in.

She dug further, and learned that—

*Je*sus. Kiptyn Llowell was a major in Marine Corps Intelligence—the MCOIB. What the hell was a *Marine* doing in China? She was pretty sure Marine Corps Intelligence concerned itself almost exclusively with war theater recon. And as far as she knew there were no impending U.S. battles in China.

The whole thing smelled fishy to her, start to finish.

"I still say we hijack the transport," Alex Zane was saying, continuing the debate on mission strategy, "before the AUV reaches the navy base. It's the only reasonable option."

"I agree," Walker said. "Once it passes through security at Yulin, kiss it goodbye."

"There's not enough time to prepare," Quinn argued, shaking his head. "The truck has already left the factory." He held up a hand to forestall Zane's response. "Yeah, it's up north near Shanghai. It'll take another day to get to Yulin, but that's still too short a time to put together a plan with any chance of success and getting away alive."

They'd gone around and around on that same argument at least ten times.

Commander Bridger had stayed silent for the most part, leaning back in his chair, ankles crossed, keeping one ear on the conversation while devoting most of his attention to his tablet. Darcy assumed he was getting constant reports on the other ops STORM Corps was conducting worldwide. It was highly unusual for Bridger to be out on a mission at all, let alone hanging about for so long. Especially with another STORM Board of Command member already on the team. She wondered about that.

Bobby Lee was coming up to his two-year mark as a commander. Maybe Bridger was here to do an eval on his performance.

Rand Jaeger was also staying quiet, but that was par for the course. The South African Jaeger was terse and more than a little mysterious. Like her, he was a computer geek of the first order and grand master of anything high-tech. Tall, rangy, and sandy-haired, he had wire-rimmed glasses framing eyes that missed nothing. If he'd spend more than five minutes a year outside and put a little color onto that pale skin, he'd be a great-looking guy.

For a com spec, Jaeger rarely spoke, just fixed it so others could. So when he suddenly sat up at his laptop and said in his quirky Afrikaans accent, "Hey. That spy. He drove off a cliff and got killed," everyone turned to him in surprise.

"What spy?" Zane asked, clueless.

"He's got a girl with him, too. Some woman from the State Department he kidnapped at a village market."

"Is she dead, too?" Bridger asked, fingers poised over his tablet.

"Looks that way."

"What fucking spy?" repeated Zane.

Just then, Captain Jenson strode up to the table looking annoyed. "He's not a real spy. He's an MCOIB operator we sent in as a decoy for your op. Some damn idiot in D.C. leaked his cover a day early," he muttered, slashing a hand through his hair. "What a damn goatfuck."

Stunned, Darcy didn't even see Commander Bridger get to his feet. But all at once he was towering over the much shorter Jenson, scowling down at him.

Uh-oh. Speaking of idiots . . .

Darcy kept her face scrupulously neutral. If she weren't sitting, she'd be taking a giant step backward. Bridger had been her boss for more than six years and she knew the man did not suffer fools.

This guy was definitely a fool.

"Are you actually saying," the commander said deceptively mildly, "that you sent a U.S. Marine into a high risk area inside enemy territory on a *ghost mission*? And then deliberately *blew his cover*?"

Bridger's expression was so unreadable the oblivious idiot had no idea he was about to get an ass-whooping of epic proportions.

"You know as well as I do, Commander, that good military strategy sometimes requires sacrifices from the men on the ground." Jenson waved it off. "Major Llowell volunteered for this mission. He knew the risks, Commander."

She could see Bridger's jaw work. Just a little. He said, "Apparently he *didn't* know the risks."

Jenson continued to dig his career grave. "The point is, his part of the plan was critical. He was creating a diversion. Drawing fire so your men could sneak in and do the real job." The navy captain's eyes narrowed, jumping to all the wrong conclusions at Bridger's interrogation. "A job STORM Corps already took, along with the hefty government check that came with it. I trust you're not trying to back out, Commander, now that you see how difficult it's going to be."

The sudden silence was deafening.

Darcy snorted into it. Aloud. She couldn't help it. What a freaking ass-hat.

Bridger darted her a hard look.

"Sorry, sir. Just slipped out." She knew better than to smile.

The job may be complicated, but the team totally had this. Hell, they'd only just started brainstorming. They were damn good at what they did. The best in the world. They'd get that AUV, there wasn't a doubt in her mind. And the navy knew it, too, or she wouldn't be sitting here now in the South China Sea getting the rundown on a mission the navy wanted to maintain deniability on.

"Would you come with me for a moment?" the Commander said to Jenson and strode out of the room without a backward glance. The captain huffed indignantly at being ordered around by a PMC, regardless of his rank, but stalked after him nonetheless.

"It's not nice to annoy the clients, sugar," Quinn said, no doubt referring to the escaped snort, but there was a steel edge to his slow drawl.

"The guy must not value his balls," she muttered. "I'd hate to be him right about now. Or the brain trust who gave that order. When the Commander gets back to D.C. it'll be soprano city."

Zane and Jaeger singsonged in unison, "Dog-meat."

Clint Walker looked positively grim. "Fuckers," he growled. "Don't know about you all, but I am now officially angry."

"That makes five of us." Bobby Lee turned to face them all, his tired eyes burning with purpose. "All right, people, time to get serious."

8

DeAnne and Kip had walked for over an hour when they reached the crest of a rise. He halted suddenly and she nearly ran into him.

"What is it?" she asked, catching her breath. She hoped he intended to stop for a break. He'd been driving them relentlessly on their trek up the mountain, through the dense lower jungles and up into the higher elevations of the evergreen forests above the fields and valleys. She wasn't used to this much exercise all in one dose. She wasn't complaining, though. The more distance they put between themselves and those maniacs with the machine guns, the better.

He just gave her a smile and indicated the view. He slipped off his backpack and to her surprise, pulled out a camera.

She stepped up next to him in a small clearing at the very top of the rise. People must have stopped here to admire the view for centuries. Heck, millennia.

He fiddled with the camera.

"Gee, you really are taking pictures."

"Yep. Well, hopefully. The camera was damaged, so I'm still testing it under different conditions. Want to make sure it works correctly."

He raised it to his eye, and she turned to the view, taking it all in as he started to click away.

Before them, the lush, emerald hillside cascaded downward, curving elegantly away from the high, amethyst mountains that framed it perfectly to either side, and dipping down to a crisp, meandering valley. Every acre below the ridge was covered either in a fluttering white blanket of flowering fruit trees, or carved into stair-step terraces overflowing with a patchwork of verdant green fields. The warm breeze carried the scents of peach blossoms and freshly turned soil. Small flocks of birds soared and swooped through the valley calling to one another, and the sound of cowbells jingled softly in the distance.

You could almost reach out and touch the tranquility.

"Oh!" she whispered on a sigh, completely enchanted.

This was the China she loved.

But deep down, she knew it was more than the beauty that drew her. It was what the scene below represented. The snug, simple normalcy of it.

A perfection that for her was at once both achingly familiar . . . and achingly elusive. Unobtainable.

"Beautiful, isn't it?" he said, and let the camera dangle by a strap around his neck. He pulled a bottle of water from his backpack. With a smile, he cracked the top off and handed it to her.

"Incredibly. And so peaceful." It was hard to imagine that just two hours ago they'd been driving like madmen, being pursued by angry soldiers determined to kill them.

"Calm before the storm," he murmured.

"Don't you mean after?" She tipped back the bottle gratefully and drank.

He lifted his camera and clicked several pictures of her drinking, then slanted her a look. "Doubtful."

She matched his wry expression and handed him back the bottle. "We'll see."

He just grunted, but didn't appear particularly concerned. He tipped the bottle to his lips, closed his eyes, and drank heavily. Under his square jaw, the cords in his throat stood out and his Adam's apple bobbed. She watched, mesmerized by the raw sensuality of the man, until he lowered the bottle and wiped his lips with the back of his hand.

He could slip seamlessly into the scene below. Honest. Uncomplicated. Elemental.

He caught her staring, and gave her a lazy smile. "Penny for your thoughts."

She fought a blush but couldn't look away to save her life. "You'd be overpaying," she managed lightly.

He held her gaze for a long moment and his eyes said he didn't agree. But he didn't push it.

"Why don't you try the cell phone?" He reached into his pocket and handed it to her.

"Hmm?" She gave herself a mental shake, emerging from her brain fog. Phone? "Oh. Right." Good grief, what was wrong with her today?

Then she realized what he'd just done. She frowned. "Wait. This is *my* phone!"

"Uh-huh." He lifted the camera and snapped her picture.

"You took it out of *your* pocket."

"Uh-huh." The camera whirred again.

"Would you stop that!" She was flabbergasted. "You *stole* my phone?"

He lowered the camera and the look on his face was singularly unrepentant. "I prefer the term 'borrowed.' "

Her jaw dropped. "*Permanently* borrowed! Why would you do that?"

He shrugged. "I needed a phone, and I thought we were about to part company. The soldiers would have taken it from you at the checkpoint, anyway, when you turned yourself in."

Of all the—

She snapped her mouth shut. Oddly disappointed. "You could just have asked."

"Next time." He winked, and stuffed the camera back in his backpack. When she didn't smile, he said, "Princess, I'm sorry. You're right. I should have asked."

Princess?

She jerked her attention back to the phone in her hand. With an exhale, she gave up and turned it on. "No. You have no reason to be. You had more important things to think about than—"

"DeAnne."

Reluctantly, she looked up at him.

His eyes were gentle. Sincere. "Next time I'll trust you."

She felt a little twist in her heart. She wanted to nod, but couldn't. "Okay," she said, her voice sounding embarrassingly vulnerable. She cleared her throat, shook herself out of it, and said lightly, "I'm kind of hoping there won't be a next time."

He turned back to the view, banded his arms over his chest, one hand still clutching the water bottle, and said, "Yeah. Me, too."

She held the phone up higher—as if *that* would make a difference—and checked for bars, pointing it at the mountain he'd indicated with a cell tower sprouting from the top. She could just make it out, a vertical silver glint against the robin's egg sky in the fading sunlight.

A bar flickered onto the screen. Success! Sort of.

"The signal's very weak, but it might go through."

"I assume it's your throwaway?" he suddenly asked.

She nodded as she punched numbers. "Yeah."

Every FSO had an official duty phone while in-country, but they were also encouraged to obtain a couple of prepaid—therefore untraceable—phones for their private use and for emergencies. The Chinese government was notorious for carefully monitoring all phone and Internet traffic within its borders. No right to privacy here.

She listened closely, but the signal kept breaking up, and finally cut off completely. "Nope," she said. "No luck."

"Didn't think so," he said, watching her with an unreadable expression. "We have to get higher up the mountain, closer to the tower."

She groaned inwardly, but forced a smile. "Yeah."

His intent gaze scanned her from head to toe, then lingered on her legs. "You okay to go on? That was quite a hill we just climbed."

"I'm good," she assured him.

As if she'd say otherwise. The truth was, her thighs were on fire and her feet were about to fall off. But she'd asked to come along on this jaunt, and she had her pride.

"Mm-hmm."

She searched the crest of the next ridge for the path. "How much farther do you think we should go?"

"I'm thinking," he said slowly, "we should go all the way."

A shift in his tone made her look back at him. He was still studying her body, his arms folded over his chest. His expression hadn't changed a millimeter. But his eyes . . .

Ho-boy.

His eyes were dark as sin. Slumberous. *Hungry.*

A sudden ache of sexual awareness flared in her throat.

"Definitely all the way," he murmured, his voice low and suggestive. "Here. Drink." He pulled his gaze up and handed her back the water bottle, which still contained an inch or two of liquid. "You need to stay hydrated."

A vivid memory of his lips caressing the plastic rim as he drank rushed through her whole body. She swallowed down a burst of desire.

His eyes held hers as the shadow of a challenge passed through them.

A spear of heat arrowed straight to the tips of her breasts. The languid invitation was unmistakable.

He wanted her.

Her pulse thundered.

Should she accept? *Or run like hell?*

She would never consider a serious relationship with this man. She knew his type all too well; she'd never inflict that kind of misery on herself. Eighteen years had been plenty, thankyouverymuch.

But . . .

She knew exactly what Major Llowell was asking her for.

And it wasn't a relationship.

They had more chemistry together than she'd ever felt before in her life. More than she'd ever known was even possible. They were stuck on a mountain, thrown together by fate, kept together by necessity, but once she'd negotiated his safe passage out of the country, they'd likely never see each other again.

Did that matter?

The thought produced a prick of disappointment in her chest. But despite that— No, it was better this way.

He seemed nice. Considerate. Stable. But that could all be a mask hiding the real man underneath. Nice, considerate men did not become military spec operators or spies. Those men were aggressive thrill-seekers who needed a constant adrenaline rush, however they had to find it.

Which didn't make for a good relationship.

Other than the kind he was offering.

The rush of male adrenaline could make *that* kind of relationship very, very good.

Thrilling. Exciting. *Breathless.*

But this wasn't like her.

And yet, he was so darn sexy he made her toes curl.

They were both adults.

And she wanted this. Just once in her life, she wanted to experience the rush of sexual adrenaline. Be the object of that kind of explosive desire.

Just once.

What was the harm?

Without letting herself think, she reached out and took the bottle from him.

Deliberately letting her tongue touch the rim of the opening, she raised it to her lips. And savored the rest of the water. It was probably her imagination—which was definitely working overtime—but she swore she could taste him on it.

Musty, spicy, male.

His eyes darkened as he watched her drink, his lids lowering. She gathered up the last drop with her tongue, then slowly handed the bottle back to him.

The intensity of his regard made her knees weaken. Goose bumps shivered over her breasts.

"Okay," he said, his voice deep and low.

Then, he turned and started to walk, heading up toward the next mountain. Where God alone knew what would happen between them.

"Okay," she whispered.

Terrified.

Exhilarated.

And wondered if she'd just made the very worst decision of her entire life.

Or . . . quite possibly . . . the very best?

9

The woman was seriously messing with his head.

Hell. *Both* heads.

Kip ground his teeth in frustration. One had been in a constant state of turmoil and the other in a constant state of arousal since meeting the unexpectedly tempting DeAnne Lovejoy.

Hell.

As they continued trudging their way up the steep trail, he attempted to make himself see reason. He did not *need* any more complications right now. This mission had already been compromised enough. First the destructive parachute landing. Then his cover being mysteriously blown. Getting chased and shot at. *And* he'd deliberately made it look like he'd kidnapped a U.S. State Department official—which had been the right thing to do to keep her career out of trouble . . . but not great for his. Having sex with her on top of all that would probably put Colonel

Jackson right over the edge. And get Kip yanked from the field and stuck behind a desk so fast his head would spin.

Which was the absolute last thing Kip wanted.

He'd wanted this op.

More like needed it.

He was sliding down the back side of his thirties, and was nervous about keeping his position as a field intelligence operator. For the past couple of years he'd been volunteering for the toughest, most dangerous ops that came up. Just to prove he still had it in him.

In his younger days in Force Recon, and later when he was promoted into the new Marine Special Operations Intelligence Battalion, his reputation for keen instincts, reckless daring, and a velvet hand as a team leader had earned him a fast track up through the ranks. But covert reconnaissance was a young man's game. He'd been feeling the pressure from on high for a while now to accept one of the more sedentary, less risky jobs with SOCOM—Special Ops Command.

You're too good an analyst and advisor to be wasted in the field, Llowell. We need you alive and planning the ops, not chasing around the world putting your neck on the line.

Sure, it would be a good promotion, but the thought of sitting behind a desk for the rest of his career made Kip break out in hives.

Luckily, this time he was also the best man for the job.

His skill with a camera was the one thing that gave him an edge over his younger colleagues. The young smartasses called him Zoom. But they were just jealous because the old man could still whip their butts on every level.

This op was critical. The navy rep had warned that failure was not an option. But Kip's unlucky landing while parachuting in had as good as doomed the mission before it started. A sudden wind shear had whipped him off course, right up the rugged side of the mountain instead of the softer jungle vegetation at the foot of it, tossing him and his equipment like confetti into the thick forest at the top. It had taken all his skill to avoid the dagger-like pine trees and not impale himself, but he hadn't been able to avoid the jumble of boulders he'd landed on. His backpack had fared even worse.

The camera had survived, but not the telephoto lens. With that damaged, there'd be no close-up of the cutting-edge AUV the Chinese would soon be using to spy on U.S. military installations and commercial ports—and anything else they wanted to—along America's coastlines. The U.S. Navy scientists working on countermeasures would be designing blind. *Not good.*

Which was why Kip had been so hell-bent on getting a ride back down to Sanya. There was no way he'd leave China without completing his mission. So he'd arranged for Jake Warner, his second in command in the unit, to meet him in the busy tourist town with a hastily scrounged replacement lens.

But somehow, Kip's cover had been blown. Sanya would now be crawling with cops and soldiers searching for him.

He needed to make contact with Jake and move their rendezvous point before either of them was caught.

DeAnne's State Department intervention could prove a useful distraction. There wasn't a chance in hell her plan to get him out would work. But it might just pull the dogs off him long enough to meet Jake and get what he needed.

As long as he didn't let *himself* get any more distracted than he already was.

Jesus. He'd really gone off the rails this time. His behavior was so out of character he didn't even recognize himself.

On the other hand . . . Damn, it would be so insanely sweet to have DeAnne Lovejoy.

Naked.

Moaning his name . . .

A vibrant image of her bare body moving rhythmically under his almost made him groan out loud. Somewhere along the line Ms. Practical had turned into Ms. Practically Irresistible.

Make that Totally Irresistible.

Damn, the woman was really getting under his skin, making him itch in ways he hadn't itched in years.

Of all the inappropriate times to regress into a hormonal teenager. How had that *happened*?

Indecision had him waffling back and forth between being smart and employed . . . or being happily sated.

Should he, or should he not, drag the delectable Ms. Lovejoy down on the ground, ruck up her sensible skirt, and fuck her till she screamed his name? That was the burning question.

He'd more or less promised. And she'd more or less accepted.

Didn't seem right not to follow through . . .

His mind went round and round.

But before he had a chance to decide one way or another, the sound of voices drifted down from the trail ahead.

Shit.

He turned swiftly and DeAnne looked up. He put a finger to his lips. "Someone's coming," he silently mouthed, and reached for her hand. Tugging her off the path, he pulled her up into the cover of the thick forest vegetation. She stumbled, swallowing a gasp, and he caught her around the waist to keep her from falling. She grabbed him for balance and ended up plastered against his chest.

A potent mixture of needing to find a safe hiding place . . . and liking the feel of her body against his . . . made him sweep her up in his arms to carry her.

"Kip!" she squeaked in a whisper. "Put me—"

"Shhh," he admonished as he moved quietly up the slope at a fast, if slightly uneven, clip.

The voices were approaching quickly.

After a short hesitation, she slid her arms around his neck and hung on. "Soldiers?" she asked in the barest of whispers.

His mouth brushed close to her ear. "Probably locals. We may have been spotted on the trail."

She tipped her head back to meet his gaze, her eyes filled with alarm.

He shook his head. "They won't find us," he barely whispered.

Her hold on him tightened, and a rush of protectiveness flooded through him. Whatever happened, he would not let any harm come to her.

He ducked behind an evergreen and stepped into the thick tangle of its low, spreading branches. They were instantly enveloped by the prickly feel of stiff, fragrant needles and the pungent scent of pine sap.

He carefully released her legs and let her slide to her feet, but kept his arms around her, tucking her head against his shoulder. She stayed there, holding him close.

It felt good. Really good.

So good he almost missed the voices and footsteps of a man and woman hurrying past.

A moment later, DeAnne whispered, "They were arguing over what kind of seeds to plant."

Right. She spoke Chinese. At her translation, his shoulders notched down a bit. But he made no move to release her. And she made no move to pull away.

He circled his arms more snugly around her. He loved how her curves pressed into his body, soft and warm. Perfect. He spread his feet apart and urged her into the V of his legs, bringing them center to center.

He felt her inhale sharply. But she didn't resist. She melted against him. He went hard again, thick and pulsing with want. He could tell she noticed. Her body adjusted with a subtle undulation of her hips, pressing against him. *Jesus.* Did she know what she was doing to him?

He grasped her practical ponytail and wound it around his palm, pulling her head back so her face was forced to tip up to his.

"Kip," she whispered, her voice a silken thread, her eyes molten.

It was nearly his undoing.

He loved the sound of his name on her lips. And the blush of desire on her cheeks. *Desire for him.* His cock thickened even more. His nostrils flared, drinking in the scent of her skin, dewy with the sweet, honest sweat of exertion, more intoxicating than any frilly perfume.

He wanted to kiss her so badly he almost shook with the self-restraint it took not to lower his mouth and take what he wanted.

He held her head immobile, slowly dipped his lips to her ear, and murmured, "God, I want you naked."

He felt a tremor go through her. Several heartbeats went by. "You mean . . . here? Now?" she whispered shakily.

The corner of his lip curled. *Scared, but willing.* He ran his hand over her ass, pressing his fingers deep into the dips in her skirt formed by the contours of her bottom. Her heartbeat quickened. He could feel its *thump a-thump a-thump* against his chest.

"No," he said, brushing his mouth over the shell of her ear. "I want to take all night with you. Fuck you breathless. But we still have ground to cover today."

Her lips parted against his throat and she swallowed, making a soft, incoherent sound.

"I'm not going to kiss you," he said. "If I do, it'll be all over."

She shuddered out an exhale, sounding strangled and breathy.

"Okay?" he asked. He wanted to hear her voice. To be sure she felt the same crazy need.

"Okay," she whispered.

She did.

He held her tight for another few seconds, then somehow found the strength of will to grasp her by the arms and set her away from him. He met her gaze one last time, sharing a look that could have powered New York for a week.

Then he took her hand again and helped her down the slope and back to the trail. "There's a cell tower on the next mountaintop over," he told her. "We should be able to make that phone call once we reach the crest up ahead."

She nodded, her expression a potent blend of desire, frustration, and fear. "All right."

Then she seemed to gather herself. "We— We're twelve hours ahead here. So it'll be"—she slid her hand from his and checked her watch—"around four a.m. in Washington." Her lips twitched. Not exactly a smile, but close. "Roger will be thrilled."

Hold on. "Roger?" An unbidden bolt of jealousy lanced through him.

She blinked. "Roger Achity, Deputy Assistant Secretary. My boss."

He took an involuntary step toward her. "You call your boss by his first name?"

She backed up. "Don't you?"

He scowled. "I call my boss colonel or sir."

This time she held her ground. "Well, the State Department is less formal than the military, I guess."

He was seized with an overwhelming urge to interrogate her about her exact relationship with this Roger Achity guy. With difficulty, he reined it in.

None of your damn business, he told himself.

"No doubt," he gritted out.

He shut his mouth before something completely inappropriate came out of it, then turned and continued up the trail.

Like he said, totally messing with his heads.

And every other damn part of him, too.

"Kip!"

He halted, looked back, and realized DeAnne must have called him several times. She'd stopped a ways back on the trail, and was holding her cell phone in her hand.

He saw to his surprise that they'd reached the top of the ridge.

"Sorry," he called back. "Gathering wool. What's up?"

"I got a signal."

Ah. "That's good," he said, and backtracked to where she was standing.

At least he hoped it was good.

Suddenly, he wasn't so sure anymore. State Department personnel were notorious for being officious rule followers. What if instead of negotiating on his behalf, they ordered her to turn him in to the Chinese authorities? What if she refused, and got fired for trying to help him instead? For aligning herself with a known spy? Her mandate to help U.S. citizens abroad only applied to those citizens who weren't embroiled in international espionage.

She put the phone to her ear. "It's ringing."

They could both be in big trouble.

"Wait!" he said, and covered the last few yards to her in two steps. "I—"

But she held up a finger at him and nodded.

Too late.

"It's DeAnne."

He just had to pray she knew what she was doing.

"Hi Roger."

And that he didn't end up strangling that Roger Achity.

10

"De*Anne*?"

Roger's voice halted for a stunned second, then burst through the connection loud and clear. "Christ have *mercy*, woman! We all thought you were *dead*!"

"Oh, gosh no, I'm—"

"Where the *hell* are you and why haven't you called in before now? I'm over the Pacific on a frigging Air Force transport plane on my way to China to find your damn dead body."

"There's no— I'm not—" He was on his way to *China*?

"We've all been sick about this. My God, DeAnne! What the *fuck* happened to you?"

DeAnne cringed at the tirade. She'd never heard her boss swear so much in under five seconds. "I'm sorry, Roger. We've been out of signal range, and—"

"*We?* Who the hell's we?" he demanded.

Leave it to Roger to zero in instantly on the one important detail. He also sounded suspiciously like he already knew who the other half of the "we" was, and just needed a confirmation.

She decided to play along. Circumspectly. In case the call was being monitored. "Um. You remember that certain citizen we were speculating about the day before I left?" She glanced at Kip, who was watching her, stone-faced, arms crossed over his broad chest.

"I'm listening." No surprise in Roger's voice. Of course, there wouldn't be. If he thought she'd died when the SUV went over the cliff, then obviously she must be with the spy.

"Well, I um, happened across him . . . that is, he happened across me and Ms. Tanner—Chrissie, you know the art dealer I was escorting?—in a marketplace and—"

"He's with you now?" Roger interrupted.

"Yes."

"I'm hanging up now. Stand by for instructions. Ten minutes."

"Wait! Rog—"

The connection cut off.

She held out the phone, looked at it, and blew out a breath of frustration. "Well, *that* was rude." And unusual for Roger. He was a consummate diplomat. Something must really have rattled him. "He thought I was dead," she said to Kip, who was still staring at her through narrowed eyes.

"Good. Our plan worked," he said. "What's going on now?"

"Heck if I know. He's on his way over here." Not exactly the reaction she'd expected from her boss, that was for sure. Although, she supposed . . . Darn, she hadn't really considered the embassy's reaction to the SUV accident. She hoped her "death" hadn't caused any trouble.

"To China?"

"Yeah." She bit her lip. "I think he's calling Washington. He said to stand by for instructions."

Kip paused for a beat, then said, "I don't like it. Instructions for what?"

She ventured, "For bringing you in, I suppose."

"Or *turning* me in. What if he's calling the Chinese authorities?" he said, his voice tight. He searched her face. "What if he orders you to hand me over to them?"

"I'd never do that!" she exclaimed.

"Even if it meant losing your job?"

"Of c—" She faltered halfway through the protest.

His mouth thinned and he started to turn away.

In that second, she knew she could never betray this man.

She reached out and grasped his forearm. "Yes," she said with conviction. "Even if it means my job. I said I'd help you. I keep my promises."

The taut edges in his face slowly eased. "You don't have to do that. Just promise you'll tell me if that's what he wants."

"I promise," she said, looking him straight in the eye.

He inhaled and nodded. "Okay. I trust you." Then he pointed to the phone. "My turn."

DeAnne handed Kip the phone and asked, "Who are you going to call?"

"Friend of mine." She didn't know who he worked for, and he meant to keep it that way. The less she knew, the better.

Just in case.

He punched in Jake Warner's number. Fun and games were over. Time to get the real show on the road.

"Joe's Bar and Grill," came the reply after three rings. SOP when a strange or blocked number came up.

"I need to change a takeaway order I phoned in yesterday," Kip said.

There was a rustle, then Jake said, "Thank God you

called." He sounded agitated. "That takeaway order is—Fuck it," he said, jettisoning the code-speak. "You were set up, man. You need to get the fucking hell out of there."

Kip straightened. "What are you talking about?"

"Tony was scanning for chatter, keeping tabs on the situation over there, and came across some encrypted e-mails referring to the 'decoy' on Hainan and how someone had jumped the gun on blowing his cover."

Kip felt a jolt of shock, then a thick core of ice drilled down the center of his body. That explained a lot. "Who?" he asked.

"Tony couldn't decipher where the e-mails originated."

If Tony couldn't, no one could.

Kip digested for a moment. If he was just a decoy, something else was going down. "What's the real op?"

"Seems to be the same objective," Jake said. "Or close. But apparently some team has been sent out. Not one of ours, though." He sounded somewhat mystified.

So was Kip. If the objective was the same, why send a whole team to do something one man could do much more quietly and efficiently?

"Get down to the coast," Jake told him. "One of the big hotels with lots of foreigners. We'll arrange an extraction."

Which Kip knew was code for the team would go AWOL and come get him. He was also well aware of the repercussions that action would likely result in for all of them. "Stay put," he ordered. "I'm serious. No sense all of us getting in trouble. I'll figure something out."

There was a pause. "You sure?"

"Absolutely."

He could hear the reluctance in his friend's voice when he said, "All right. But I'll keep this channel open. Ping if you need us."

"I will." *He wouldn't.* "Thanks. And thank Tony for the heads-up."

"Be safe, bro."

Kip hit the "off" button and wordlessly handed the phone back to DeAnne. Her eyes were glued to his face, worry etched on her own.

"What's happened?" she asked.

He considered keeping his mouth shut. Or even lying. But she had just given him a promise to be straight with him. It was the least he could do to be honest with her in return.

"Looks like I'm on my own out here," he said, his feelings walking a thin line between betrayal and fury. Her gaze held his, brimming with concern, and he felt a complicated knot of emotion tighten in his chest. "Other than you," he added. And hoped that came out tender and appreciative, not whiney like a two-year-old.

"I don't understand," she said, sounding confused.

"Hell, neither do I." He paced away from her, rubbing a hand over his short-cropped hair. A dozen possibilities logjammed in his mind. "Someone deliberately blew my cover. Someone from *our* side."

Her eyes widened. "Who? Why would they do that?"

"That's a damn good question," he gritted out. "Believe me, I intend to get some answers."

She swallowed, watched him pace for a few moments, then asked, "What should we do?"

He halted and took in the sight of her—her practical clothes and sensible shoes all disheveled and dusty from hiking, her ponytail all sagging and crooked so tendrils of chestnut hair had escaped to feather around her face and neck. He'd never seen anyone more beautiful in his life. And she looked so earnest and upset for him, his heart completely melted. Another flood of protectiveness washed over him, ten times stronger than the first.

There wasn't a chance in hell he'd drag her any further into this . . . whatever the hell this was.

He limped over to her and gently took her face between his hands. "You need to go back to your embassy and forget about me," he said. She started to protest, but he moved a thumb over her lips. "I'm so damn sorry I got you mixed up in this shit, DeAnne. You're so— Damn, princess, I really wish—" He cut off what he was about to say. *No sense going there.* "You need to get back to where it's safe. Away from me."

"Kip—"

"No arguing. I mean it."

She wanted to argue, he could tell. But just then her phone rang. She glanced down at it and puffed out a breath.

"Tell Roger what's-his-name you need to be picked up. I'll take you as far as the main road."

She looked mutinous. The phone rang again.

She checked the number, hit the "talk" button, and without preamble said, "So what's the plan for getting him off this island?"

Kip hiked his brows. Had she not heard a word he said?

She listened impatiently on the phone for a few moments, then said, "I understand that. So what's the plan?"

A muscled twitched in her jaw. *Uh-oh.* But for once her face was unreadable.

"I see." She listened. "Oh?" She listened some more, and the muscle twitched again. "Trust me, yes, I do know. So what are you going to *do* about it?"

Kip had heard enough. "Tell him you need transport, DeAnne."

She glared at him. "Roger? What are you not telling me about this situation?"

Somewhere along the line her voice had acquired a razor-sharp edge. As she listened, the edge shifted to her eyes.

"No," she said in growing agitation. Then, "No!" And, "I said *no*." Then she got very, very calm.

It was downright scary how she did that.

"Roger?" She smiled serenely at Kip, her face a one-eighty from seconds before. "Roger, listen. Will you please listen to me?"

Finally. She was finally going to ask to be picked up.

"Rog— Roger—"

Kip began to relax. She'd soon be out of here and safe.

"*Roger!* Will you shut up and *listen*, for Pete's sake?" she snapped. She took a breath, and said, "Because I am only going to say this once."

She smiled at Kip again when his eyes went big at her strident tone.

"Thank you. Are you listening?" She lifted her chin and spoke very succinctly. "Roger. I. *Quit.*"

Wait.

What?

She pressed the phone's "off" button very firmly and exhaled. "Lord, that felt good."

But Kip was feeling the opposite of good. What had she just *done*? "Are you *nuts*? You can't quit!" he exploded.

"Oh, but I just did."

He was horrified. "But why? Call him back. Tell him you were kidding."

"Not going to happen."

"What the *fuck*?"

This time her smile was genuine, if tremulous. Those guileless blue eyes looked up at him, filling with the uncertain reality of what she'd just done. She cleared her throat. "Well, Major Llowell. Looks like you're stuck with me for the foreseeable future."

11

Darcy was feeling restless again.

It happened every now and then. More so lately.

She opened her eyes and checked her watch, careful not to wake Bobby Lee. They were sharing the narrow bottom bunk and, as always for the past two years, he was spooned up against her, his back to the door, one arm thrown protectively around her, his Ruger P345 tucked under the pillow.

She still hadn't gotten used to sleeping with him. Well, with anybody, really. *Sleeping* sleeping. This close. All of the time. There were nights she thought she'd never get used to it.

As much as she loved him.

The team had decided to grab a couple precious hours of shut-eye before resuming the heated debate over how best to execute their mission. Despite her head spinning from exhaustion, Darcy had woken up several times. Now the alarm was about to go off, and she felt even more drained than she had before lying down.

"What is it, sugar?" Bobby Lee whispered in her ear. "I could bounce quarters off your muscles. Why so tense?"

She had an inkling, but it wasn't something she wanted to discuss. Not with Bobby Lee. And certainly not with Jaeger and Zane sleeping in the other bunks six feet away. Even though her soft whisper was unlikely to be heard above the steady, ambient rumble of the ship's engines.

"Can't stop thinking," she said quietly, knowing he'd assume she meant about the mission. Bobby Lee was laser focused while on an op.

"It's a bitch," he agreed, his soft Alabama drawl smooth as Southern Comfort. "But we'll figure somethin'."

"Yeah."

"Meanwhile, you need to relax." His voice was barely a whisper as he slid his hand up under her tank top to her breast.

She stifled a small gasp that turned to a breathy moan as his long fingers gently grasped her nipple and squeezed.

"Stop," she said on an inhale, but her body reacted all on its own. Her backside wriggled against him, finding the hard erection she'd known would be there and pressing into it.

She felt his breath quicken, stirring her hair.

He found her other breast and tugged at that nipple, making electric streaks of need stab through her. "Bobby . . ."

"Hush now, baby. Just relax," he soothed, his hand on her breasts having the opposite effect.

His other hand slipped down the front of her PJ shorts. She wanted to move away. She wasn't into public exhibition. But his fingers found her and she was lost. He'd always known just how to melt her body and her willpower to warm molasses. A soft moan escaped.

"That's right," he quietly urged.

His fingertips teased and slid, circling the slick center of need that instantly throbbed for his touch. She writhed a little, seeking more, her mind a blissful blank, absorbed in the pleasure only he could give her.

She felt his head lift and his lips trailed over her temple, warm and moist and loving. His hand enveloped her breast, powerful and possessive. She felt totally secure, completely loved, and hopelessly in love.

So why couldn't she give him what he wanted?

A date. That's all he wanted from her.

A wedding date.

He held her tighter, and increased the pressure of his fingertips. He twisted a nipple, and she had to bite her lip to keep from crying out.

His tongue trailed down the shell of her ear and pulled her earlobe into his mouth. He sucked on the sensitive lobe, making her writhe. He knew that always drove her mad with want.

He was relentless, and it didn't take long for the first trembles of orgasm to take over her body. His fingers flicked over her need, around the aching nub, driving her deeper toward the hurtling climax.

It hit hard, just as his hand clamped over her mouth.

Her body quaked in a silent explosion of pleasure, and she rode it to the very end, letting herself go, absorbing the pure, sweet ecstasy of Bobby Lee's touch, knowing he held her in his powerful arms, and that she was safe in his care.

When she'd finally stilled, he kissed her hair and lowered his hand from her mouth, but held her fast when she tried to turn to face him.

"Sleep, sugar. We've still got a few minutes."

She let out a sigh and drifted on the sea of contentment, lulled by the rumbling of the engines.

And resolved that tomorrow she'd do it for sure.

She'd pick her wedding date.

She really would.

"It's getting too dark to see the trail," DeAnne said from behind Kip.

He had pushed them longer than he'd planned, but he'd wanted to get as far as possible down toward the coast, now that they'd made their phone calls.

"Yeah. I've been looking for a place to stop," he told her. He'd taken a different route down the mountain, so wasn't totally sure of the possibilities.

Not only was it getting too dark to see, but they were also approaching the lower valleys where more and more villages would start to spring up along their path. If he were alone, he'd take full advantage of the nighttime to get past them unseen, but he didn't want to risk DeAnne falling in the darkness and getting injured.

"We should find something soon."

"Um . . ." she glanced around hesitantly. "You mean . . . like, here? Outside?"

Right. She definitely looked like a city girl, from a family that stayed in fancy hotels when they traveled, not makeshift campsites. He slanted her an apologetic grimace. "Not a lot of choice, I'm afraid. By now everyone's probably heard about the dangerous American spy on the loose." He made a face. "I don't think we dare ask for shelter, even if you do speak the lingo."

She blinked a few times and nibbled on her lip. "Okay."

"We'll be all right. Nights are warm this time of year. And I saw you put a jacket in your shoulder bag, right?"

She was resting her hands on it in front of her. She looked down, as if she'd forgotten all about it. "Oh. Yeah. It's a down jac— The thing is, I'm not really . . ." Her words trailed off.

She suddenly looked so damn vulnerable. Not like the strong spitfire he'd come to know.

"Not a camper, eh?"

She shook her head.

"Come here." He reached out and pulled her into his arms, nestling her close against his chest. "You are amazing, you know that?"

She made a snorting noise into his peasant jacket.

"I'm serious, DeAnne. You're incredibly brave, and haven't complained once, even though I'm making you hike through the jungle in a damn business suit and camp in the middle of nowhere, all while being chased by nasty guys with big guns. Jesus, princess, you even gave up your damn *job* for me. I'd call that fucking amazing."

He felt her breath sough onto his chest in a puff of warmth. "I didn't quit for you. It was on principle."

Which was a good thing. He didn't need *that* on his conscience, too. "You quit because your boss was disregarding his prime directive, to protect American citizens."

"Exactly."

She'd told him what Roger Achity had said when she'd called. That they couldn't help Kip because of some order they'd received from higher up. Ol' Roger's hands were tied. Have a nice day. Just as he'd thought.

And in light of what Jake had said, it made perfect sense.

But DeAnne hadn't seen it that way. She'd been outraged.

His little warrior princess.

Okay, not so little. She was tall and curvy, her breasts round and full as they pillowed into his chest.

Which reminded him . . .

He lifted her chin up with a finger, brushed his lips across her cheek, and murmured, "Well, I think you're amazing." *Amazingly desirable . . .*

Her cornflower eyes glistened, like the darkening sky reflected in a clear pool. She looked almost fragile. "Thank you," she whispered. "I . . ."

He bent down and kissed her. She did a tiny intake of breath, then melted into him. She opened to his kiss, warm and willing, and all sensual woman. He raked his fingers into her hair and pulled out the rest of her bedraggled ponytail, luxuriating in the silky feel of the strands as he spread them over her shoulders. And kissed her some more.

Finally, he drew back. "Amazing kisser, too," he murmured, his voice rough with want of her.

She blushed. "Just following your lead."

He liked the sound of that. A lot. But he made himself kiss her forehead, and gathered his willpower to step away from her. They were still on the trail, out in the open and exposed.

"There's a place up ahead I'm hoping will work for us," he said. "And we need to find some food, too. Come on. Just a little farther."

They walked another couple of miles, and he spotted what he'd been looking for. He'd remembered a farm on the map, an outlier that had several outbuildings. With any luck they'd find food and potable water, as well as shelter where they could tuck themselves out of sight to sleep.

And whatever else was going to happen between them.

He hadn't forgotten that part.

She hadn't either, judging by that intense kiss.

"This is it," he said, taking her off the path to a small clearing hidden by a hedge of dense foliage. "You stay here while I take a look around. See what I can scrounge up."

She looked instantly alarmed. "Can't we stay together?"

"I just want to make sure it's safe. I'll be right back."

She reluctantly nodded. He slid off his rucksack, patted the M9 in his shoulder holster and the extra clip in his pocket, and slipped out past the hedge.

He went to check the outbuildings. The first was filled with burlap bags stuffed with manure. He nearly fell over backward from the stench. He'd rather be captured by the PLA than sleep in there.

The next one had chickens. Lots of chickens. He didn't even approach that one. He knew from experience the ruckus those birds would make if anyone invaded their home. They didn't need eggs that bad.

The third shack was better. It was a toolshed, small and

weather-tight with an earthen floor. The four walls and a small table were laden with ancient but pristine iron tools with well-worn wooden handles. Sacks of seed stood in one corner.

This would do. They just needed to be gone before daybreak in case the farmer came looking for his tools or seed.

Now Kip just had to find some food.

It was tempting to grab one of those chickens. A few had escaped the coop and were strutting around pecking at the ground. He'd leave money, of course. But no. The noise factor scared him too much. Then there was the neck wringing and the feather plucking. Not his favorite jobs. And he couldn't even imagine how DeAnne would react to that mess. He grinned in spite of himself. But the real clincher was the fact they'd need to light a fire to cook it. That would be a dead giveaway to the enemy. Not a bright idea.

Good thing he liked fruit. He hoped DeAnne did, too.

Or maybe there was a root cellar around.

It was completely dark by now. But there was a sliver of moon up, giving off just enough light to see the dim outlines of his surroundings. He scanned the orchards and the farm and the hills behind it. *Bingo.*

He made his way carefully through the groves to a wooden door built into the hillside. The underground cellar where the farmer's food stores were kept, if he wasn't mistaken. Kip assumed there wasn't much crime in these parts because it wasn't locked.

Inside, it was cool and dark, and smelled of damp earth and ripe vegetables. He risked turning on his pocket flashlight, and found stacked woven baskets of apples and carrots, potatoes and radishes, and several vegetables he couldn't identify. Bags of rice, beans, and peas were lined up in an orderly row. There were even a few hanging slabs of dried meat. He helped himself to a few of the things that wouldn't need cooking, and sliced off a small portion of the dried meat, filling the roomy pockets of his peasant jacket with enough for tonight and for breakfast in the morning.

After leaving the farmer a generous payment, he cracked open the cellar door and peeked out.

He was greeted by two glowing amber eyes and a deep, throaty growl.

12

Ah, hell.

The dog was big and brown with black spots on its rump and ragged ears. With long, nasty teeth. Every one of which was bared at him.

"Nice doggie," Kip muttered.

He liked dogs. He did. *Usually.* He'd had to deal with many of them over his years of boots-on-ground. Farm dogs could be a bit on the territorial side.

He swiped a hand over his mouth. Bribes sometimes worked.

He dug the slices of meat out of his pocket and tossed one to the growling beast.

It totally ignored the treat.

Figured.

It growled again.

He ducked back into the cellar and shone his flashlight around, grabbing a coil of rope lying on the floor. He tied several large knots in one end, then stretched it taut between his hands, wrapping the other end around his palm, and snapped it a couple of times for good measure. Returning to the door, he opened it wide, took aim at the growling dog, and tossed the rope's knotted end to it.

It lunged at the knots, seizing one between its jaws and started to pull, shaking its head viciously. Its growls sank deeper in its throat as Kip began to yank back on the rope.

No dog he'd ever met could resist playing tug.

He egged it on, teasing it into playing instead of attacking. It didn't take long. The dog wasn't vicious. It had just been doing its job guarding the farm. Now it figured Kip must be a friend, since he was taking the time to play.

"Good doggie," he murmured encouragingly, slowly tugging it toward the cellar door. A few minutes later he'd gotten it past the threshold. This time, when he tossed the sliver of meat, the dog dropped the knotted rope and went to sniff at it.

Kip took the opportunity to make a hasty exit. He closed the door but made sure it would swing open when the dog tried to get out, and took off at a lope in case the dog started barking. But it didn't. Not yet, anyway.

The night was warm and the sky clear. The fields smelled fertile and green, the heavy leaves of the plants whispered against his legs as he brushed past them on his way back to DeAnne.

She was sitting on the ground, bare legs curled under her, holding something between her hands. She looked up sharply when he stepped through the hedge, but her shoulders notched down when she saw it was him.

"There you are. Thank God! I heard a dog growling like crazy earlier. I thought . . ."

He dropped down beside her. "Nah. It was a pussy cat."

Apprehension chased through her eyes. "You ran into a guard dog?"

"More like it ran into me." He winked, and produced the

apples, carrots, and assorted other goodies from his pockets. "Our feast. It's not much, but—"

She held up the object in her hands, a large tin cup. It was filled with— "Milk?" he asked in surprise.

"I ran into a cow in the field over there." She waved a hand, then held out the cup to him. "This is your share." She gave him a pixie smile. "Sorry. I couldn't wait."

He accepted the cup in astonishment. "You milked a friggin' *cow*?" Never mind venturing out into the fields.

Her smile grew, her white teeth shining in the moonlight. "One learns the most unlikely things in the name of goodwill and diplomacy." At his hiked brows, she explained, "A few of us from the consulate visited a market fair last year. The men declined to try milking." A million stars twinkled in her eyes. "I had to uphold the honor of the delegation."

"Well. Thank goodness for that," he said, raised the cup to her in a salute, then drank. The fresh milk was still warm, pungent and creamy thick, and he could taste the bursts of sweetness on his tongue. "Mmm," he said appreciatively. "Good."

She scooped up a handful of strange-looking fruit from a dip in her skirt. "I found some dragon fruit and a few goji berries, too."

"Wow," he said, even more impressed. He traded her a few for an apple. "And here I thought *I'd* be the sole breadwinner."

"Bread would be nice," she said wistfully. "And a glass of wine."

They shared a chuckle.

"Tomorrow," he promised. Then immediately regretted it. *He wouldn't be with her tomorrow.* She might have quit her job, but Roger wouldn't leave her high and dry. As soon as they were near the coast Kip would make her call the consulate to be picked up. He wouldn't allow her to be in danger a minute longer than necessary. Roger might be a jerk, but he could protect her.

And he'd better, if he valued his life.

She munched on her apple. "So, what is the plan for tomorrow?"

He set the cup aside and grabbed a carrot. "Same as today. Get down to the coast without being caught."

"Or shot," she added.

"Yeah. That, too."

"Then what happens?"

He pushed out a breath, and told a half-truth. "I meet up with my buddies. You meet up with yours. Roger will take you back."

She regarded him, the sparkle in her eyes fading. "You're abandoning me."

He choked on a bite of carrot. "Abandoning? No. That's not—"

"Sorry." She waved it off. "Lord, what a stupid thing to say." Her tone strove for wry humor. It failed miserably. "So, you'll be going your separate way, then, is what I meant."

No she hadn't. She'd meant exactly what she'd said.

For a split second he wondered what kind of jerk had abandoned her in the past and broken her heart, causing the shadows that now dimmed those beautiful blue eyes.

Then he came to his senses.

He said earnestly, "You have to know you can't stay with me. You think this morning's shoot-out was hairy? That was child's play compared to what I've got in store. When my unit arrives to—"

She held up a hand. "Kip. I was there when you talked with your men. You told them not to come."

Ah. Right.

Her muscle twitched. "You don't have to lie to me, Major Llowell. I'd much rather have the unvarnished truth."

Major Llowell again.

"Occupational hazard, I'm afraid," he said truthfully.

"Yes," she replied evenly. "I know."

There was a whole universe of bitterness in those three quiet words.

It bothered the hell out of him. Not the bitterness itself. But the fact that it was there. Evidence that someone had messed with this smart, generous, sexy woman so badly that it had left enduring scars. Kip knew all about scars. There were the trophies of battle he carried on his skin . . . but also the invisible kind that dwelled deep in your soul. The kind only those you loved most could give you.

His protective instincts reared up again, but he told himself firmly that her pain was none of his business. Tomorrow she'd be gone.

End of story.

And even if she weren't going to be gone tomorrow, he would still not be getting involved in any of that stuff. Or with her. He would not be getting involved, period. He had his own issues to contend with. Of which the principal issue was the serious and unwanted consequences of becoming involved, *really* involved, with any woman.

He'd tried it a couple of times when he was younger—getting involved. Because he loved women. He truly did. He loved being with them. Touching them. Yeah, even loved the feeling of falling in love with them, the closeness of having someone all your own.

But inevitably, it got to the point where the woman he was with expected more. Like a ring. And a picket fence. Kids and a dog.

A dog would be good, he conceded. And he had nothing against fences. Kids? Maybe someday . . .

The ring? Not so much.

But the women never understood that. They'd call him commitment phobic and other equally flattering names.

Well . . . if the combat boot fit . . .

Yeah. It was a fact, he *was* commitment phobic. For a very good reason.

There was no way in hell he was getting married. Not anytime soon, anyway.

Because getting married would trigger a very real legal consequence for Kiptyn Llowell III. One he was not remotely ready to confront.

His trust fund.

And all the family drama that came with it.

Darcy woke a split second before the alarm was set to buzz. She reached out to hit the off button, but Bobby Lee beat her to it by a hair.

"Rise and shine, ladies," he called out, waking Jaeger and Zane. As the others started to stir, Bobby Lee leaned over and gave her a lingering kiss. "Naptime's over, sweet thing."

Across the room, Zane groaned, but she didn't know if it was over having to get up, or having to listen to Bobby Lee's endearments. Zane had been captured and tortured for sixteen long months by fanatical Islamic terrorists a few years back. Alex Zane was not a sentimental man.

Well, except where it concerned Rebel, his wife of two years and the light of his life. His beautiful angel, he called her. So he really didn't have any room to complain about sappy endearments.

They all dragged themselves out of bed, made themselves presentable, and headed back to the wardroom to continue planning their strategy for the op. Darcy needed a massive infusion of caffeine, so she went straight for the urn and filled four mugs, carrying them to the table where the guys had already started up the debate again. She set the mugs down and three hands shot out to grab one.

"Hey! Those are mine!" she protested.

To a man, they froze, hands suspended in midair, and looked at her. All of them knew she could kill a man seven different ways before he knew what hit him, and under certain circumstances wouldn't hesitate to do so. What they weren't sure about was whether stealing her coffee was among them.

She smiled in satisfaction. "Ha. Had you going." She grabbed a mug with a grin and leaned back in her chair, indicating they should do likewise.

The three men let out curses and did eye-rolls.

"You are such a punk," Zane grumbled.

But they hadn't touched the mugs until she gave permission. Good to know one had the respect of one's colleagues.

"Not nice to scare the boys like that, baby," Quinn drawled over his mug . . . ignoring the fact that his hand had stopped just as quickly.

"Hell, I don't scare that easy," Zane retorted lightly. A bit of dark humor. He still suffered terrible PTSD from his ordeal at the hands of those terrorists, and had been known to wake up cowering in the corner from the nightmares. Not that anyone would ever mention it out loud.

"She scares *me*," Jaeger said with feeling, then went on with what he was doing on his laptop. That was about as long-winded as Jaeger got.

She smiled.

"Okay, people," Quinn said, getting them down to business. "I'm tired of arguing. We need to start making some decisions. Everyone put together a skeleton plan for the strategy you think will work best. We'll compare and then vote." He checked his watch. "We've got three hours till zero-hundred. Bridger's going to want some solids on the mission before he leaves tonight."

During an op, a sit-rep meeting was always held at midnight to keep each other informed of progress made that day. Assuming they weren't in the thick of things. Commander Bridger was taking off right afterward for parts unknown.

As if summoned by the speaking of his name, Bridger suddenly materialized next to the table, startling the heck out of her. "Commander. Miss Zimmerman."

Sweet Jesus. The man was like a ghost.

He nodded at the others. And pretended not to notice that all four of them had nearly gone for their weapons at his sudden appearance. She was sure he did it on purpose as some kind of perverted test.

She suddenly noticed he had two other men with him. One was Clint Walker, the other an older guy, probably in his fifties or sixties, with a long, silver ponytail hanging halfway down his back and wearing a colorful Florida shirt. He had all the markings of a civilian, but definitely felt ex-military, like Walker.

Clint Walker nodded to them, gave Quinn a casual salute, and grabbed a chair.

Bridger said, "People, this is Master Chief Rufus Edwards, USN retired. Sonar spec."

She quirked a brow. Sonar?

"We get to have a submarine, too?" she asked.

"You want one?" Bridger returned.

God, he was serious.

She pursed her lips speculatively. "Really?"

"Chief Edwards will be rounding out the team."

And that made six.

Everyone introduced themselves and shook hands. When Edwards got to her, he said, "I can hear cogs turning in that pretty head of yours. You got a plan yet?"

"Give me a minute," she said, and he smiled broadly.

She could tell they were going to get along just fine.

13

The night was balmy and the stars were twinkling overhead. But DeAnne was not in the mood to enjoy them. She had been so looking forward to being close to Kip tonight. But the mood was spoiled. She knew he was right, she couldn't stay with him once they got back to civilization, but that didn't make her feel any better.

She couldn't believe she'd quit her job over the man. Well, no, actually she could. It was the principle of the thing. The ethics. And she was pretty sure she'd made her point with Roger. He'd probably take her back if she asked. He probably thought she'd lost her mind.

He wasn't the only one.

She was making a fool of herself over Kiptyn Llowell, even if she was the only one who knew it.

Why would a man like him possibly want her, anyway?

More to the point, why would she want a man like him?

He was brash, egotistical, and insensitive. And he was a U.S. Marine. Everything she hated in a man.

If only she could get her body to believe that.

The problem was, every time she came near to him, her body sizzled with awareness. She couldn't forget those kisses. He kissed like a god. And he'd taken her breath away when he'd whispered in her ear he wanted to see her naked.

She was so torn.

No. She wasn't. He'd reminded her in no uncertain terms that he had no interest in her, other than the obvious.

She'd thought earlier she could do that, but she'd changed her mind. Who needed the heartache?

Not that her heart was involved. It was just—

"You're quiet," Kip said, interrupting her unhappy thoughts.

A while ago, he'd gone to fill their water bottles at a nearby pump, then sat down beside her. She'd lain back on the grass with her down jacket under her head and shoulders, and gazed up at the night sky as they ate their supper of vegetables and fruit.

"Just tired," she said now.

He threw an apple core into the darkness. "You're angry with me."

"No. Just disappointed."

He lay down next to her, turning onto his side with elbow bent, and propped his head on his hand to look at her. "The last thing I want to do is hurt you, DeAnne."

"I believe you." And she did. That was never their goal, the men in her life. It always just happened.

"I have every intention of seeing that you're safe before leaving you. But coming with me is just not possible."

Still on her back, she rolled her head to gaze at him. "I know. I'm not saying I'm being rational." Not looking at it from the outside. But from in here . . .

His lips curved, just a little. "I get that."

Did he?

He reached out and traced a finger lightly down her arm. Despite herself, her body reacted instantly, a spill of goose bumps shivering over her. An ache of longing curled through in her center.

"Kip . . ."

"That's better." He shifted a little closer. "I don't like it when you call me Major Llowell."

She didn't know what to say to that, so she didn't say anything. Her disappointment at being jettisoned might be less than logical, but her anger had been totally reasonable. Anger at herself. For forgetting what was real and what was simply wishful thinking.

Even if Kip hadn't wanted to get rid of her at the first possible opportunity, which clearly he did, it would never work between them. For a myriad reasons.

So why bother starting anything?

He scooted closer still, their bodies almost touching. His hand was warm on her skin as he brushed it up and down her arm. "What are you feeling, princess?"

A tingle of arousal went through her.

"Not like a princess."

She righted her head to gaze up at the stars and tried to shift away from him. She hated that her body was reacting to his touch. It made her want things best left undone. For some inexplicable reason, she was more attracted to this man than she'd been to any other in a long, long time. If ever. But he was so wrong for her.

His hand on her arm wouldn't let her escape. But his voice was gentle and sincere. "What can I do to make it better?"

She squeezed her eyes closed. She didn't want him to be nice.

He slid his hand across her midriff as he moved closer still, his body pressing intimately against her side. "How about this?" he suggested.

He was big and warm and solid. He felt so good. Her willpower wavered.

"Not a good idea," she whispered desperately as his hand drifted upward. Trying to convince herself more than him.

"Oh, I disagree." He toyed with a lock of her hair. He'd pulled out her ponytail earlier and she suddenly wished she'd put it back up. He lifted the strand to his nose and breathed in.

A wire of need tightened through her belly, and lower.

"What happened to the woman who was flirting with me all day?" he murmured.

She turned her face to gaze up at him, barely hanging on to her sanity. "She got hit with a dose of reality."

His fingers brushed over her cheek. "The reality is we both want this. It doesn't have to be any more complicated than that."

It was hard to argue against such simple reasoning. Especially since she'd been thinking the same thing for most of the day. She'd never done mindless hookups or one-night stands with strangers. That just wasn't her. But somehow, the thought of giving herself to this stranger, under these circumstances, had felt heady and exciting, not sordid.

Now that she'd gotten to know him, though, that had changed. Now, it just felt . . . dangerous.

"But it *is* more complicated," she refuted.

The fact was, she was afraid of her unexpected feelings for him. Afraid if she slept with him, it would mean more to her than just casual sex. Because, somehow, she knew it would.

How had this happened?

His hand cupped her face, his thumb moving slowly over her cheekbone. His arm rested across her torso, just below her breasts, touching their undersides. "Yeah. We actually like each other. A lot. What a shock."

She managed a smile. *He had no idea.* Her breasts felt as though an electric current were going through them. "Kip—"

He cut her off by leaning over for a kiss. His fingers slid around to the back of her head, holding her immobile for him. She had no choice but to kiss him back.

She opened her mouth and let him invade her. His tongue swept in and took command, plunging deep, tasting of sweet apple and hot man. She moaned and felt herself weaken.

He felt it, too. And took advantage.

He canted his body over hers and deepened the kiss. It was wet, thorough, and thrilling. His tongue laved her, exploring every corner of her mouth, his lips covering hers completely. *Oh, yes.*

She squirmed under him, wanting more. Wanting everything he was promising with that total ravishment of her mouth.

"More," she pleaded in a swallowed whisper. "More."

He made a sound deep in his throat and his free hand found her breast. His fingers squeezed her nipple through the layers of her clothes, and he drank down her gasp at the shock of pleasure.

He quickly undid the buttons of her blouse, spreading it wide, and pulled down the edges of her bra. His hand cupped her bare breast, grasping the pebbled nipple between his finger and thumb. He gently twisted, and she came up off the ground in an agony of pleasure.

She cried out, but his mouth still covered hers and the sound was muffled by his groan. He lifted and cursed. "I want you. Now. I want to be inside you."

Her hands were clinging to his shoulders, her fingers digging into his flesh. "Yes," she breathed. She moved to find the buttons of his peasant jacket.

He caught her wrist. "Not yet. You first."

She felt her cheeks heat. "You do it." If she was really going to do this, she wanted the full fantasy.

He lifted her shoulders and tugged off her blouse, then made quick work of her bra. With a growl he straddled her, raising her up so her back arched, feeding her breasts into his mouth. He licked at them and his tongue curled around one tip, drawing it out, sucking it hungrily.

She cried out. Writhed at the stinging pleasure.

He switched to the other and did the same, only harder. He licked and sucked until she thought she would go mad with desire. She felt empty and needy. And nothing would help but his thick cock thrusting into her.

"Please," she moaned, pulling at his shirt.

Suddenly her skirt and panties were gone, her shoes tossed aside. He was on all fours, looming above her, still fully clothed.

She was completely naked.

Her pulse thundered. She shivered in the heat of the night, and burned in the smolder of his moonlit regard.

She was exquisitely, mortifyingly aroused. Her body was ready to detonate.

"You take my breath, princess." His voice was low and gritty, his expression dark.

He spread her thighs wide and slid down between them. His mouth found her center and an explosion of sensation engulfed her. Never before had she felt the like. Her entire body was consumed in flames of pleasure. Almost at once she came. And came. And came.

He kept at her until she nearly died of the pleasure.

Afterward, she felt his weight lift, but she was too spent to open her eyes. She heard the rustle of clothes, and a crinkle and snap.

And then he was on top of her. His huge male body pressed down onto her, squashing her breasts and fitting her curves with his firm, muscular frame.

14

Zane and Bobby Lee were still going at it, arguing over when was the best time to run the op—before the AUV arrived on Hainan Island, or after.

Darcy leaned back in her chair, sipped coffee, and wondered if they would ever agree. Not that there seemed to be any good solution to agree *on*.

Before he left to take care of other business, Commander Bridger had informed them he'd had word from the embassy that both that Marine decoy, Major Llowell, and the female foreign service officer he'd kidnapped were still alive. Apparently, the two had staged the accident to throw off their Chinese pursuers. Smart.

At her "death," State Department had released her name as Ann Barrett, but Jaeger's research had proved that to be a false identity, probably to give her a better chance of avoiding unpleasantness in case she had actually been detained.

Whoever she was, the woman had contacted the deputy

assistant secretary in D.C. via cell phone, but then for some reason she'd quit her job. The DAS was convinced she was being threatened and coerced by Llowell. For leverage.

But that didn't smell right to Darcy. Even though it might make sense on the surface. The FSO hadn't called back, and her phone went straight to voice mail, so Llowell might have taken her phone away from her. Or she may actually have meant it when she quit and just didn't want to talk to her former boss. Darcy's vote was on the latter.

Still. That whole situation was a wild card the STORM team didn't need.

She glanced around at the others.

Jaeger was busy on his laptop, doing a deep background on the Marine. Just in case he became a factor down the line. Too bad the consulate was being so tight-lipped about the attaché's identity. It was always best to be prepared.

After that, Jaeger'd be looking for some kind of angle that would give them more than an ice cube's chance at success. He generally didn't share until he had something worth sharing.

She hoped he'd find something good. Failure wasn't an option on this one. Not only because it was such a vital mission for the security of their country, but also because everyone on the team would do just about anything to avoid letting down the client. Or themselves. She'd been on a failed mission once. Just before she joined STORM. It hadn't been pretty. In addition to not securing vital information on a terrorist, one of the guys, Marc Lafayette, had ended up in a Turkish prison for a year. She herself had been fired from her job at CIA. Well. Okay, she'd quit. But she'd seen the writing on the wall.

Of course, she'd also met Bobby Lee Quinn on that op, and within hours had been in bed with him having the most incredible sex of her life—up until that point, anyway—and the rest, as they say, was history. He'd gotten her a job at STORM, and she'd never looked back. Marc had gotten out of prison, not too much worse for wear, and was now a happily married man, off with his wife on a rescue mission somewhere in South America.

Hmmm. Marc and Tara's wedding had been in November. The ceremony and celebration had been really nice, if a little chilly. Maybe November would be a good month . . .

Clint Walker drew her attention when he came back with more coffee and topped up her mug. He had been mostly silent this whole time. He sided with Zane in that he did not even want to try breaking into a secure Chinese military base like Yulin. He thought it would be the height of insanity. She agreed about that. But she also agreed with Bobby Lee that the less than twenty-four hours left wasn't enough time to plan a foolproof hijacking in a hostile foreign country. Not with any certainty of getting away. This was not some Chinese orange team in a training exercise they were dealing with. It was the real McCoy. If they got caught, the Chinese would throw away the key. If they were lucky. The only speedy trial guaranteed in this country was up against a wall in front of a firing squad.

They had to come up with a workable plan.

But what?

She caught Chief Edwards watching her. She smiled and rolled her eyes, jerking her head at the heated discussion. He winked back at her. The man looked singularly untroubled. He was one cool customer, that was for damn sure. Either that, or he didn't plan on leaving the ship with them.

She tapped a fingernail against her mug and idly wondered why Edwards had been chosen for the team. Obviously chill under fire, he seemed nice enough, and certainly intelligent, but at his age he was hardly a warrior. Not the boots-on-ground kind, anyway.

What had they said his specialty was? Sonar. Of all the weird things. She supposed it made a kind of sense since they were dealing with an autonomous underwater vehicle. But the team wasn't going to be underwater. And sonar wasn't used on land. It was a puzzle.

She raised her mug to her lips. So why the hell did they need—

A sudden thought came to her, and she almost choked on her coffee. She darted a look back at Chief Edwards, but he was now studying the map of Hainan's coastline that Bobby Lee had spread out on the table. She skimmed a look over at Walker. Edwards and Walker knew each other from before. They'd said they met a couple of years ago on a scientific mission in the Arctic.

What was Walker's specialty again? She narrowed her eyes. They hadn't said what his specialty was. He'd only told them he was retired navy, just like Chief Edwards.

She had a sudden feeling it was important to find out. She turned to him. "Hey, Walker. What did you do in the navy, anyway?"

Quinn and Zane paused briefly in their discussion to listen.

He answered without hesitation. "UUVs were my specialty. Both ROVs and AUVs."

All things unmanned and underwater.

Okay. Again, it sort of made sense. "Any aspect in particular?" she asked.

He lifted a casual shoulder. "All aspects. Mechanical, programming, payload, pilot."

She contemplated him for a long moment, then darted a glance at Chief Edwards, who was still fussing with the map.

She was starting to see a pattern here.

"Who put you on the team, Chief?" she asked Edwards.

He looked up. "Your Commander Bridger."

That surprised her. "You know Bridger?"

He shook his head. "Nope. I understand Clint, here, recommended me to him."

Bobby Lee shot her a questioning look, which she ignored.

"Who recommended *you*?" she asked Walker.

He pursed his lips. "I believe it was Captain Romanov."

Which made total sense. *Not*.

But it did remind her . . . "Speaking of which. Would someone care to enlighten me as to what the freaking hell a Russian submarine pilot has to do with this mission?"

"Driver," Walker said.

"Huh?"

"Submarine driver, AUV pilot."

"Right. Whatever. But what is his role in all this? Or was that just a casual, meaningless introduction earlier?"

But everyone knew Bridger never did anything casual or meaningless.

By now, she had everyone's full attention. Good. Something was going on here, and she wanted to find out what.

Walker blew out a breath. "I believe Bridger's idea is to send him into Yulin Naval Base on a goodwill tour in full regalia, to split their attention when we launch the op."

"Send him *in*? As in—"

"Through the gates. Right into the jaws of the tiger. Some sort of diplomatic exchange, or some such thing. Hopefully all those medals will keep him from being eaten alive."

She wouldn't count on it. The Chinese were going to be more than suspicious. First an American spy on their soil, then a sudden visit from a Russian dignitary? They wouldn't buy that as coincidence, not if it came with hot fudge and a cherry on top.

"And Romanov's fiancée?" she asked. "She going in as arm candy, or what?"

"Julie?" Walker grinned. "Nah, she just wanted to work on her tan. This is a tropical South Seas island, after all."

"Uh-huh. And being with CIA had nothing to do with her tagging along, I suppose."

He made a your-guess-is-as-good-as-mine-but-I-won't-be-taking-any-bets face.

She wouldn't either. But she was getting off track.

She contemplated Walker and Edwards. She could sense Bridger's fine hand in this. The man was brilliant . . . and subtle. He would never tell his operators how to run their missions. But he'd provide the key ingredients if he saw a good solution, and just kick back and watch. And here these guys sat—an AUV pilot, and a sonar spec.

Earlier, did Bridger not seriously offer to get her a submarine? She narrowed her eyes. And then there was that Romanov dude . . .

Definitely a pattern.

By now, Edwards was smiling inscrutably at her. Either he saw it, too, or he *was* the damn pattern.

All at once, all the pieces fell neatly into place.

Slowly, she smiled back.

Oh. Freaking. Yeah.

She tapped Quinn's arm, interrupting the resumed debate. "Hey."

"What?" They all looked over at her.

"I do believe," she said, a buzz of excitement starting to hum through her veins, "we've been going about this plan all wrong."

The man surely loved to kiss.

DeAnne was floating on a cloud of bliss. They'd made love twice, but Kip was still holding her in his arms and kissing her. Not aggressively. Sweetly and sensually. And enjoying it. She'd never met a man who loved to kiss like this, after the sex was over.

Or maybe it wasn't . . .

She, for one, could go on doing this forever.

She loved being kissed by him. And she loved touching his body, so strong and muscular, with its intriguing male planes and angles, and just the right smattering of coarse, curly hair.

He seemed to like touching her, too. His hands constantly roamed, as if memorizing every inch of her as his lips and his tongue made sweet love to her mouth.

He'd rolled her so she lay on top of him. His big body was warm against her skin, but the night was rapidly cooling.

As his hand caressed her back, he frowned. "You're cold." He wrapped his arms around her. "We should move into the hut where we'll be sheltered."

"Mmm. I don't know if I can walk," she mused, feeling wonderfully boneless.

His lips tilted, and he brushed them over hers. "From all the hiking, I assume."

"Yeah, that must be it," she agreed.

"It really was a long day, and a longer hike," he said. "I'm frankly amazed you're still awake."

"I'm awake?" She feigned surprise. "I was sure this was all just an incredible dream."

"If it was, then I'm dreaming, too, thank God." He gave her another delicious, lingering kiss. "Come here."

Eventually they stopped kissing long enough to rise and gather their clothes. When she hesitated to put back on her dirty skirt and severely wilted blouse, Kip tossed her a clean T-shirt he dug out of his backpack, then handed her his sturdy peasant pants. "They're no cleaner than your skirt, but at least they'll cover your legs."

She took them gratefully. "What about you?"

"I had on jeans and a T-shirt under them. Those'll do for me. As you pointed out, it's not like I was fooling anyone with my clever disguise anyway."

They quickly dressed, grabbed their other things, and made their way to the little hut Kip had scoped out earlier.

"Hang on," he said, approached the door, and carefully peeked in. "Okay, it's clear."

Inside, it was cozy and not too stuffy. It smelled pleasantly of linseed oil and wood shavings. He pulled a space blanket out of his backpack and unrolled it to sleep on. He seemed to have all the essentials in that backpack. Obviously, he'd done this before.

"We have to be gone before dawn," he warned as they settled down.

She nodded, snuggling up against him. "Mm-hmm."

Lord, it felt good lying next to him, even on the hard ground with nothing but a micron-thin sheet of silver whatever-it-was wrapped around them. But being in his embrace was so much better than any wooly blanket. The sex had been incredible, but what she was feeling was more than just the happy contentment that came from good sex.

He made her feel cherished. And so . . . protected.

She let out a long sigh as she drifted toward sleep. Too bad it was all just an illusion.

This moment was fleetingly temporary. She knew that. Tomorrow he'd be dumping her by the side of the road—even if it was in the driveway of the Sanya Hilton or Ritz-Carlton with Roger waiting there to welcome her back to the fold—and she'd never see Kip again.

She told herself that was a good thing. A very good thing.

Because this Marine was just plain dangerous. Dangerous *because* of the illusion. She knew better—she did *not* want to end up like her mother!—but the temptation to delude herself into thinking Kiptyn Llowell was different, *must* be different, from her father, was perilously strong. Quite possibly strong enough to blind her to the consequences if she gave in to the allure of being with him for longer than one night.

The consequences to her heart.

Her father was a strapping, handsome charmer, too . . . when he wanted to be. He could sweet-talk his way into anyone's heart, or bed, and frequently did. But under all that smooth affability, he was a restless soul whose only real joy was the adrenaline rush of the fight, whether it be strategical on the battlefield, or physical at the local bar.

When DeAnne was little and still adored and looked up to him, she'd sit on his lap and gingerly touch his many scars, one by one, and he'd boast to her about how he'd acquired each of them. It wasn't until much later she'd understood why her mother got so upset by that ritual.

Making love with Kip, her fingertips had skimmed over the familiar hard, smooth ridges of flesh.

She'd ignored them tonight. But she wouldn't tomorrow.

If it quacked like a duck . . .

So, yeah. It was a very good thing he was leaving her behind when they reached the coast. She would let him go, and she wouldn't even watch him walk away. Because if she did, she had the terrified, sinking feeling she'd run after him.

And beg him to stay.

15

Kip jerked awake, instantly alert.

And knew at once he'd fucked up.

Sunlight was streaming in through the cracks all around the shed's primitive wooden door.

"*Shit*," he cursed under his breath.

And a dog was barking its fool head off. The sound was coming closer by the second.

"God *damn* it."

By his side, DeAnne stirred to life. "Kip? What's wrong?"

He slid from her arms and rolled up to a crouch, noting thankfully that he only felt a twinge from his leg. He reached for his rucksack. "We overslept. I think we've got company coming."

She blinked the sleep from her eyes and sat up, checking to make sure her clothes were all fastened. "What do we do?"

She looked so adorable with her hair all mussed and her face still flushed from their long night of lovemaking, he almost forgot the danger. He wanted to rip those ugly peasant pants right off her and go down—

Damn it! That was exactly the kind of thinking that had gotten them into this predicament in the first place. Or rather, *not* thinking.

Apparently she didn't suffer from the same stars in her eyes. She was already on her feet and rolling up the space blanket. He slipped into his shoulder holster, tucked the M9 into the pocket, and pulled his T-shirt over it. The gun was a last resort. No way would he use it on a civilian.

He just hoped it was a civilian coming for them.

He only heard one dog barking. Presumably his old pal. With any luck the mutt was full of carrots and dried meat after spending the night in the food storage cellar, and feeling less than feisty. Though it didn't exactly sound that way.

He could hear the farmer yelling at the dog. Maybe the human hadn't yet realized there were intruders in his shed.

"We need to get out of here, pronto," Kip said, keeping his voice low. He put an eye to a crack in the door, scanning the fields for a visual on the farmer and his dog. There was the dog. No farmer yet.

"Ready when you are," DeAnne said from behind him. He glanced back and saw she'd put the peasant jacket on over his spare T-shirt and her puffy shoulder bag was strapped across her chest. That was quick.

She handed him his rucksack, all packed up.

Ready for what, was the question.

He took it, hiking it onto his shoulders as he cracked the door open. The baying dog was coming at them full tilt, his brown spotted coat shining in the morning sun. The farmer was still out of sight, though his shouts were getting louder.

They'd have to take their chances with the dog.

He slid his sheathed knife out of its pocket on the side of the rucksack, and handed it to her. "Here. Put this in your bag."

She shook her head. "I'm not hurting a dog."

"I'll try to draw it off. But use the knife if it attacks you. Think about the rabies shots you'll need otherwise."

She made a horrified face.

"Exactly." He thrust the weapon at her, then grabbed her other hand as they slipped out the door as unobtrusively as possible, hurried around the shed's corner, and took off at a sprint toward the orchards.

Running from a dog was never a good idea. He could hear it gaining speed, barking nonstop, its big paws crunching leaves and scattering dirt as it pounded after them.

They made it to the sheltering grove of fruit trees and plunged into the shady wood, the canopy above heavy with sweet-smelling blossoms and thick with late spring growth. Tangles of low bushes screened them from view as they ran a zigzag path through the orchard, heading down the slope of the mountain. Kip hoped the undergrowth would discourage the dog from following. No such luck. It slowed down but kept coming.

They'd have to stop and make a stand against the beast. They'd left the farmer far behind, but the dog's infernal racket would eventually lead him right to them. Along with family and neighbors and the local constabulary, no doubt. Kip was hoping the authorities would believe for a day or two longer that he'd perished in the cliff accident. Or at least long enough to get DeAnne back to Sanya and safety. Which wasn't going to happen if that farmer found them.

No choice. The dog had to be neutralized.

He shifted the Beretta to the front of his waistband as they ran.

DeAnne glanced at it aghast.

"Only if it's us or the dog," he assured her.

"But the noise," she puffed. "Take the knife back." She reached into her bouncing shoulder bag.

He put a hand to her wrist as they ran. "No. You keep it."

"But how are you—"

"I'll think of something."

Hopefully.

The dog had almost caught up to them.

Kip spotted a fallen tree lying on the ground next to the path up ahead, its branches still fairly intact, if sideways. "How good are you at climbing trees?" he asked, veering toward it.

"What?" she asked between panted breaths.

Slowing to a halt, he pushed her toward a thick, sturdy limb that jutted up into the air. "Climb as high up as you can," he ordered, then in a single motion slid his rucksack around to shield his front, scooped up a broken-off tree branch as a weapon, and spun around to meet the dog head on.

It came at him like a hellhound, paws pumping and tongue lolling sideways from its open mouth. Its eyes were bright and ears pricked. He heard DeAnne start to scream his name, then slap her hands over her mouth.

Kip swung the branch upward in defense, but the dog was faster. With a howl, it lunged, hitting him square on the backpack, then tumbled away on impact.

Kip went over backward, landing flat on his back. *"Oof!"* The branch flew from his hand.

He cursed. Prepared to be ripped to shreds by long teeth and sharp claws.

The dog leapt on top of him. Its drooling jaws opened.

DeAnne started to scream.

Kip grabbed for its neck . . . just as its long, sandpapery tongue slobbered happily up his cheek and over his nose.

It was *licking* him.

DeAnne's scream morphed into a muffled squeal of surprise. Kip was shocked mute, then started to laugh as his face became covered in dog glop.

"Hey! Ew, gross! Hey! Down, boy! Off! Get the—"

Between stifled peals of laughter, DeAnne called out

something in Chinese, and threw a stick several yards away. Immediately, the dog hopped off his chest and bounded after it.

Kip jumped to his feet, wiping the slime off his face with his T-shirt. "Jesus. I was so *not* expecting that."

She was still laughing. "You'd maybe prefer big chunks of your flesh missing?"

"Ha ha." He glanced in relief at the dog retrieving the stick. "What did you say to it, anyway?"

"Fetch. I think. I may have told it to adopt us."

He wheezed out a laugh. "Uh-oh."

The dog bounced back with the stick in its mouth, doing a full-body tail-wag as he offered it up to Kip. But when he tried to take it to throw, the dog hung on, daring him with its eyes.

"Really? *Really?* After you scare the crap out of me you expect me to play?"

"Awww. He likes you."

But who could resist an ugly mug like that?

"Fine," he grumbled. "Just for a minute." He pulled on the stick, yanking it back and forth, and broke into a smile playing tug with the dog again. Yeah, he could definitely go for having a dog. "Poor ol' boy. Doesn't that farmer ever play with you?"

He managed to get the stick away from it, and tossed it as far away as he could through the trees. The dog took off after it.

"We should get moving," he said to DeAnne as he watched it disappear into the underbrush. "It may follow us for a while, but at least it's not barking anymore." He glanced over at her.

He froze. *Oh, God.*

She had *The Look* on her face. Gazing at him with sweet adoration, pink hearts embroidered on her imaginary white satin sleeves. He could practically hear the picket fence being hammered into place around him.

Oh, no.

He wagged a finger at her. "Whatever you're thinking, don't." Picking up his rucksack, he swung it back onto his shoulders. "I am not that guy."

The Look evaporated. "I have no idea what you're talking about."

"Sure you do. But don't go there. I'm just saying." He started to walk. "Last night was fun—" He halted abruptly, turned to her, and grasped her arms. "Hell. Not fun. Last night was incredible." He pulled her against his chest and put his lips to her forehead. "I can't remember ever being quite that turned on before in my life. You were— Ah, hell."

Suddenly swamped by the sensual memory of her melting into him, under him, around him, he swallowed heavily, wrapped his hand around her jaw, and kissed her. Instantly, he was hard. And instantly he wanted her again. *And again.*

The dog pranced up with the stick, butting its nose into their legs, startling him back to reality. *And saving him from himself.*

She was far too tempting. He broke the kiss and held her mouth away from his. Just inches, but enough that his lips couldn't reach her. She looked a little shell-shocked. About the same way he felt. He reached down with his other hand, grabbed the stick from the dog, and whipped it back into the underbrush. The dog charged off.

"Princess," he began.

"No." She shook her head free from his hold. "Kip— You seem to have gotten the wrong impression about me, somehow. About us. About . . . whatever this is between us."

He narrowed his eyes. "I don't think so."

"Well." She took a step back from him. "Just in case, let me set the record straight."

"All right." Mentally, he prepared his usual let-her-down-easy lecture. He really liked DeAnne—*a lot*—and didn't want to see her hurt. Or even disappointed. Though that was probably inevitable at this point.

She took a breath. "Truly, I have no interest in pursuing any kind of relationship with you."

"I'm sorry," he began on autopilot, "I—"

Wait.

What?

"Don't take it the wrong way. You are very handsome and sexy, and smart, and you obviously love dogs," she said with a lopsided grin, glancing after the mutt.

She turned back, and before he could even think of a response to that, she continued. "And you're right. Last night was . . . far more than amazing." Her cheeks blazed pink for a quick second. "But, um, you're not really my type. So you don't have to worry about me having any inappropriate fantasies about you. Or us." Her nose twitched. "And by inappropriate, I mean anything involving exchanging keys, or phone numbers, and the like." She smiled. "So rest easy."

If he weren't such a seasoned intelligence officer, trained to hold his face perfectly neutral when taken unawares, he was pretty sure his jaw would have dropped.

He wasn't so egotistical as to think he was— Okay, maybe he was that egotistical. After last night, and the way she'd given him The Look, naturally he thought . . .

Clearly, he was wrong.

"Okay," he managed, praying his voice sounded normal and relieved. Which was absolutely, unequivocally, what he felt. Total relief. "That, um, that works for me."

She nodded pleasantly. "I had a feeling it would."

With that, she turned and started downhill, heading for the path that would take them off the mountain and eventually down to the coast. Where they would part company.

The dog bounded up, sans stick, and ran an excited circle around him, then trotted off to tag along beside DeAnne.

Traitor.

Kip huffed out a breath, feeling unreasonably irritated—and imprudently challenged—as he struck out after her.

What the hell was *that* all about?

He couldn't imagine why he was feeling so damn annoyed. This was a dream scenario. A hot woman and hotter sex, with literally zero strings attached. What more could a man ask for?

Nothing, that's what.

This was good.

He was good.

It was all good.

And there was no way in hell he was going to demand an explanation. He would just smile like hell and count his damn blessings.

Fuck.

"Hey!" he called, striding off after her. "What the hell do you mean, I'm not your type?"

16

Oh, dear. Now she'd done it.

DeAnne cringed inwardly. In her attempt to set the record straight, she'd gone and involved Kip's male ego. That had been a colossal mistake. Almost as colossal as his ego.

She did not slow her pace.

Well, he could just deal with it like an adult. As he had expected *her* to do. She rubbed her cheek to keep it from twitching. *Last night was fun, princess*, she mimicked in her head. *But I am not that guy.*

No darn kidding.

"Princess, wait." He strode up beside her and reached for her hand.

She glared at him. "I am *not* a princess."

"Whoa." He held up his palms. "Okay, baby, I—"

She glared harder. He was really pressing his luck.

"Okay, *DeAnne*, sweetheart . . . I can call you that, right? Considering how well we know each other now?"

She stopped abruptly, and he followed suit. The dog did

so, too, then sat down, tail wagging in the dirt, and peered up at them.

Realizing her hands were balled into fists, she uncurled them, crossed her arms over her abdomen, and stuck her hands under her armpits. She didn't know why he was upsetting her so much.

Okay, fine. She did. She hated that he was right, and saw right through her façade. And yet *he* was angry, just because she was honest? *She* was the one who should be angry!

Instead, she was just hurt.

She schooled her features. "Yes, Kip. We do know each other quite well now. At least physically. And yes, being with you was undoubtedly the best—"

Again, she stopped abruptly. No sense inflating his colossal ego any more than it already was. "But none of that has any bearing on the future—our future. Of which we have none. You've made that clear. Correct?"

His eyes grew stormy. Make that *more* stormy. "Correct. But that still doesn't answer my question."

Why did he keep picking at this? Whether or not he was her type was completely irrelevant.

She turned and started trekking down the mountain again. "I don't see that it has any bearing."

"I do." He didn't miss a step. "Because you're lying."

"I. Don't. Lie," she enunciated. *Unlike some people.*

"All right. Deluding yourself, then. I am *exactly* your type, and you know it."

She snorted.

"You like me, princess. You *more* than like me. You're just afraid to admit it out loud. Why?"

Suddenly, the dog's ears pricked up, it gave a yip, and bounded off, heading back the way they'd come. She turned and watched it go, walking backward for a few steps, then swung back around to continue downhill out of the forest, back toward the steamy jungle below.

Lord. This was not a discussion she wanted to have. She exhaled. "Let's just say there are issues there, and leave it at that."

He kept pace with her. "Let's not. What issues?"

She shot him an exasperated glance. "I can't see that my issues are any of your business."

"Of course they're my business, when they affect our relationship. I'm your lover, DeAnne, and—"

"You have got to be kidding!" she said, almost choking. "Just thirty seconds ago you were all don't-even-go-there-I'm-not-that-guy with me."

He said, irked, "Yeah, well, it was the look you were giving me. Like you were already planning our wedding."

"Oh, puh-*lease*."

"I have no interest in getting married. Not now. Probably not ever."

"Doesn't affect me."

"It could."

"No, it couldn't." She was about to tell him to just leave it alone, already, when he dropped a bomb.

"What if I wanted it to? Affect you. I mean, what if I want to keep seeing you? Later. After all this is over and we're back in the States?"

She whipped her head around and stared over at him, openmouthed. And tripped.

He caught her by the arms and kept her from tumbling, dragging her to a halt.

A billion thoughts crashed through her mind in those few seconds, a chaotic soup of conflicting emotions.

"Why?" she finally demanded. "For the great, no-strings sex, I suppose?"

He regarded her evenly, but his eyes were anything but calm. She knew just as many conflicting thoughts were going through his mind. He just didn't want to show it.

Why?

At length, he said, "What's the right answer, princess? Yes or no?"

"The truth," she shot back.

But did she really want to hear the truth? Probably not. Either way was an epic trap.

"No," he said, and her heart sank. "Not just for the great sex. Though that's certainly part of it. I like you, DeAnne. You intrigue me. And we seem to agree on certain key issues."

Her heart sank further. A ringing endorsement if ever she'd heard one. "Such as marriage," she stated.

"For instance."

Wow. He could at least try to lie to her at the right time.

She took a deep breath. "But you're wrong. I'm not against marriage." She tore her gaze away from his, looked down at her dusty shoes, and admitted, "I'd really like to get married. Someday."

He was silent for several long moments. "Okay. So, just not to me." It wasn't a question. "Why? What's wrong with me?"

He was like that darn dog and the stick. Always coming back to that. Maybe his ego was more fragile than colossal.

"Kip, believe me, it's not you, it's—"

"Oh, *God*, spare me the it's-not-you-it's-me speech," he said impatiently. "What's the real, no-bullshit, no psychobabble reason?"

He actually sounded upset. Why, she couldn't fathom. He'd just told her he had no interest in a real relationship with her! But if he wanted a straight answer, she'd give him one. Not that he'd accept it.

"Because," she said, "you're a Marine."

He snorted. Then he saw that she was serious. His face went stony. "I asked you that once before. You denied having a problem with the Marines."

"No, I denied having a problem with *you*."

His eyes narrowed to slits. "All right, then. Spill it. What's so terrible about the Marines?"

"*The* Marines? Not a thing. *Men* in the Marines?" She battled back a flood of emotions. Mostly bad ones. "Plenty."

She did *not* want to talk about this with him. With anyone, really. She whirled, and started marching through the underbrush. "When are we going to get to the trail again? Is this even the right direction?"

He was in front of her, blocking her path, before she could draw a breath.

"Okay, so what have you got against *men* in the Marines?" he said between his teeth. "Because I sure as hell didn't notice any aversion on your part last night."

"I do *not* want to talk about it."

"Well, I do! Is it because we're too low class for you? Is that it? A wealthy socialite FSO is too good for the likes of us lowly grunts? Except to fuck, of course. We're good enough for that."

Her face burned with indignation. "Kip, move aside."

"No."

"I mean it. I don't want to talk about this."

He leaned way down into her personal space. "And I don't give a flying shit what you want. Answer the goddamn question!"

His words, his tone, even his posture, were all sickeningly familiar. She swallowed down the bile and drew a sharp breath.

"And *that*"—she poked her finger into his chest hard enough to push him back—"is *exactly* what I have against Marine men. You are nasty, violent"—she poked again—"arrogant thrill seekers"—another poke—"who just can't *wait* for the next battle, so you're always picking fights"—poke—"and you *lie*—"

"DeAnne, what the—"

An even harder poke. "And you *cheat* on your wife"—poke—"and you *desert* your kids." She gave him one last, big, five-finger poke that was more like a shove. "All you Marines do is *hurt* the people you're supposed to *love* and take *care* of." Her voice cracked when she finished with, "And *that's* what I have against men who are Marines!"

Kip gaped down at her, stunned speechless.

To her horror, she realized there were tears streaming down her face. "Damn it," she muttered, and swiped them off. She whirled away from him and started running blindly.

Immediately, she felt his hands on her shoulders from behind, pulling her to a gentle halt. "Sweetheart, stop. You're heading right into the bushes."

She swiped at her face again, which was just as wet this time, and shuddered out a mortified sob. "Told you I had issues."

He didn't try to turn her, just tugged her gently back against his chest and put his arms around her from behind. He pushed out a long breath, stirring her hair.

"Your husband?"

Had she been so transparent? *Well, duh.*

"No. Father."

He grunted. "Bastard."

"Yeah."

"You understand, not all Marines are like that."

Tears continued to leak out, and she sniffed them away. "In my head, yes. My heart, not so much."

He made a noise low in his throat. "Well. That explains a lot."

She couldn't believe she'd just tossed her emotional cookies all over him. She had to get hold of herself. This was not his problem.

She hiccoughed. "And for the record, I'm not a wealthy socialite. I was raised by a mom who had to work two jobs just to pay the rent."

His breath stirred her hair again. "Sorry. I made assumptions based on your appearance. Stupid of me."

She thought about that. She'd worked so hard all her life to project that false image of herself—to appear privileged, sophisticated, well-educated. And had worked even harder to achieve it in reality. So she wouldn't be tainted in people's minds by her crummy past. Funny, she'd never considered that image might be doing the opposite with some people—driving them away from her. Isolating her. Was that why she always felt alone?

Maybe it was time to downgrade the picture a little.

"It's true about the fucking, though," she said, shocking them both. "You are good at that."

After a wry cough, he asked, "You talking about me, or Marines in general?"

"You," she whispered, her cheeks flaming. She turned in his embrace, putting her arms around him and burying her face against his chest. "I'm sorry I'm such a mess. You don't need this right now."

He laid his cheek on the top of her head. "Sounds like you've had a rough go. That sucks."

"Good thing you're getting rid of me today once we reach Sanya, huh?"

She felt his lips brush her hair. "Not how I look at it. DeAnne, I meant what I said about seeing you later, in the States."

What could she say to that? Every warning bell in her head was going off.

And yet, she was torn. She really had loved sleeping with him. And he did seem different from her father, for the most part. But . . .

"Kip, just because my issues are out in the open doesn't mean they went away. And we haven't even started talking about yours." She held up a hand. "Not that I want to. The point is, why start something we both know isn't going anywhere?"

He kissed her hair. "Why does it have to go anywhere? It's nice right where it is."

"We're back to the great, no-strings sex, aren't we." But this time there was no heat in the accusation. Not the angry kind, anyway.

She felt his smile against her temple. "Maybe."

"You are such a m—"

"Watch it."

"Man."

"Hmm. I seem to recall you liking that part about me . . ."

She smiled against his chest. "Maybe."

They fell silent, and for a few minutes just stood there under a canopy of sweet-fragrant white blossoms in an orchard in China, holding each other. So much potential; so little future.

But no matter what happened, she knew she would remember this moment for the rest of her life.

"Anyway," he said at length, "who knows if I'll even make it off this island. I could be spending the next twenty, thirty years in a Chinese prison. Dating may be a moot point."

She knew it was a very real possibility. The Chinese didn't take kindly to spies. But she just couldn't allow herself to think of him locked away in one of those awful places.

"Don't say that. You'll make it back to the States."

"Tell you what. If I do, promise me one date. We can both make up our minds then."

She swallowed. It seemed a small concession. An added incentive for both of them to make it out of here. "One date?"

"Dinner and a movie." He bent to whisper in her ear. "And breakfast. What do you say?"

But before she even had a chance to think about her answer, they suddenly heard shouts in the distance. Male voices, harsh and excited. And a dog barking.

She and Kip jerked apart, their eyes meeting in alarm.

"Damn it to hell," he ground out. "I knew that dog was trouble."

"But how could it—?"

"Doesn't matter. They found us."

"What'll we do?"

He grabbed her hand. "I vote for run like hell."

17

Kip and DeAnne ran through the forest for nearly a mile, dodging trees and doing their best not to leave a visible trail. All the while Kip could hear the shouts behind them. The good news was, it wasn't the PLA guys in Jeeps, and no guns were blasting. Yet, anyway. Their pursuers were on foot and didn't seem to be getting any closer. The bad news was they weren't losing them, either. And Kip could hear their pal the dog bellowing in the lead.

Shit.

He scoured his memory of the map for a possible route to escape. They were heading down to the more populated jungle lowlands where they would find roads and villages with structures where they could hide, scattered among the orchards and fields. That held promise. But they had to throw that damn dog off their scent first.

"Kip, I can't run much farther," DeAnne gasped between ragged pants of breath.

"There," he said, pointing to a place up ahead where the

terrain dipped and he could hear the faint sound of water tumbling over cobbles. "Make for the stream. We need to lose the dog."

It could work. Maybe. Or at least give them a little more lead time. Hopefully their pursuers were simple farmers who didn't do a lot of hunting. Or watch TV.

They sprinted to the edge of the stream and DeAnne halted, sucking in lungfuls of air. Kip whipped his rucksack around to his front and turned his back to her, bending his knees. "Climb up, piggyback."

"No, I can—"

"The bottom is treacherous. It'll go faster this way."

She hesitated a moment, then did as he asked. She was still breathing heavily, and her hands were shaking, but she managed to grab his shoulders and he boosted her up, grabbing her around the legs.

Their pursuers would most likely expect them to go downstream toward the coast and Sanya, so he turned upstream instead. He'd backtrack just far enough to shake them.

"Hang on."

He plunged into the water. It wasn't too deep, but the bottom was all smooth and slippery river cobbles. He was wearing his combat boots, so the treads helped keep him upright as he picked his way upstream as fast as he dared.

"I'm holding you back," DeAnne said when her breathing slowed enough to speak. "You should leave me here. I can distract—"

"Hell, no," he said gruffly. "I'm not leaving you anywhere."

"I'll be fine. It's not the PLA, and these people don't have guns. I can speak to them and—"

"No."

"I don't want you to get caught."

"Me, neither. But no."

She stopped talking when he hit a stretch of sandy bottom and picked up speed, jogging as fast as he could manage through the water. He could still hear their pursuers, but they'd halted, and the sounds of a heated discussion rang through the trees. The dog was barking nonstop, frustrated. They must have reached the stream.

He sent up a prayer they'd fall for his simple ruse.

Sure enough, the shouts turned downstream, getting more and more distant, and eventually the noise of their pursuers ceased.

Kip let out a breath of relief, and climbed up the bank. Back on dry land, he eased DeAnne down to her feet.

"I'm so sorry," she said in consternation as she rearranged herself. "You really didn't have to—I must weigh a ton."

"Nah, I'm used to carrying much heavier packs," he said easily. He was barely winded. "You've obviously never been a Marine."

He winced. *Damn.*

"No, thank goodness."

He grabbed her hand. "Come on. Let's get moving. We've fooled them for a while, but they'll catch on quick."

"How do we get past them?"

He surveyed the vee of mountains surrounding the small valley, and oriented himself on his mental map. He pointed at a nearby hill. "On the other side we should hit a footpath down to the main road to the coast. It's more populated over there, though, so we'll have to be careful."

She nodded. "What about checkpoints?"

"There's only one left between us and Sanya. We should be able to avoid it if we stick to the smaller paths."

They struck out at a fast clip, his waterlogged boots squishing underfoot, and in an hour they were standing on top of the hill. Below them, an undulating checkerboard of fields spread out in the morning sun. As they rested, ate some fruit, and drank water, he got out his camera and took some shots.

"Wish I had the telephoto lens," he murmured, taking in the sweeping panorama. "Nothing's going to show up."

She watched him, a mildly puzzled look on her face. When he asked her what she was wondering about, she just shook her head. But he knew what she was thinking. He was used to the reaction.

"What? Can't a Marine be artistic?" he asked, aiming the camera at her.

Her eyes widened in alarm. "Don't you dare take my photo!" She turned her face and covered it with the water bottle she was holding. "I'm a mess!"

He grinned, clicking away. "A beautiful mess. I love how you look."

She peeked out from behind the bottle, her eyes soft and vulnerable behind a façade of skepticism. "You're such a liar."

He clicked off a series of shots. "Am not." He reached out and shifted aside a tangle of chestnut curls from her flushed cheek. "Mmm. Like you just got out of bed after a night of making love. Makes me hard just looking at you."

He fired off some more shots as she dropped the bottle to her lap, forgotten. "You are so bad," she murmured in embarrassment, but he could tell she secretly liked it.

He winked. "Hell, no. Bad would be if I asked you to take off your clothes and let me photograph you naked."

She let out a small gasp. "Kip!"

"Maybe when we're not running from bad guys," he said with a mock sigh, and stowed the camera in his rucksack. "Ready?"

Nodding, she capped the water bottle and slid it into her shoulder bag. As she turned to him, he gathered her in his arms and kissed her.

It was their first kiss since they'd awakened and had to

start the day running for their lives. He made the kiss long and deep, mating their mouths as he'd mated their bodies last night. She melted into him like she belonged there. He liked that. A lot.

After the long, sensual kiss, she moaned and pulled away. "Kip—"

"I know. We need to get going. I just had to do that first. It's been too long since I tasted you."

She licked her lips, uncertainty shining in her eyes. "You're complicating things."

He touched the tip of her nose. "No. You are."

With that, he turned, hefted his rucksack, and started down the other side of the hill, his lover following on his heels.

His lover.

It had a nice ring to it. He liked thinking of DeAnne that way. As his lover. *His* lover.

No one else's. Just his.

Except that it was, he reminded himself, not true.

But it could be. She'd already agreed to see him again when they got back stateside. How hard would it be to talk her into being his steady lover? A hot, undemanding relationship they could both enjoy.

Of course, there was her job to consider. She'd no doubt change her mind about quitting the State Department, so she'd be posted God knew where out in the world. Getting together could be tough.

And then, there was that whole crazy Marine thing. Not that he was too worried about that part. Her father sounded like a real bastard, but Kip was *not* a bastard, and he was sure she'd see that pretty quickly.

It could work.

Assuming he made it out of this godforsaken country alive.

Which led him back to thinking about his mission. Ever

since Jake had clued him in to its true nature, he'd been getting more and more steamed about the situation. Had Colonel Jackson known Kip was sent in merely as a decoy for the real mission? He didn't think so. The colonel could be hot-headed, demanding, and severely old-school, but he was a straight-shooter. And he respected his men. He'd never send his troops into battle without all the facts.

One thing was for damn sure, if Kip ever met up with that navy jerk again, the guy was toast.

But that would only happen if they could get down to Sanya, and he could find a way off the island.

"Kip! Slow down!"

At DeAnne's winded call, he halted and turned. And realized he'd been double-timing it down the path, leaving her in his dust.

Whoops.

"Sorry," he told her when she caught up.

"Gathering wool again?" she asked with a little smile.

"Something like that." He looked around and saw they were nearly at the foot of the hills, approaching a small village.

"How much farther?" She wiped a sheen of sweat from her brow.

He did a quick calculation. "Barring trouble, five or six more hours on foot."

Her face fell and she looked as though she wanted to groan, but she didn't. She just let out a long breath. "Five or six. Okay. But I swear, you better make sure I get a long, hot—"

Suddenly, he spotted something that put a big smile on his face. "Hello."

She broke off, frowned, and glanced around. "What?"

"That."

He indicated the narrow dirt road that wound out from amid the ramshackle buildings. Along its verge, leaning precariously on a rusty kickstand, was an equally dilapidated motorcycle.

Hallelujah. Transpo.

"Oh, yeah," he said. "That'll do quite nicely."

"So, you really think Llowell kidnapped that diplomat?" Darcy asked Captain Jenson, then shook her head. Sounded like a real stretch to her.

Last night at the midnight sit-rep, the team had managed to impress Commander Bridger with their daring mission plan. At least he'd pretended to be impressed. She still wasn't convinced he hadn't manipulated the whole operation himself.

After a long night at the drawing board, finally satisfied with the plan, the STORM team had fallen into their bunks just as the sun came up. Only to be awakened about five minutes later for an eight a.m. meeting with the client.

Maybe it was their continued lack of sleep, but no one on the team was remotely happy with Captain Jenson's orders for the day, to be carried out while they waited for the submarine that Commander Bridger had requisitioned to arrive.

A submarine! How cool was that?

"Why else would an educated, well-respected deputy director for the U.S. State Department ally herself with a roughneck spy running for his life?" Jenson insisted, bringing Darcy back to her question. "And quit her job to boot? Hell, no. Major Llowell's got to be threatening her. Or worse."

Darcy lifted a brow. "Worse?"

Captain Jenson gave her a knowing look. "A defenseless woman alone in the wilderness with a desperate fugitive?"

Based on the woman's behavior thus far, Darcy had her doubts she was all that defenseless.

But Captain Ass-hat had his mind made up.

All right. Whatever. He was the client.

Darcy would keep her mouth shut, but she still wasn't buying it. And from Jaeger's profile of Llowell, he didn't seem the type to go around kidnapping and threatening random women, either. The guy had a chest full of medals for valor, and he was an artist to boot. Some of his photographs had been featured in an online gallery, and they were frikkin' good.

"Desperate fugitive?" Clint Walker put in. "You realize Major Llowell's on *our* side, right?"

Exactly.

"And *you* sent him in to be captured," Zane reminded Jenson with a bitter note to his voice.

The captain bristled, at the same time looking guilty as hell. "That was *not* the intent. And he hasn't been captured."

"That we know of," Darcy muttered at the same time Zane muttered, "Yet." They looked at each other and grimaced.

Jenson slashed a hand through the air. "We're talking about the woman now. The embassy is more than concerned for her safety. Regardless of her exact status, they want her back at the compound and out of danger. And I want to debrief her."

"Why?" Commander Bridger asked. He'd been pensively silent up until this point. Now even he was looking irritated.

Jenson's face hardened. "The Pentagon needs Llowell taken out of the picture, ASAP. With his cover being blown way too early, they're worried in his present status as a fugitive he'll interfere in your operation instead of leading the Chinese away from it as originally planned. Jeopardize the outcome. That's not acceptable."

"So why aren't we going after *him* instead?" Quinn asked.

"You really think a seasoned operator like Llowell will

just waltz into town and announce himself?" Jenson shook his head. "He'll have her dropped off somewhere we can find her, but he'll no doubt be long gone. At this point she's just a liability he needs to be rid of. But trust me, you won't see a shadow of the guy."

Darcy pursed her lips. Apparently the client didn't have much confidence in the team's abilities.

"And you think the woman will lead you to him," Quinn speculated without betraying the disdain she sensed emanating from every pore in his body.

"If she wants her job back."

Hmm. The job she'd just quit in protest over being asked to betray the major? Darcy could only think of one reason to give up your job for a man, and it wasn't altruism.

Darcy said, "I definitely do not think he's holding her against her will."

"The navy isn't paying you to think, missy," Jenson retorted.

Around the table, spines went rigid.

"No call for being rude," Chief Edwards said levelly. He turned to her. "For what it's worth, I agree with you."

"Regardless, you have your orders," Jenson snapped. "Here's her photo." He tossed down a woman's publicity headshot. The name on the back had been redacted, and "Ann Barrett" written above it with the same black marker. Nothing like being obvious.

"I suggest you draw up a plan and get moving. She could reach Sanya any minute." With that, Jenson stalked from the room.

"Fucker," Zane muttered.

Bridger got to his feet. "Well, I'll leave you to it, then."

"Sir, do we really have to grab the diplomat?" Darcy asked as he left. She was the only one who'd question his orders on this. Okay, not really question, more like clarify. He hadn't actually given the order.

The commander halted at the door. "You heard the client. He wants Major Llowell taken out of the picture, and he thinks she can make that happen."

Which wasn't really an answer.

Okay.

Think subtle.

She narrowed her eyes at him. "So you're saying our true objective is to neutralize the major, not necessarily to secure the woman."

He gave a neutral smile. "I'm sure you'll come up with an appropriate solution. In the meantime, I have to see a man about a submarine."

The team watched mutely as he strode out of the wardroom, checking his tablet. They remained silent for a full minute.

"What the hell was that supposed to mean?" Zane grumbled finally.

She exchanged a look with Quinn. He cleared his throat. "Well," he drawled. "That puts an interesting slant on things, now, doesn't it? Ideas, people?"

"Are you serious?" asked Walker incredulously, as it dawned on him what they were thinking. "You really believe you can take down an operator with over a dozen years experience in eluding the enemy?"

Quinn shrugged. "I guess we'll find out."

No one on the team so much as cracked a smile, but she knew exactly what they were all thinking. *Well, duh.* Those kinds of odds weren't the least bit intimidating to this crew.

"Janson's right though," Chief Edwards put in, and they all swung around to look at him.

"How so?" Darcy asked.

Edwards leaned back in his chair and steepled his fingers. "The woman is the key to pulling in the major. We really do need to go after her."

18

DeAnne clung to Kip's waist and burrowed her face against his back. She'd never been on a motorcycle before. This was a small one and they were not going very fast, but even so, she kept her eyes squeezed tightly closed. The roads were bumpy and winding, and she hadn't quite got that leaning thing down yet. When Kip took a curve, her body instinctively wanted to lean in the opposite direction, but he made her lean with it. She was convinced they'd tip over on their side and end up a bloody smear in the dirt. He assured her that wouldn't happen, but she had her doubts. And she definitely didn't want to see how close her legs got to doing a slide into home plate—minus the plate.

Still, it was infinitely preferable to walking. She wasn't sure her feet would ever recover from the last twenty-four hours.

She sighed.

Kind of like her heart . . .

She couldn't believe how quickly they were approaching

Sanya. Soon Kip would drop her off, then he'd ride away into the sunset. Possibly never to be seen again. By her, anyway.

It was shocking how much that thought hurt.

How had this happened to her? Had she really *fallen* for the man? A man who wanted nothing to do with a real relationship? A man so wildly inappropriate for her that it made her stomach knot? Of all things, a *Marine*?

Yep. She really had.

Oh, Lord. She was in such trouble.

They worked their way down the mountain, Kip keeping to the small paths that ran between the verdant fields and orchards, until finally they were forced to travel on the main paved road.

Her fingers dug into his muscled flesh as he took the turn onto the pavement, bringing them closer to the moment of truth.

She knew what he wanted from her. A casual, friends-with-benefits, see-each-other-when-we-can relationship. But she didn't think she could do that.

Sure, she'd slept with him after knowing him less than twenty-four hours . . . but the circumstances had been extraordinary. Not something she'd normally do. Not by a long shot. She'd wanted a taste of the wild side, to throw caution to the wind with an incredibly hot man, to live for the moment because she'd come so close to death yesterday. And because she'd been so ridiculously attracted to him. Still was . . .

He hadn't led her on, hadn't pretended to offer any more than what it was. Which was fine. She could handle that. A brief fling, then he'd walk away and it would be over.

But now he wanted to keep seeing her.

And her darn heart had gotten involved.

It would be better to end things here and now. And spare herself the inevitable heartache.

Because she was pretty sure it was going to hurt like the

dickens when he left her and moved on. Which he would, sooner or later. That was inevitable, too.

The motorcycle zoomed around one last sweeping curve, and suddenly the trees and hills fell away and a wide, blue expanse of ocean stretched along the horizon. Before them, the first crowded tendrils of modern development reached up into the foothills, melding into the full-blown jumble of the big coastal city of Sanya.

Kip pulled the bike off onto the side of the road, took out his camera and snapped a few shots. Then he half turned to her. "Let me see your phone."

She dug it out of her shoulder bag and handed it to him, along with the battery and SIM card he'd removed the day before. "Calling your men to come pick us up?"

He gave her a neutral smile, reinserted the card and battery, and punched a few buttons, bringing up her list of contacts. "Something like that."

She frowned as he hit one of the numbers. "Who are you—"

He kissed her forehead as the phone rang, and put his finger lightly on her lips. "Hush."

"But—"

He angled away from her, gazing out toward the sea. "I'm sure you know who this is," he said when someone picked up on the other end, "so just shut up and listen. I'll be dropping her off at the Sanya Hilton in two hours. Be there with a protective detail, and get her off this island immediately. She wasn't serious about quitting her job, I forced her to say that. None of this was her doing."

Then he hung up and plucked the battery and SIM card out again, and handed it all back to her.

She gaped at him. "Why did you do that?"

"You didn't really think I'd leave you wanted by the Chinese authorities and unprotected?" he asked mildly.

Her heart sank. *So he really was going to leave her behind.*

"Um . . ." No, she hadn't actually thought about what would happen to her when they parted ways. It had been such an impulsive move to quit her job, and deep down she knew Roger probably didn't take her seriously. But still, it should have been *her* decision whether or not to ask Roger for help, not Kip's. She'd hoped Kip would . . .

Never mind what she'd hoped. It wasn't going to happen.

He steered the bike back onto the road and gave it gas. "And you can tell ol' Roger that if he doesn't put you on the first plane out of China, he'll have me to answer to."

Her heart did a little flutter at the hardened steel in those words. He sounded deadly serious. He laid his hand over hers and squeezed. The protectiveness his whole body was projecting nearly took her breath away.

But he was leaving her.

"Kip, you should come with me," she called over the whine of the motorcycle and the rush of the wind. "Let Roger protect you, too. I'm sure he can get you out if—"

He cut her off. "Not a good idea. I know how international diplomacy works. You guys have to play by the rules, and I sure as hell don't want to end up rotting in a Chinese prison just so some idiot politician can save face or get a better trade deal on Chinese widgets."

She couldn't come up with a good argument against that reasoning, so she kept silent, pressing her body against the heat of his back. Seeking his comfort while she could.

What would become of him? Would he find a way off the island? Or would he be lost forever, buried alive in some horrible Chinese prison.

She felt tears well in her eyes. Which was silly. This was his job, just another day at the office. He'd be fine.

At least that's what she kept telling herself, all the way to Sanya.

They stopped at a small open market on the outskirts of town, and bought food and a bottle of wine, a pretty native sarong-like outfit for DeAnne, and a cartoon T-shirt and conical straw China hat for Kip. All the while, Kip took photos of everything. Just a couple of tourists. Then they headed for the international district on the bay, where they would blend in with the masses of other sun-worshiping tourists from all over the world.

A few blocks away, they parked the motorcycle, ducked into a doorway and changed clothes, then strolled hand in hand through the district entry checkpoint speaking German to each other.

Well. She spoke German, and he responded using his rather impressive vocabulary of German swearwords.

"I did a stint with MARFOREUR—our European operations in Germany," he explained with a wink.

Her pulse was hammering as they approached, but the Chinese guards hardly looked up, just gave them a wave through.

There was still over an hour until the appointed drop-off time at the Hilton, so they took a rickshaw down to the beach and had a picnic on the sand amid the crowd of vacationing families and honeymooners.

They spread out the space blanket for a tablecloth and feasted on the delicacies they'd bought, drinking the wine right from the bottle, laughing and talking about everything under the sun. Everything except what was really on DeAnne's mind.

No sense going there.

"Tell me about your father," Kip said when the bottle was nearly empty and the remains of their meal lay scattered on the foil blanket. They'd lain down right on the warm sand, her head on his chest and his arm wrapped around her.

The last thing she wanted to discuss was her father.

She sighed. "Not much to tell. He wasn't around all that often."

"Because he was sent overseas a lot?"

"That, and he preferred to spend his time with his Marine buddies and their groupies rather than his family." She gave a humorless chuckle. "Probably a good thing, though. He was a mean drunk. We were better off without him."

Kip's arm tightened around her as he digested that. He gave her temple a tight, lingering kiss. "I'm sorry your dad was such an ass."

She smiled weakly. "Yeah. Me, too."

She could feel the muscles of his jaw work against her hair. "We're not all like that, you know."

No, she didn't, actually. Kip was far more honorable, and gentle and loving, but he still had a phobia against commitment, just like her dad. He'd made it clear he preferred the nomadic, adrenaline-charged life of a soldier over settling down and having a family. How different was that from her dad, when push came to shove?

But she didn't feel like spoiling the moment pointing that out.

"Mmm," she hummed noncommittally. She exhaled, drawing her fingers through the sand, pouring a little pile on the thigh of his jeans. "So what about your dad? Tell me about your family."

She felt his body go tense. "I don't really—" He swallowed and took a deep breath. "We haven't spoken in years."

She turned to look up at him. For a split second his expression was filled with pain and regret. "Oh, Kip, I'm so sorry. What happened?"

His face went blank, though she could tell there was a wealth of emotion roiling behind his storm-blue eyes. He shrugged. "He didn't approve of my choice of profession."

She hiked a brow. "He didn't want you to be a Marine?"

A crack formed in the granite and a brief smile appeared. "No, that came later. I wanted to be a photographer."

Okay, no surprise there. He'd been taking pictures like crazy the whole time she'd known him. But—

"I don't understand. How could anyone possibly object to your being a photographer?"

He exhaled. "The big plan for me was to follow in daddy's footsteps."

Daddy? Footsteps? That sounded very . . . um, Upper East Side.

"I take it you didn't agree."

"Nothing in the world is more boring than commercial land development."

She blinked. *Whoa.* He must be . . . wealthy?

In one fell swoop, her entire perception of Kiptyn Llowell turned on its head. She'd assumed . . . Well, whatever she'd assumed, it hadn't involved having a rich family.

"Yeah," she managed. "That does sound . . . not terribly exciting." Of course, neither was being a photographer. Clearly, there was a story there. "So, you left home to make it on your own?"

He gave a short snort. "You could say that."

Definitely a story there. "How did you—"

But he looked at his watch and interrupted. "Time's up. We better get going."

His entire mood had shifted. He was now as closed up as one of the oysters they harvested in the shallows up north, his family history apparently kept buried deep inside—the irritation he'd built the layers of his life and career around. She was intrigued, but at the same time dismayed that she'd unwittingly shattered the feelings of closeness they'd been sharing. She didn't want things with him to end like this.

But his movements were swift and efficient as he tossed the remnants of their picnic and packed his belongings into his rucksack. He'd shut her out.

She took a deep breath. Okay. Probably for the best. It would make parting with him a tiny bit easier.

When they were ready, she turned to cross the wide band of sand in the direction of the road.

"Not that way," he said, and tipped his chin down along the shore. "The Hilton's down there. We'll go in the back way, from the beach side."

"Oh." She hesitated, then nodded. "All right."

They started walking, and she saw he was back in soldier mode, casually but intently scoping out their surroundings, his eyes never resting, missing nothing. *What was he looking for?*

Along the sandy shore, they passed people lounging on towels, kids building sand castles and playing in the water, teenagers chasing Frisbees and kicking soccer balls. There was no sign of police or army personnel, nothing out of the ordinary for a crowded beach resort.

He stopped a half block from the hotel property, and pretended to watch some windsurfers on the water. "This is where I leave you," he said.

Shocked, she drew in a sharp breath. *So soon?* She'd known it was coming, but the reality hit her like a kick in the gut.

"Please, Kip. Come in with me. Roger will—"

"No. I know you mean well, but I can't trust anyone right now except myself." He turned to her, reaching a hand out to run his fingers down her cheek. "And you. I trust you, DeAnne. But you're not the one making the decisions for the State Department."

She swallowed back her emotions, a thick lump forming in her throat. "So this is it, then."

His thumb brushed over her lips, his stony façade softening for a brief moment. "I hope not. I'll find you when this is over. I'm not forgetting about that date you promised me."

It was now or never. She had to do it. For her own good.

"Kip, I . . ."

At her expression of misery, his face fell, along with his hand. The stone wall was back.

"Or not," he said, his voice rife with irony. After a moment he lifted her chin with his fingers, leaned in, and gave her a hard kiss. The tender lover of last night was gone. "It's been good, princess. Take care of yourself."

With that, he turned on his boot heel and strode away. Leaving her with an aching heart and an overwhelming urge to run after him and tell him, "Yes! I'll be your sometimes lover! If only you promise not to break my heart . . ."

Too late.

Somehow, she held herself back.

She straightened her spine and forced herself to turn and walk toward the Hilton without a backward glance. She got as far as the hotel pool without breaking down, but once safely there, she collapsed into a deck chair, battling back the overwhelming emotions. Eyes shut, she breathed deeply, collecting herself for several minutes before she could get her legs to carry her into the hotel lobby.

She walked in slowly, and saw her boss right away. Roger Achity was pacing back and forth in front of the concierge desk.

She could do this. It was what Kip wanted. She'd be safe now.

She straightened her spine and waved to Roger, and he halted, waving back in relief, bee-lining it in her direction.

He'd only taken a few steps when a tall man approached him from one side, grasped his arm, and jerked him to a stop. He held something to his ribs. Something long and black, like a—

What the—

Her steps faltered. *Oh, God.* That was a *gun*!

She had to get out of there!

She spun, and started to run. And ran smack into an even bigger man. He was older, with a kindly face and long, silver hair. But he had a gun, too, covered by a beach towel draped over his arm. He pointed the pistol at her chest. "Don't," he said.

A blond woman appeared at her side, took her arm, and greeted her as though they were old friends, steering her off toward the outside exit.

"I'm sorry, ma'am," she said softly, "but you'll need to come with us. And do not even *think* of trying to get away."

19

God. *Damn.* It.

He should *not* have let her go in alone.

Kip had smelled a rat the whole time they were walking up the beach to the Hilton. Something hadn't felt right. It was too calm. The drop-off had seemed too easy. He was a wanted man, a foreigner with every law enforcement official in China hunting him; he would have expected some kind of checkpoints set up in the tourist areas. But there'd been no sign of troops.

He'd been so dismayed by DeAnne's refusal to see him again that he'd not paid enough attention to his instincts.

And now three armed tangos had kidnapped her right from under that idiot Achity's nose.

Where the hell was that protective security detail he'd asked for?

God *fucking* damn it.

Kip didn't stop to think about what he was doing. The second he realized what was happening, he launched himself out of his hiding place behind the pool cabana, reaching for the weapon tucked in his shoulder holster.

A half bottle of wine had never taken the edge off his reflexes before. But apparently that, combined with the terror coursing through his heart at seeing the woman he loved being threatened, must have paralyzed every one of his instincts for a few precious seconds.

Before he could take even one step, he felt the iron grip of two hands clamp onto his arms. "I wouldn't do that if I were you," a voice drawled, and the prick of a hypodermic needle touched his neck. It didn't penetrate, but it had the desired effect. He froze in his tracks. He was instantly relieved of his weapon.

He tried to jerk in the opposite direction and twist free, but it was no use. His reaction came too late. These guys were gorillas, and that needle had him breaking out in a cold sweat. Besides, the last thing he wanted was to start a fight, drawing the Chinese security police.

Frying pan or fire?

He could see Roger Achity standing inside the lobby, watching in horror as DeAnne was led away by an amazon in a slick pantomime of friendliness, powerless to help her because his own captor kept him firmly in place.

So, Achity wasn't part of this?

"Who the fuck *are* you?" Kip growled, weighing the odds of getting shot full of tranqs if he tried one of his more lethal moves to escape their hold. He could probably do it. The only question was the consequences, and who would suffer them.

"Don't even think about it," the other guy said, reading his mind. "We don't want to hurt her."

They started weaving him back through the crowded pool area, laughing, talking loud, pretending to be a rowdy trio of drunken tourists.

"Let her go," Kip bit out. "She's got nothing to do with any of this."

"I don't think so," came the deceptively lazy answer. Deceptive, because he could hear the steel beneath the words. Not to mention feel it in his arms. The guy was a blond Rambo type, short hair, bulging muscles, military commando written all over him.

Shit.

"Come along now, nice and easy, and no one gets hurt."

Was he kidding? "What is this," Kip asked with a snort, "a bad spaghetti western?"

Nevertheless, he went along with them nice and easy, mainly because he could see DeAnne being ushered his way, her eyes huge and filled with fear. The female kidnapper had an arm around her, best friends, a weapon digging into DeAnne's side. The old guy trailing them had one, too.

Fury streaked through Kip's whole body. "If you've hurt her, I'll—"

"Are you that blind?" his second captor said, voice calm and sardonic. "Her fear is for you, bro."

Kip turned his head to scowl at him. Tall and broad-shouldered like a swimmer, the man was young, still in his twenties. But his eyes were as old as Kip had ever seen. "What the hell are you talking about?"

The kid just smiled, those ancient eyes seeing straight through him. Which made Kip so angry he tried again to jerk away from the two assholes, which just landed him with both arms yanked high up his back and excruciating pain searing through them.

DeAnne gave a small cry of dismay, which razored straight through his heart.

"I *said* nice and easy," the first guy drawled, casually showing him the hypodermic.

Kip gritted his teeth. He was getting really sick of that

obnoxious Southern accent. "Lighten the fuck up," he ground out. "You've got me, okay?"

They were walking past the pool area now, heading with surprising speed toward the parking lot at the side of the hotel.

"Be good," the young guy said, and at some unseen signal they both let Kip's arms down a few inches. "We're on your side, Major. Just gotta put on a good show for the natives."

With a surprised glance, Kip scanned their surroundings. Sure enough, a pair of uniformed PLA muscle stood just outside the parking lot, watching their progress. *Shit.* He ducked his head and decided it was best to play along for the moment. At least these guys spoke the right language.

God knew what he was getting himself into, but it had to be better than a Chinese prison.

DeAnne's trio joined them at the perimeter of the parking lot. She looked frantic, her cheeks flushed, her pretty blue eyes rimmed with red. "Oh, Kip, I'm so sorry. I never meant—"

"Hush, princess. I know. It'll be all right. Please don't cry."

To his surprise, the gorillas pushed him to her side. Then they encircled the two of them in a moving formation that to anyone else would just look like a bunch of inebriated friends having a good time.

She clutched his waist, trembling, and Rambo actually let one of his arms go so he could put it around her and hold her close.

"Who are you people?" he demanded quietly. He was starting to think—*hope?*—maybe he'd misjudged the situation. "Where are you taking us?"

"We're the good guys," the Southerner returned. "And we're getting you the hell out of here. So shut the fuck up and let us do our job."

A white panel van pulled up with a squeal of brakes and

the side door slid open with a bang. A tall, rangy man with a black ponytail and the features of a Native American hopped out and held it open for them.

He took one look at DeAnne and his serious expression melted away.

She looked back at the man and let out a loud gasp. “My God. *Clint?*”

A huge grin broke over the guy’s face. “Hello, DeAnne. I thought it might be you.”

20

Wait.

For a moment, Kip just stood there, dumbfounded. *What was going on?*

He wasn't the only one. The rest of his captors looked equally taken aback. Everyone except DeAnne and the man she'd called Clint.

Before Kip could tighten his arm around her, she threw herself into the other man's embrace and he swung her around in a big hug, both of them laughing and talking over each other.

Kip folded his arms and glared. "You *know* this guy?" he demanded, confusion battling with a totally irrational desire to pound the man into the pavement.

"Oh, Kip!" she said, her entire face lit up with surprised joy. She stood grinning and hugging the other man, his arm wrapped around her shoulder. "This is Lieutenant Commander Clint Walker. He—"

"Not anymore," Walker interrupted. "Don't forget, I'm a civilian now."

"Whatever." She waved him off with a smile. "Clint was—I helped him—" Her mouth opened and shut a couple of times, then her eyes clouded with consternation. "Oh, dear. I'm not really supposed to talk about that, am I?"

Kip narrowed his eyes. "Talk about what?"

"But I can," Clint said, giving her a much-too-affectionate look. "DeAnne helped get me out of a real jam last year. My wife's ship was hijacked by pirates. Well, a Chinese PLA assassination squad, actually. Needless to say, I was their target. DeAnne negotiated with the Chinese government to call them off. She did a great job, as you can see. I'm still alive."

By now, everyone's jaws had dropped almost to the pavement. Including Kip's. But he'd fastened on to two words that managed to wipe the red haze from his vision.

My wife.

Relief twisted through him like a tornado. He didn't know what he would have done if he'd had to watch her with some old—

No. He wasn't going there.

Besides, she didn't want Kip. Didn't want to go on seeing him. She'd as good as said so less than fifteen minutes ago. He *shouldn't* care.

He eased out the breath he'd been holding and let himself be crammed into the corner of the third-row bench seat in the patiently idling panel van. DeAnne climbed in after him, followed by Clint Walker, joining them in the back row.

"Where are you taking us?" Kip asked no one in particular as the van pulled out of the hotel parking lot.

"The harbor," Walker said, then DeAnne asked him about his wife, and he said she was pregnant, and DeAnne exclaimed and hugged him again, and that's when Kip tuned them out.

Weddings and babies. The thought made him shudder.

He did a quick assessment of the others in the van. *Captors or rescuers?* Despite DeAnne's relationship with one of them, Kip still wasn't completely convinced.

There were six operators. Walker sat on the far side of DeAnne. Occupying the middle bench seat were Rambo, who seemed to be the team leader, the amazon, and the young guy with the eyes that had seen too much—who also looked as though he hadn't slept in a week. The older guy with the ponytail was the front passenger, and the driver was a somber, silent man who hadn't been part of the kidnapping. *Getaway driver.* Even with his geeky glasses and pasty complexion, Kip would definitely not want to meet that one in a dark alley.

When they were on the road, the woman reached into a cooler and tossed drinks all around. She looked at him and DeAnne. "We've got Coke, Fanta, or water."

Grateful, he took a bottle of water. He had to admit, this was about as far as it got from what he'd expected when he felt that first prick of a tranq needle against his carotid artery.

He wondered if Jake had somehow sent this crew to rescue them. It was obvious this was some flavor of spec ops team. They might look like misfits, but everything they did was coordinated and on point.

But why the kidnapping ruse?

Or was this friendly hospitality the ruse?

"Thanks," he said, cracking the cap of his water after surreptitiously inspecting it for tampering. "But will somebody please tell me what the hell is going on?"

DeAnne and Walker looked up from their conversation.

There was a long moment of silence in the van, broken only by the crunch of the vehicle's tires on the uneven pavement.

"Fair enough," Rambo said, and everyone turned to him. "You've already met Walker. I'm Commander Bobby Lee Quinn." He touched the woman's shoulder. "This is Darcy Zimmerman, and that's Alex Zane." He tossed a thumb over his shoulder at the younger man, then pointed to the front of the van. "Up front we have Master Chief Rufus Edwards, retired"—the old guy saluted him—"and our esteemed driver is Rand Jaeger."

"Okay," Kip said. "And?"

Quinn said, "Ever heard of a PMC called STORM Corps?"

Kip nodded. Working intelligence behind the lines, he'd run across most of the private military companies whose specialty was recovering hostages and defending assets in war-torn regions of the world. There weren't many of them. STORM—Strategic Technical Operations and Rescue Missions Corporation, if he wasn't mistaken—was one of the best-known, with an excellent reputation for getting the job done right, with minimum fallout.

He opened his mouth to probe further, but DeAnne beat him to it. She sat up, nearly dropping the Coke bottle the woman, Darcy, had handed her. "You're from STORM? The outfit that rescued those three kids from the terrorist camp in Indonesia?" Her eyes darted to Walker.

He shrugged. "Don't ask me. I was just brought on two days ago."

Darcy smiled at Quinn as if remembering the op, then nodded at DeAnne. "Yeah. That was us. A good outcome."

"I'll say," DeAnne said, her expression morphing from hesitancy to admiration. "You really are the good guys."

He shouldn't be too surprised that a State Department official knew about PMCs. No doubt State often had to deal with private companies hired by families horning into cases involving everything from kidnapped American businessmen to foreign-born parents taking children out of the

U.S. without proper custody. The Indonesian incident, for instance, had been all over the news . . . though STORM hadn't been mentioned by the media, apparently preferring to remain under the radar. The State Department had taken all the public credit for that rescue.

"So you're all with STORM?" he asked.

"Yeah," Quinn answered without hesitation. "Except Walker and the master chief. They're on loan."

Kip looked around at the six operators, something still niggling at him. What exactly was the agenda here?

"Who sent you to help us?" he asked, cutting to the chase.

Every one of the six shifted slightly in their seat.

Ah, hell. And just like that, the rescuers turned back into captors. "You weren't sent to help us." He should have fucking known.

The master chief cleared his throat. "Truth is, we were sent to neutralize you."

"Neutralize?" DeAnne squeaked. Fear crept back across her face.

Walker patted her hand. "Don't worry. That doesn't mean we're supposed to shoot you."

Kip wanted to rip the guy's hand off. He had to physically restrain himself from putting a proprietary arm around her, pulling her away from the jerk, and telling him to back the hell off his woman.

Except, of course, she wasn't his woman.

"That would be a waste of a perfectly good Marine," Quinn drawled, and flashed a smile at DeAnne. "And a pretty lady."

That earned Quinn an elbow in the ribs from Darcy. *Good.* Kip decided he liked her.

"Sent by whom?" he pressed.

"Sorry. That's privileged information," Quinn said.

DeAnne frowned, and Kip muttered, "Give me a fucking break."

"Goddamn navy, that's who," Alex Zane piped up, a large dose of bitterness coloring his tone.

The navy.

Kip was shocked. *Shocked.*

Jake had said Kip had been sent in as a decoy, never intended to complete his mission to photograph the prototype of the new Chinese AUV being tested at Yulin Submarine Base. The whole ridiculous decoy plan had clearly turned into one big political clusterfuck, so it made sense they'd want him off the playing field.

What *didn't* make sense was this too-obvious, broad-daylight kidnapping charade. Not the navy's usual style.

"If you're not going to shoot us," he asked, leveling a penetrating look at the STORM commander, "what *do* you intend to do with us?"

The cocky Southerner sent him an irreverent grin. "Why, Major, I think that's fairly obvious. Send you back into the fray, of course. But this time, you'll be working for us."

21

The team had one more thing to do before boarding the fishing trawler that would take them back to the navy ship, USNS *Impeccable*. Quinn had arranged to meet up with the Russian submarine captain, Nikolai Romanov, to discuss the new plan. The Russian had become an integral part of it, more than just the mere distraction he'd previously been meant to play.

Darcy hadn't ever thought using Romanov as a distraction would work, because of the coincidence factor. The Chinese would be expecting something to happen and would be ready for it. But now Darcy wondered if Commander Bridger had predicted all along the need for an operative inside the Chinese naval base, and somehow orchestrated Romanov's timely tour of the facility. The man was scary brilliant. Hell, the man was just plain scary.

The van pulled up to a busy pedestrian square surrounded by sidewalk restaurants and craft vendors. In the middle of the square, a troupe of street performers was juggling and doing gymnastics to the delight of the crowd.

Darcy hopped out of the van, and at a signal from Quinn, Clint Walker climbed out after her. Darcy would recognize Romanov, but wasn't sure he'd know her after only seeing her that one brief time on the ship. However, Walker was his friend, so there wouldn't be any question from either side as to who they were dealing with.

"Take Alex, too," Quinn ordered, and glanced at his watch as Zane slid from the vehicle. "We'll be back for you in ten."

The three of them melted into the crowd, searching for the Russian.

"There," Walker said, tipping his chin toward a European couple standing on the opposite side of the troupe. "He's with Julie."

Julie the CIA officer. Darcy wondered what her bosses at Langley thought about their upcoming nuptials. Detente to the extreme. Although they did make a really pretty couple, with Julie's flame-haired elegance and Nikolai's studly imperial bearing.

They worked their way over to them through the crowd. "Nick! Julie!" she said cheerfully, putting on her "tourist" persona. "What a gorgeous day, huh?"

The pair turned to them, all smiles. "Hey, girl, how are you?" Julie greeted her with a kiss on the cheek, Euro-style, then gave Walker a big hug. "Wolf! So good to see you!"

Wolf?

Nikolai shook hands with them, said "hi" to Alex, and they all chitchatted for a few moments about the jugglers. Then he glanced around and said, "Shall we grab an ice cream?"

They broke off from the crowd, and as they made their way across the square, Darcy said, "The plan's changed a bit, sir. We've decided instead of staging the mission on land, we're going to divert it during a blue-water test, right into our waiting hands."

Romanov's steps faltered for a split second. "Blue water?"

"Blue water" meant deep ocean, as opposed to "green water," which referred to littoral shallows.

"Apparently Bridger has friends in deep places," she said. "He got us a Kilo."

For a moment, Romanov's expression went positively nostalgic.

Julie, on the other hand, looked horrified. "Please tell me it's not a Russian boat."

Darcy shrugged. "Not sure. Why?"

Julie shook a finger at her fiancé. "You are not stepping foot on that submarine, do you hear me?"

Uh-oh. Darcy held up her hands. "Don't worry. That's not in the plan."

"Explain to me," Romanov said, "how you plan to 'divert' a sophisticated, tightly controlled, remotely steered vessel underwater?"

"We've got the new guidance system, remember?" This from Walker.

Stunned, Darcy asked, "How do you know that?"

Bridger had gotten the guidance system software from the client under Top Secret confidentiality—everyone at STORM had Top Secret clearance—and she'd gotten it from Bridger. The two of them were the only people in STORM Corps who knew they had a copy of the cutting-edge Chinese guidance system software.

"Well?" she demanded, battling to keep her voice low.

Walker smiled. "Julie was the spy who stole it last year. Afterward, I delivered the storage disk to the navy."

Darcy's eyes bugged out in shock.

"I did not steal anything!" Julie huffed indignantly. Her lips twitched. "I found it."

"Yeah. On my damn boat. Right before they blew it up," Romanov groused, but his eyes were twinkling.

"And I am *not* an s-p-y," she spelled out under her breath. "I'm an analyst."

Speechless, Darcy gaped from one to the other. Were they for freaking real?

Alex snorted. "And they accused the Marine of being a spy."

All three of them shushed him.

"So anyway," Romanov said, turning to Darcy, who'd somehow managed to snap her mouth shut, "what do you need from me?"

She gave herself a mental boot and dragged herself back to the present situation. "Right. We need you to go through with your planned diplomatic tour of the naval base. And while you're inside . . ." She pulled a pack of gum from her jeans pocket and casually passed it to him. "There's a thumb drive in there. I need you to stick it into any USB port that you can get to on any mainframe terminal on the base."

He regarded the gum warily. "What's on it?"

"A nifty little app that will call home one time with the log-in info I need to access their system, then wipe itself clean."

STORM's extensive server-side databases included log-in data for dozens of U.S. and international systems—they had done missions for nearly every major government in the world, and inclusion in the country's security data pool was a nonnegotiable condition of their services. Unfortunately, they'd never done work for Beijing.

Every vestige of humor had fled Julie's stricken face. "You know what will happen to Nikolai if they catch him."

Darcy knew. They all knew. It was the accepted risk in the game they played.

Romanov leaned over and kissed her hair, murmuring a few words in Russian to her. Julie nodded, her eyes glistening. They were so in love it was downright painful to watch.

Darcy turned away. God, she was becoming a sentimental fool.

"Be sure to take the gum wrapper off when it's in place," she told him, "so you don't leave any fingerprints."

Romanov gave a nod. "Anything else?"

"Nope. That's it. And thanks, Captain. We appreciate what you're doing for us."

He gave a regal incline of his head. "Think nothing of it." He tipped his head at Walker. "Clint, you can really do this spoof?"

Walker winked. "Rufus and I'll give it a hell of a shot, Kapitan."

The Russian's lips quirked. "I trust he brought the Ukrainian balalaika music?"

Walker gave a belly laugh. "I'm sure he did."

Darcy blinked. Okay, *that* must be a hell of a story.

Julie rolled her eyes. "Watch those two," she muttered to her. "They are complete lunatics. Thank God Nikolai won't be with them."

But Darcy had the feeling she wished he were, rather than doing what had been asked of him.

Romanov gave Walker a slap on the back. "Keep it hot, straight, and normal, my friend."

"No crazy Ivans, I promise." Walker gave his shoulder a squeeze. "Stay safe, Nikolai. Don't take any chances."

"Nor you." With that, he hooked his arm around his fiancée's shoulder, and they strolled away.

Okay.

After a moment, Darcy looked at Walker. "You're good friends."

He nodded. "Yeah. Almost dying together tends to do that."

How well she knew.

"You'll have to tell me about it sometime."

As they walked back to meet the van, she thought about Quinn, and how many times they'd faced death together over the years. A whole bunch. It had brought them closer than most people would ever be with another human being.

Was that why they loved each other so much? Because no one else could understand what it meant to stare mortality in the face on a regular basis?

No. She'd faced death with any number of STORM operators. But Bobby Lee Quinn was the only one she was in love with.

So why couldn't she bring herself to set a date to marry the man?

With a sigh, she thought of her adoptive parents, and for the millionth time silently cursed them.

Deep inside, she knew exactly why.

They'd taken her in, made a legal commitment to her, then two years later had replaced her with their own much-wanted children, leaving her in a loveless, emotional wasteland to fend for herself.

But knowing the reason didn't help the deep-seated, totally irrational fear that Quinn would do the same thing to her as they'd done.

It was the legal commitment part that terrified her, down to her very toes. Without that, if he left, she could always tell herself it hadn't been real, wasn't official, so it didn't matter so much if he left her for someone else. Replaced her. But after they were married . . . if he discarded her that way, it would kill her. Literally. She wouldn't be able to take it. She'd be devastated, lose her concentration completely, and make a mistake. In this job if you made a mistake you were dead.

The ultimate replacement.

She saw the white van coming up the road, approaching the square, and shook off her distressing thoughts. She really needed to get a grip. And stop being so damn paranoid.

And just pick a frikkin' date.

"Everything go okay?" Quinn asked when they'd all climbed into the van.

She gave him a very unprofessional kiss on the cheek. "Yep. I gave him the thumb drive and he agreed to place it. We're all set."

"Excellent." He turned to Jaeger, who was still at the wheel. "Okay, let's head for the harbor. It's high time we got off this damn island."

Fifteen minutes later, they were all sprawled out below decks in the crew lounge of a nondescript fishing trawler, heading out to sea.

DeAnne couldn't decide whether to celebrate or to start worrying again. The good news was, Kip was safely out of China—or he would be as soon as they hit international waters—and could no longer be arrested for espionage. That was a huge relief.

Okay, yeah, she'd nearly had a heart attack when they were abducted at gunpoint, but Bobby Lee Quinn had explained it had all just been for show, in front of witnesses, so U.S. officials could say the accused spy and his accomplice had been swiftly and quietly dealt with, and there would be evidence.

While Walker and the two others were gone and the van was just driving around, Kip had asked Bobby Lee Quinn what he'd meant when he'd said he was sending Kip back into the fray but he'd be working for STORM. DeAnne had been more than a little alarmed when he'd said that, and also wanted to know what he'd meant.

Kip had never actually told her what his mission was on Hainan. Something to do with photography, she'd gathered. There were a lot of military installations on the island, so she figured it involved one of those. But exactly what he'd been sent to do, she had no idea.

Quinn hadn't been any more forthcoming. He'd told Kip to be patient, that everything would be explained once they reached their destination—a navy ship somewhere between China and the Philippines.

And then Quinn had told DeAnne that she'd be transported to the Philippines, and from there she'd be flown home.

"Wait. I'm not going with you?" Her heart had stalled.

Quinn had shaken his head. "Our orders were just to pick you up. The navy will get you back to the States. We have a mission to run."

"But Kip—Major Llowell isn't part of your team, either."

"No, but he's a Marine, ma'am."

He'd said it as if that explained everything.

Which she supposed it did. For better and for worse.

She glanced over at Kip now. He'd chosen to sit on the opposite side of the fishing trawler's salon. His eyes were closed, his head leaning against the back of the fish-stained banquette, his legs stretched out with boots crossed, arms banded over his chest.

He hadn't looked her way since boarding the trawler. Practically since being loaded into the van. He'd closed himself off from her completely.

She'd thought . . . For those terrifying moments while they were being kidnapped, he'd been so protective of her. He'd held her so close, using his own body as a shield against the danger. She'd thought he'd forgiven her for reneging at the last minute on their promised date. For in essence rejecting his offer of a relationship. Such as it was.

She supposed she'd asked for his indifference. But it still hurt.

And now they really would be going their separate ways, as soon as they got to the ship. And she'd never get a chance to tell him . . . how much he'd come to mean to her.

If only he'd look at her . . .

"Don't worry. He's just being a guy," Darcy murmured, following the direction of her gaze. The other woman had taken a seat on the same banquette as DeAnne. "Men are so totally oblivious. But trust me, he'll come around."

DeAnne felt her ears burn. Had she been that obvious? She shrugged. "Doesn't matter. No future there, anyway."

A wry smile curved Darcy's lips as she glanced at Quinn. "Yeah. That's what I said, too."

DeAnne caught her look of love. "You're with Quinn?"

"Yeah. Engaged." She stuck out her hand and DeAnne oohed over the gorgeous diamond on her finger.

"Nice. When's the happy day?"

Darcy made a face. "I can't decide. Bobby Lee's about ready to get out the shotgun and drag me to Vegas."

DeAnne smiled . . . and tamped down a twinge of jealousy. "That would be romantic."

Darcy wrinkled her nose. "Gawd. Quinn, romantic? That'll be a cold day." But she didn't seem displeased by that. In fact, she kind of glowed. "I just wish . . ." She shook her head.

"What?"

"I don't know. The idea of marriage . . ." Darcy's body gave a little shudder. "It's just so . . . I don't know . . . permanent."

DeAnne chuckled. "Well. Not really. There is such a thing as divorce." She realized what she'd said and slapped a hand over her mouth. "Oh, jeez. Sorry! I didn't mean—"

Darcy gave a strained laugh and waved a hand. "Believe me, I know. But . . ." She made a wry face. "I'm still terrified."

Their eyes met in perfect understanding. "Yeah. I get that," DeAnne said quietly.

Just then, Quinn appeared in front of them, taking up every square inch of open space. "What are you two talking about that's so funny?" he asked with a smile, and plopped himself down on the narrow banquette next to Darcy, scooping her onto his lap as he did so.

"Hey!" She swatted at him and wriggled in protest at his casual manhandling, but her eyes were sparkling with love and laughter as he kissed her on the temple.

"Well?"

"If you must know, we were discussing our wedding date."

"Yeah?" His expression softened, and for a moment he looked like a hopeful little boy at Christmas. "You finally decided?"

Her gaze slid to the diamond on her finger as she fussed with his T-shirt pocket. "Um. Not exactly. Soon, though. I promise."

He blew out a long breath. "Good thing I'm a patient man."

She kissed his cheek. "One of the many reasons I love you so much."

DeAnne watched their interaction with a bone-deep envy. She didn't know what the deal was with the wedding date, but it was obvious they were both completely in love with each other.

What would it feel like to have someone love you that much, and that openly? She couldn't even imagine. She'd only ever seen love like that in books and movies. Apparently it existed in real life, too, for a lucky few.

She slid her gaze to Kip, and was surprised to see him watching the affectionate couple, too. Before she could look away, his unreadable gaze met hers. She smiled, and his eyes narrowed, then closed.

Shut off again.

She wanted to cry.

The sound of a phone buzzed through the room. Bobby Lee jumped up after setting Darcy aside, and strode to where he'd left his jacket. "That's the sat phone."

Which apparently meant something to everyone else, because they all sat up and listened as he answered the call. Even Kip opened his eyes and rearranged himself on the banquette.

"Quinn." The big blond man listened for a long moment. "Roger that. We'll be ready." He clicked off and sent a grin around the room. "There have been developments, people. Be ready to roll in ten."

DeAnne watched several of the others get to their feet, gather their gear, and disappear up the companionway to the deck. She glanced out through a nearby porthole and saw they were still surrounded by water. She wasn't sure what she should do, and didn't relish fighting the motion of the boat pitching to and fro as it sped over the waves, so she stayed where she was.

Clint ambled over to her on legs that didn't even notice the rocking.

"What's going on?" she asked him.

"Not really sure."

"What kind of developments could Quinn be talking about? The Chinese Coast Guard or something?" She'd started getting nervous again. Had they made it into international waters yet?

"He didn't look too worried, so I doubt it. My guess is our transpo's here."

It turned out he was right.

When they went up on deck with the others a few minutes later, Clint didn't seem the least bit surprised by the sight that greeted them.

But she was. Shock slammed into her full on.

"What the heck?" she murmured under her breath.

Master Chief Edwards chortled. "*Oh*, yeah."

The others actually cheered.

DeAnne just stared. *This* was their transportation? Somebody *had* to be kidding.

Breaking the surface of the ocean with an explosion of black antennas and spumes of white spray was a huge, gray submarine.

22

"We need to make this quick," Bobby Lee Quinn said to DeAnne, Kip, and the others as the fishing trawler's crew lowered a dingy over the back end of the boat. "It'll be a squeeze with us and the equipment, but I don't want to make two trips."

DeAnne looked in horror from him to the submarine as it dawned on her what was happening. They weren't going back to USS *Impeccable*. That *submarine* was their new transportation.

Okay. This was *way* outside her comfort zone. They were literally out in the middle of the ocean with swells as big as skyscrapers, and that lunatic wanted her to get into a teensy little dingy and cross the open water to the waiting submarine.

Oh, yeah, and then she had to climb up a flimsy rope ladder one of the submariners was now tossing over the side, figure out how to walk across the slick metal deck without getting swept overboard by a rogue wave, make her way to the porthole-sized hatch, where she'd then have to climb down into the bowels of the submarine—in a sarong—and then—

God, she had no idea what came after that.

She didn't really *want* to know. And she definitely didn't want to do any of this.

But DeAnne's new motto was *never let 'em see you sweat*, so she lifted her chin, swallowed her fear, and joined the others so she could be handed down into the dingy.

Ho. Boy.

"You look a little green around the gills," Clint said with a sympathetic smile at her unease. He was standing next to her waiting his turn. Kip was in front of her, wearing his backpack.

"Big ocean, little boat," she said nervously. "Not my thing."

"Not to worry," Clint said. "If you fall in, I'll jump in and save you. I'm a former SEAL, you know."

"I remember," she said. "I also seem to recall you enjoy playing with sharks. Something I'd just as soon avoid."

One time—after several glasses of wine—his wife, Sam, had told her a story about when she and Clint were under siege on her hijacked ship. At one point he'd had to take a freezing swim in the Bering Sea to escape the bad guys, and Sam had feared the worst when he came back covered in blood. Turned out it had been shark's blood, not his, and Clint had been grinning like a fool. Afterward, the sex had been amazing, Sam had confessed sheepishly.

Clint shot DeAnne a suspicious glance. "You know about the shark?"

"Oh, yeah. I know *all* about the shark," DeAnne said, feeling a tinge of heat in her cheeks as she recalled Sam's blissful expression. She turned away in embarrassment, and her gaze collided with Kip's stony visage. Quite a contrast. He did not appear the least bit amused or embarrassed.

Wordlessly, Kip grabbed hold of the rail at the back end of the trawler, bent his knees, and leaped over the edge, making a light, perfect landing on the bench of the dingy below. It barely rocked.

He turned and indicated she should hand him her shoulder bag. After setting it down, he stretched his arms up toward her. "Jump. I'll catch you." No encouraging smile. Or hint of concern.

She hesitated, and for the briefest of nanoseconds thought he was so darn granite-faced he'd probably catch her only so he could toss her overboard.

Silly.

Clint was about to offer her a hand instead, but at some silent, primitive male communication with Kip, he backed off, palms out.

Great.

They were choosing *now* to have a pissing match?

For Pete's sake, Clint was happily married. *Blissfully* married.

Instead of rolling her eyes, she squeezed them shut, took a deep breath along with Kip's hand, and let herself be tugged down into his arms.

He caught her easily.

The shock of warmth and the dark male scent of his body surrounding hers made her want to moan in pleasure. And stay there tucked against him forever. But he eased her feet down to the bottom of the dingy and held her steady as he helped her to a seat toward the back, then let her go.

He squeezed into the seat next to her, forcing Clint to find a place in the front of the dingy.

Finally, she couldn't take it any longer.

"Are you mad at me?" she asked Kip as the last of the team climbed on board.

"Nope," he said, passing her shoulder bag over to her.

"Then why are you ignoring me?"

For the first time he looked her square in the eyes. "I thought that's how you wanted it."

"No," she said. "That's not how I—"

But she didn't get a chance to say any more, because Bobby Lee Quinn started calling out instructions to his team for after they were on board the submarine. It was all Greek to her. Something about birthing compartments and equipment and boomers and diving.

After a few thankfully short minutes of braving the huge waves, they bumped against the hull of the sub and made fast. Alex Zane scurried up the flimsy ladder first, followed by Darcy and the master chief, each carrying a large duffel bag. When it was DeAnne's turn, she gathered her courage and stood, and found herself once again enveloped by strong arms helping her to the ladder.

A hot wind whipped through her hair and her dress as she secured her shoulder bag. Foolishly, she hadn't changed out of the pretty sarong outfit they'd bought at the market. Had it really been just four short hours ago?

"I've got your back," Kip said. "Grab the ladder and go."

Easy for him to say.

Ascending was harder than it looked, mainly because the fluttering fabric of her skirt kept getting tangled in her legs, and the submarine's deck was a lot higher up than it had appeared. Somehow she made it up the never-ending rungs. True to his word, Kip remained right behind her the whole way. There was no chance she could fall off. He'd catch her before she plummeted two inches.

When they reached the top, he put a sheltering arm around her waist and jogged her over to the main hatch, where he guided her to the solid metal ladder descending into the belly of the submarine.

Halfway down, she realized he hadn't followed after her.

Darcy was at the bottom, waiting alongside a handful of submariners dressed in blue, gray, and black camo uniforms. "Welcome on board, ma'am," she was greeted by the men, along with friendly handshakes. They eyed her long skirt, but didn't comment.

They were Americans, but she'd noticed there'd been no identifying markings on the sub. She got the distinct feeling she was now on a U.S. Navy vessel that didn't officially exist.

She was dying to ask what the heck she was doing on a ghost sub in the middle of the South China Sea. But so far nobody'd given her a straight answer to any of her questions—except Bobby Lee Quinn, and she figured if he wanted to tell her anything, it would only be when he was good and ready.

Darcy hefted a small duffel in one hand, and slipped the other through DeAnne's arm, pulling her toward a round-topped metal doorway in the solid wall of instrument panels and maze of hanging pipes that crowded nearly every square inch of the claustrophobic space.

"They bunked us together," Darcy said. "Come on."

The other woman seemed to know her way around. "You've been on a submarine before?" DeAnne asked, climbing through the opening after her. The watertight door's sill was shin high and the top rim came down to her nose. A round metal handle like a steering wheel stuck out from the middle of the heavy, solid door.

"A few times. We've launched some of our ops from subs in the past. It's been a while, but the smaller ones are all pretty similar."

Smaller ones? This one had seemed huge to DeAnne. From the outside, anyway.

As they walked, Darcy gave a guided tour of her surroundings. "There are three decks on these old tubs," she explained. "The control rooms are on the main deck. On the lower deck are the living quarters. The shallow deck below that contains batteries and other yucky things that power the boat. You don't want to go down there."

DeAnne wondered about that. The small size and the presence of batteries meant they were on a diesel electric submarine, not a nuclear powered one. She didn't know a whole lot about the Pacific Fleet, but she did know that the U.S. had stopped using diesel electrics in favor of nukes a couple of decades ago. And yet, here she was on one.

Strange.

They went through two more watertight doors, passing several instrument-filled side compartments with a half-dozen submariners busy at various tasks, along with a kitchen and open dining room next to it.

"Up top," Darcy continued, "the big tower thing that sticks up from the deck is called the conning tower, or the sail. Don't ask me why."

They came to a cylindrical opening in the floor containing another steep ladder.

"Down we go," Darcy said. "Heads up below!" She tossed her duffel, grabbed the handrails, and slid down the metal ladder. "Try it!"

"You're crazy!" DeAnne took her time and managed to make it down in one piece without tearing her dress or banging her knees too badly.

They continued along the lower deck, and when they got to a very narrow section of passage punctuated by three normal doors, Darcy said, "Here we are. Home sweet home." She opened the first door wide. "You got lucky. This is officer country, so the cabin's a bit bigger."

DeAnne peeked in. *"Bigger?"* Good grief. She'd seen bungalow closets that were bigger.

She stepped inside. The room was microscopic, but they'd somehow crammed in a narrow bunk, two tall lockers on one narrow wall, a minuscule fold-down desk and a pull-down aluminum sink on the other. A conglomeration of communication devices was attached to the scant inches of bare wall space by the door.

She studied the layout for a moment, then suddenly realized—"There's only one bunk."

Darcy had remained standing just outside the door. She tipped her head to the space above it. "The other one pulls down."

"Ah. Like on a train. That should be cozy." Cozy like sardines.

Darcy's thumb fiddled with the handle of her duffel bag, which she still held in front of her. She looked uncomfortable, and cleared her throat. "Yeah. Um. About that."

DeAnne's stomach pinged at her tone. "What is it?"

"The thing is, space on a sub is at a premium. You and I are supposed to share, and Quinn and Major Llowell are supposed to share. So, um, I thought we could trade, and I'll bunk with Quinn."

Which meant—

Oh, no.

"I figured that would be okay with you. And judging by the dagger looks he's been giving Walker whenever he gets near you, the major will no doubt be fine with the arrangement, too."

"You c-can't be serious," DeAnne stammered.

"I know you've been roughing it away from civilization, so I packed you a bag with extra clothes and necessities." She handed over the duffel bag she'd been carrying.

DeAnne took it, her mind still stalled back at the first part, about sharing with Kip. "Darcy, seriously, I can't—"

Darcy pointed down the corridor. "The facilities are two doors down. Make yourself comfortable. Grab a shower. Get some rest. The team's going to do some strategizing before dinner. I'll come get you when it's time to eat."

"Darcy!"

But it was too late. The rat was already halfway down the corridor.

DeAnne swore silently, tilting her face to the ceiling

with a loud groan. She'd have to talk to Bobby Lee Quinn and find some other place to sleep. Darcy was wrong. Kip was not going to like this arrangement. They were barely on speaking terms. Sleep together?

Hardly.

With a sigh, she set the duffel on the bunk, unzipped it, and rifled through the contents. A pair of yoga pants, shorts and a sweatshirt, a pack of bikini undies, a sports bra, two T-shirts and a tank top, flip-flops, a towel, and a cosmetics bag with a few items of makeup and personal essentials. And a small cardboard box.

Curious, she pulled it out of the duffel bag. But before she could see what it contained, she heard a deep voice behind her.

"DeAnne? What are you doing in there?"

She whirled, clutching the box in her hands. "Oh! Kip. Hi."

He glanced at the metal sign on the door and frowned. "I could have sworn Bobby Lee said I was in this berth."

She bit her lip. "Yeah, um, Darcy pulled a switch on us. She thought we wouldn't mind sharing. But of course I'll speak to Bobby Lee and . . ." Her words trailed off when she noticed his gaze had dropped to her hands.

His eyes had narrowed dangerously and his whole body shifted subtly. Slowly, his gaze lifted. The look in his eyes was pure predatory male animal.

Her pulse skyrocketed. What . . . ? She looked down at her hands. And almost died when she realized what she was holding.

Oh. My. *God.*

It was a box of condoms.

23

Kip took a step into the stateroom, dropping his rucksack and duffel on the floor. What the *hell* did she think she was playing at? Fury simmered in his blood.

DeAnne took a step backward. Her tongue peeked out to wet her lower lip. "Kip. It's not what—"

"So that's not a box of condoms?" he interrupted silkily.

Her throat worked. "Um . . . I . . ."

"Planning a party? With Walker?" He'd seen how they smiled at each other.

She gave a little gasp. "No! I'm not— We're not—"

Her denial gave him a second of relief, then shifted his heat in another direction.

"Who then? Me?"

She glanced down at the box and nibbled her lip. The silence stretched.

Enough. He made up her mind for her. He shut the door behind him and shot the latch. The loud click of the lock made her jump.

"Nervous?"

She licked her lips again. The unconscious gesture was driving him nuts. *He* wanted to lick her lips. To taste that pink tongue.

"Should I be?" She swallowed. "Nervous?"

"Never." The word was just short of a growl.

This was such a bad idea. The woman did not want him. Not for more than a quick fuck, anyway. A little forbidden spice in her boring life.

He didn't care. He could work with that. His cock was already hard for her.

"Okay." But he could see her hands tremble.

"So what are you waiting for?" he growled.

She blinked a couple of times. "Um . . ."

"Take off your clothes, DeAnne." He curled the corner of his lip. "Or do you want me to do it for you?"

Her eyes widened. Her fingers convulsed, crushing the box.

In a swift move, he closed the narrow distance between them and slipped the box from her grasp. One-handed, he flipped it open, fanned the contents onto the narrow bunk, and tossed the empty box to the floor. For several seconds they regarded each other, breath quickening, blood heating. Then he reached out and with the tips of his fingers drew the sleeves of her outfit down over her shoulders.

She shivered under his touch.

"I want you naked," he murmured. "Now."

After a short hesitation, her hand went to the front buttons of her colorful blouse. Her finger toyed with the top one. "I want you, too, Kip. But you know this isn't going to solve anything, right?"

He raised a brow. "There's nothing to solve, princess." He pulled his T-shirt over his head and discarded it. "We both know what this is." He eyed her breasts under the thin cotton fabric. She wasn't wearing a bra. Her nipples had spiraled to tight points, and he could imagine the rest of her body tightening and slickening, readying itself for him. "And we both want it."

"Yes, but . . ." Her voice was soft, almost pleading. With herself?

He wrapped his hand around the back of her neck and pulled her face close to his, held his lips a tremble away from hers. "But what, DeAnne?"

He could taste her breath on his tongue. *Wine, piquant spices, Coca-Cola.* And hot, hot desire.

"Nothing." It was barely a whisper.

She slowly undid the buttons of her top, one by one.

He was salivating. He wanted his mouth on her breasts. But he made himself wait. He wanted her shivering with need. He wanted her begging. He wanted her out of her mind for want of him.

As he was for her.

Her top drifted to the floor. A blush of color tinged the pale skin above her lush breasts. A low rumble of approval surfaced from deep within him.

Perfection.

"Now the skirt," he ordered, his voice boots on gravel. His cock was a ramrod, and waiting was pure, sweet torture. He ached to thrust inside her and pound into her until she screamed his name.

But he was determined to take it slow. If this was to be their last time, it was going to be a time they'd both remember for the rest of their lives.

His free hand sought the tie of her sarong skirt and pulled it so the bow dissolved and the knot loosened, sending the gossamer fabric down her legs to pool at her feet. He could feel the filmy silk of her panties slide sensually against the denim of his jeans.

He held her head in his grasp so she couldn't move her face away, and he didn't want to relinquish that power. So instead of removing her panties, he slid his free hand down the front of them, seeking her slick heat.

His fingers found her and she moaned softly, her body undulating against his hand. He watched her eyes as he touched her, sliding his fingers around the center of her need. Circling, zeroing in. She was hot and wet, *damn, so wet*, and he could feel her pulse going out of control as he coaxed her body to yield to the pleasures he was giving her. He dipped his finger into her, then another, pushing them deep, deep inside.

She moaned breathily, and moved her face infinitesimally, so their lips brushed.

"No." He turned slightly aside. He didn't want to give her that particular pleasure yet. But when she mewled in disappointment, he let her kiss his jaw and his cheek and his neck, drawing her tongue over his stubbled skin to taste him.

It was killing him not to taste her back.

He swung their bodies around, and backed her up against the stateroom door, pinning her against it with his chest and thighs. He pressed his thumb to her and worked her flesh to a frenzy of desire, watching the conflicting emotions and the raw sexual need play across her face like a kaleidoscope.

And he realized with profound, blinding insight that he wanted to see that look of desire on her face over and over and again, for years to come. To experience for the rest of his life the searing, overwhelming passion he felt for this woman.

"Kip," she cried, her fingers digging into his shoulders, her breasts rubbing skin to skin against his bare chest with an unbearably sensual friction. "Kip. Kip. Oh, Kip."

He shoved his knee between her legs and spread them wide, opening her to him fully.

"Come for me, princess," he commanded, low and gritty.

She cried his name once more, then her eyes closed and he felt her body go rigid, convulsing into the onrushing tempest of her climax.

He kept at it until the sounds of her pleasure quieted, and the quivering ceased. Then he lifted her limp body in his arms and laid her on the bunk, scattering the small foil packets he'd strewn there earlier.

In seconds he had his boots and jeans off, and a packet ripped in two.

He lowered his body onto hers, and whispered in her ear, "You can fight it all you want, princess, but you're mine. You're mine now, DeAnne, and you'll always be mine."

She gazed up at him, her blue eyes tide pools overflowing with emotion. "Yes," she whispered. "That's what I'm so afraid of."

24

"You did *what*?"

Darcy cringed at Quinn's outburst. She'd waited for a while to tell him about the room switch, just in case she'd been wrong about DeAnne and the major. She hadn't been.

"It just made more sense this way. Llowell and DeAnne clearly have something going on."

"That is beyond unprofessional." Quinn slashed a hand through his golden hair. "Did you even bother to *ask* if they wanted to bunk together?"

"Considering he went in there over two hours ago and neither of them has come out yet, I assume the arrangement is acceptable."

She turned back to the laptop she'd been keeping her eye on, waiting for a ping to tell her Captain Romanov had planted the thumb drive on the Chinese server. His diplomatic guest tour of the Yulin Naval Base had been scheduled to begin over an hour ago, and run until four o'clock, giving him a good three-hour window. The submarine was transiting just under the surface to allow the radar and satellite communications array to poke up out of the water.

"Besides," she added, "after two days and nights of living off the land, they're probably thrilled to have a real bed. Even if it is only wide enough for a skinny swab."

Quinn made an exasperated noise. "You are beyond the pale, Zimmerman."

It was never a good sign when Bobby Lee called her by her last name. Darcy called nearly everyone by their last name. Old habit. But Quinn, being a good ol' Bama boy, wasn't usually that formal. Unless he was pissed off.

Thankfully, she was saved from further verbal flogging when Walker and Jaeger trooped into the wardroom, where the team had once again spread out their equipment.

Quinn shot her a look, eyes flashing, that plainly said, *we're not done here, woman.*

God, he turned her on.

He could yell at her all he wanted, but she knew he'd be the first one to get naked later, when they were alone. Sharing a bunk thanks to her.

Strolling in, Walker was smiling and for once Jaeger didn't look too somber, so she figured it had gone well down in the torpedo room.

"Find everything you need down there?" she asked them.

"Oh, yeah," Walker said. "The equipment the navy didn't already have, Bridger had sent over. This is going to be fun."

"Yep," Jaeger said, shocking her with his cheerful verbosity. Though his expression didn't change.

She smiled back. "Great. I just hope the plan actually works." She eyed the laptop. Still no ping.

"It'll work," Walker said confidently. "As long as Nikolai gets you into that server so we can retrieve the AUV data and test schedule."

"I assume Commander Bridger wouldn't have sent him in if he didn't think he could do it," she said.

"Bridger doesn't know him. I'd trust Nikolai with my life—and have—but he's a sub driver, not a spy," Walker said with a worried frown. "I just hope nothing goes wrong."

"He'll get it done," Quinn said. "If he doesn't, we're back to square one and he knows it."

"Let's hope," Darcy said. "Once the thumb drive is in place, we're good to go."

She had been one of STORM's top computer specs since joining the company, and thanks to her generous budget for equipment and training—and her God-given talent, thankyouverymuch—she knew tricks that would make most Silicon Valley and Beltway geeks lie down and weep. She had no doubt she could penetrate the Chinese system once Romanov had gotten her past the firewall.

The only really tricky part would be remaining undetected as she navigated through the files to get the intel they needed. Not knowing the Chinese language might prove a handicap. She could inadvertently trip alarms.

Hmm. Maybe DeAnne could help with that. Walker'd said she was fluent in Chinese. It was worth asking her, anyway.

"Say." She glanced at Quinn as something else occurred to her. "Weren't we supposed to turn Ms. Lovejoy over to Captain Asshole? How come she's still with us?"

Quinn shrugged. "No way to get her back to *Impeccable* once the sub intercepted us. Besides, there's no need for anyone to interrogate her, now that we got the major off the island."

She supposed that was true. Still, having a civilian along on a sensitive, potentially dangerous operation was not STORM's usual modus operandi. She had a feeling there was more to it.

"What aren't you telling me?" she asked him, looking up with a scowl.

But Quinn had already left.

Kip came awake with a start and had to blink a few times to remember where he was. And with whom.

DeAnne. They were spooned together, back to front, and she was sound asleep. He didn't blame her. He'd driven her hard these past couple of days. And their lovemaking had been . . . intense. He wished to God he could stay right where he was and sleep for about a hundred years, but there were things he needed to do.

Such as demand to know what the hell was going on.

A submarine? Seriously? What was this STORM team planning to do, blast the damn AUV out of the water with a torpedo? He couldn't see what that would do, other than delay the inevitable. And why the hell would they need to kidnap *him* to accomplish that? He knew squat about submarines, AUVs, or anything else underwater. He was a solid ground kind of soldier.

He slid quietly out of bed, grabbed the clothes from the duffel bag that Quinn had given him after telling him they'd be bunking together, and slipped out of the stateroom. In the matchbox shower he broke the rules and, after soaping up, let the hot water run over his body for a full three minutes. *Pure heaven.* Not the same kind of heaven as making love with DeAnne, of course, but close.

He thought of her slumbering peacefully in his bunk after giving herself to him so fully, and he almost broke down and went back for more. He'd never get enough of that.

What had happened to his famous discipline?

Over the fucking cliff, that's what. Smashed to bits with the SUV on the morning he'd met her. He hadn't been the same since, that was for damn sure.

He thought about the unsettling insight he'd had while making love to her. That he wanted to throw away the whole friends-with-benefits relationship idea. That he wanted to be with her for the rest of his life. Just her.

Did he truly want that?

The rest of his life meant a commitment.

A commitment meant marriage.

And marriage meant . . .

Having to confront his family.

And deal with the trust fund.

The whole scenario sent him into a blind panic. *No way.* He'd lived this long without his snooty family and their precious money, and he had no intention of changing that now.

He shut off the tap with a vicious twist and gulped down a steadying breath, shaking the water from his hair and eyes like an angry dog. Even after all this time, recalling the condescension on his father's face after confessing his dream of becoming a photographer still had the power to flay his soul.

It wasn't the photographer thing that made him so mad. It was the condescension. The derision of his dream. As though his father hadn't believed his only son capable of doing anything meaningful on his own, without the influence of his powerful family name behind him. Let alone succeeding at it. His father hadn't deemed such a lowly artistic endeavor as taking photos worthy of the Llowell family scion's efforts, and refused even to consider the possibility.

It was his way or the highway. As it always had been with his father, and his grandfather, and all the fathers before them.

Thus the Llowell trust fund that he would be forced to inherit upon marriage, and the pressure to spend a lifetime managing and increasing it.

Kip had chosen the highway, and hadn't looked back.

Little had they known that ironclad clause would be Kip's escape hatch, rather than the ideal way to keep him tied to their purse strings, and ensure the family name continued.

The idea of caving in now went against every cell in his body.

He'd just have to figure out something else to do about DeAnne. Marriage was simply not an option. He did not want to fall under his family's influence again. Because it would happen. That would be inevitable. All that money would need to be channeled, and he knew himself too well to think he could just ignore his responsibilities, however unwanted and unwelcome. Which would be fine if his family—his father—weren't so damn controlling. He would no doubt want to tell Kip exactly how to run the trust, what to spend the money on. And if he didn't go along with the family's plan, there'd be hell to pay. It wasn't worth it. Kip hated being dictated to. Being marginalized and condescended to. It infuriated him.

Which reminded him all too vividly of his present situation—being manipulated, lied to, and given no choice in his own fate.

He dried himself off, got dressed, and stalked toward the ladder to the upper deck, ready to confront the STORM commander about his role in their operation.

And he was in no mood to take any shit from anybody.

He shot up the metal rungs and stormed into the wardroom, which had been taken over as mission central.

"All right, Quinn," he gritted out. "I want to know what this operation is all about. And I want to know now."

25

"It's real simple," Commander Quinn said after Kip had been talked into taking a seat at the table and accepted a cup of coffee from the kid with the ancient eyes. "We're going to hijack the AUV you were supposedly sent to photograph. Then we're going to take it apart and let you photograph it—for real this time—inside and out, and download all the juicy software that we don't already have. Then we'll put it back together all nice and neat, and send it back to its mama. With any luck, the PLAN—the Chinese navy—will never know we had it." He actually grinned.

Incredulous, Kip glanced around at the six STORM operators. "Are you kidding me right now?"

Nope. They weren't kidding him. Even the old guy, who definitely should know better, was looking pleased with the outrageous plan.

Kip let out a laugh. Then he laughed some more. He hadn't heard anything so funny in years.

"You got a better idea?" Walker asked calmly, after Kip's mirth had subsided to chuckles.

"Hell, no," Kip said wryly, hands upraised in mock surrender. "I'm just a boots-on-ground grunt. What do I know from autonomous underwater vehicles?"

"Quite a bit, I'd wager, being in Intelligence," Quinn returned evenly. "I served in the Corps and so did Zane. Jaeger, here, was in the South African NDF. We're all pretty knowledgeable about AUVs, UUVs, ROVs, UAVs, and every other kind of Vs out there. So don't even try that lowly grunt bit on us."

Kip's respect for them took an upward swing. "Fair enough," he said, though still far from convinced. "But you don't honestly think you can pull this off?"

"We do," Quinn said. And proceeded to tell him how.

Ten minutes later Kip's skepticism was waning. After twenty minutes he was nearly won over. Their plan was an elegant blend of old-school wits and high-tech savvy—totally dependent on the dexterity and skill of the operators and how well they coordinated their efforts as a team. Which was clearly outstanding.

He liked it.

Hell, he liked them.

Which shocked the snot out of him.

"Okay," he said. "There's just one little problem."

"What's that?" the big Southerner drawled.

"I can't take the photos. My camera's broken. Bad parachute landing." He ground his teeth in frustration. He never had arranged to meet up with Jake to get the replacement. After learning the true nature of his mission, he hadn't thought he'd need it.

The cute blonde popped out of her seat as if it had springs. "Oh, we got that covered." She pulled a rigid aluminum case from under the table, set it down in front of him, and snapped the locks. "Figured you'd lost your equipment somewhere along the way."

When she opened the lid it was as if a chorus of angels had gathered over her head and sang just for him.

Nestled inside the case on a bed of sleek black foam was a top-of-the-line Nikon DSLR, five insane interchangeable lenses, ten three-gig storage disks, and a whole mini-rack of assorted Koken filters.

Jesus. The whole package must have cost well over fifteen grand.

"Holy shit," he murmured, running his fingers reverently over the pristine equipment. The gear he got through MSOIB was good, but, wow. "This stuff is sick." He looked to Quinn, a bit awestruck. "I actually get to use this?"

"It's yours," Quinn said with a flick of his hand. "Consider it compensation for the trauma we put you through this morning."

Kip stared, not quite understanding. "You can't mean—"

"And for the shitty way you were used and betrayed by the fuckers who set you up," threw in the kid with the eyes. There was a fire burning in them that Kip recognized as fury-tinged empathy.

He suddenly wondered what kind of terrible betrayal the young man had suffered to put that amount of bitterness in them.

"Thanks," he told Zane sincerely, then looked to Quinn. "I'm happy to help, but I can't take this stuff, if that's what you mean. I don't like being in debt, and I'd definitely owe you."

"Not me. STORM Corps. But that remains to be seen." Quinn roused himself and strolled over to the coffee urn. "We'll talk again when the entire PLAN submarine fleet is on our six and the torpedoes start whizzing past us like locusts."

He might have a point.

A soft gasp sounded from the entry door. DeAnne stood there, fresh and pink from her nap, bedroom-eyed from their lovemaking, and still damp from a recent shower. She'd changed into a pair of clingy black pants and a U.S. Navy T-shirt. His heart turned over in his chest at the sight of her.

"They're shooting torpedoes at us?" she asked, her voice an octave higher than normal.

"Not yet, but give 'em time," Zane said with a sardonic grin.

"Alex Zane!" Darcy scolded. "You're scaring her!"

"No one's going to be shooting at us," Walker assured her. "They're never going to know we're here. Kilos are the stealthiest, quietest subs ever made."

She looked more than skeptical.

"Hi, princess," Kip said softly as he stood to put an arm around her, and kissed her hair. He hadn't even realized he'd moved, and he certainly hadn't thought it out. He'd just pretty much exposed their relationship to the whole team. Not that it would have stayed a secret for long—there was no such thing as a secret in such close quarters. "Have a good nap?" he asked her.

She gave a smile just for him. "Mm-hmm." Then she looked a little embarrassed, glanced around, and asked, "What was that about torpedoes?"

"Just a joke," Quinn said. "Grab some coffee and take a seat. We'll bring you up to speed."

"I'll get it," Kip volunteered, and took his own cup to refill at the same time, while Walker gave her the abridged version of the plans.

Kip worked really hard to keep a pleasant look on his face, and even somehow resisted putting a proprietary arm around her when he sat down again next to her. She'd told him she was not interested in Walker, and he believed her.

But for some reason, those primitive, caveman instincts kept rearing up out of nowhere within him.

Mine. You're mine now, DeAnne.

With impeccable timing, just as Walker was finishing up laying out the plan, Darcy gave a whoop. "Yes! We're in!"

Everyone came to attention.

She started typing furiously on her laptop. "Score one for Kapitan Romanov!"

Quinn strode behind her and peered over her shoulder at the screen. "Excellent. How long till you can get the intel we need?"

She shot Quinn an exasperated look. "Jeez, babe, give me a freakin' minute or two!"

"Sorry, Zimmie. Didn't mean to push."

She harrumphed. "You're forgiven. But only because you're so damn cute."

His eyebrows flickered. "I live to be cute, darlin'."

Kip stifled a smile. Then changed his mind and let it break through. He slipped his fingers under DeAnne's hair and caressed the back of her neck. These people were clearly consummate professionals, but he liked that they felt at ease enough to tease and show each other true affection without reservation. It felt relaxed. Real.

Or maybe a total fantasy.

He withdrew his hand. "So what happens now?"

Darcy gave the keyboard a final flourish. "I had one of the language experts at STORM Command throw together a translation macro so I could navigate to where I need to be . . ." She squinted at the screen and jetted out a breath. "I've got the AUV blue-water testing schedule. I'm pretty sure, anyway. DeAnne? Can you take a look and confirm?"

"Sure." DeAnne left his side to sit next to Darcy and study the screen. "Yes. And it looks like the first test run is . . . tomorrow morning at high tide." She glanced up. "Wow. They're not wasting any time, are they?"

"All the quicker to spy on us," Master Chief Edwards said grimly. "Clint, will we be ready for the intercept by morning?"

Walker's lips curved with satisfaction. "Absolutely. We just need to upload the software and your sound library into our decoy AUV."

"Sound library?" DeAnne asked as Darcy concentrated on downloading the files they needed from the PLAN computers.

Edwards sat back in his chair. "I was a sonar operator on submarines for nearly three decades. Nowadays it's largely a visual and digital technology—the sonar tech identifies the ambient sounds around the submarine by their digital signature on a color monitor. But back in the day it was all about the ears and the headphones. The navy has an amazing collection of underwater sound recordings thanks to SOSUS. And I made a few myself during my time in the shack."

"He's being modest," Walker said. "Chief Edwards has one of the largest private sonar libraries in the world. He has recordings of everything from rare fish noises to German U-boats from World War Two."

"Copied from Smithsonian recordings," Edwards qualified with a chuckle when DeAnne's brows went up at the U-boats. "I'm old, but not *that* old."

Suddenly there was a loud ping from Darcy's laptop and she literally jumped back. "Whoa."

Quinn was instantly back at her side. "What happened?"

"The signal cut off." She stared at the laptop. "It shouldn't have done that. The files were not quite finished downloading."

"What does that mean?"

"Damn!" She looked up, her expression not happy. "It means they must have found the thumb drive."

As one, every set of eyes turned to the big clock on the wardroom bulkhead. It read 3:27.

"When was Nikolai's tour of the base supposed to end?" Walker asked.

"Four o'clock," Darcy said apprehensively.

Even Kip understood the implications. And they weren't good.

Nobody had counted on the Chinese finding the thumb drive before Darcy could download the needed files and wipe it clean and harmless. Ten minutes, max, start to finish.

Something must have gone terribly wrong.

"We have to get Nikolai out of there," DeAnne said anxiously, rising to her feet. "How do we reach him?"

"I don't think we can," Quinn said with a frown. "I doubt they let him keep his cell phone inside the base."

Jaeger had been quiet as usual this whole time. But now he looked up from his computer screen and somberly said, "It's too late. They just arrested him."

26

Everybody started talking at once. Except Bobby Lee, who ignored the heated discussion, his eyes getting narrower and narrower as the cogs turned inside his head. Darcy was terrified. Because she knew exactly what he was thinking.

His team. His responsibility. *Leave no one behind.*

And he'd do it, too, with or without the team's agreement.

"I'm going in." Quinn's three clipped words cut through the cacophony like a machete.

Darcy's heart sank. Sometimes she hated being right.

"Baby, that's crazy," she argued. "What will you do? Grab him in court? Break him out of jail?"

"If I have to. Romanov was helping us. We take care of our own. You know that."

She did. True, not too many of the countless rescue missions she'd taken part in were for their own operators, but STORM had never left any of its people out in the cold. There had been a few prison sentences—including Marc Lafayette on her own disastrous first joint mission—but as soon as the political fallout had settled, STORM had negotiated or bribed every one of its people to freedom. Marc had gotten out after just a year of a twenty-five-year sentence.

But this was different. Nikolai Romanov didn't work for STORM. He was also a Russian national, and the case was bound to attract massive international attention. Especially on top of the "American spy" media hoopla.

"You're just one man, Bobby Lee Quinn," she reminded him, "and your blond head will stick out like a damn sore thumb. You don't think they'll see you coming a mile away?" She didn't even want to think about what could happen to him if he was arrested.

"I'll figure it out," he said, stubborn as the Alabama mule he was.

"I'll go with you," Major Llowell announced, surprising everyone into momentary silence.

"What? You can't go back there!" DeAnne exclaimed. "If they catch you in China, they'll—" She clapped a hand over her mouth, a groan of distress escaping between her fingers.

Oh, yeah, Darcy thought. She had it bad.

The major reached out and stroked DeAnne's hand with his thumb. "I know. They'll do to me what they'll likely do to Captain Romanov if someone doesn't help him. Could you live with that? Letting him twist in the wind?"

DeAnne blinked, her eyes glistening. Darcy could tell she badly wanted to say yes, but those expressive eyes gave away her good heart.

Before she could say anything, Zane jumped in. "Don't put yourself in danger, Major. I'll go with Quinn. You stay here with your lady."

For a nanosecond Llowell didn't move a muscle.

Darcy winced inwardly. She knew he was reacting to the "your lady" part. But frankly, she was more worried about Zane's neck than Llowell's commitment issues.

Alex still suffered PTSD from his two-year ordeal of torture and abuse at the hands of terrorists. He was doing a lot better now, especially after marrying his longtime secret crush last year. But he still had moments of panic, freezing up at the least appropriate times. True, they hadn't found him for a while curled up on the floor in a fetal position after a bad night, but he had yet to be allowed out on a truly dangerous op. Such as breaking someone out of a secure Chinese prison.

"Nope," Quinn said, shaking his head. "You haven't been cleared for hazardous duty yet. Bridger would have a fit."

"This is an emergency," Zane argued. "I can handle it."

Quinn regarded Zane assessingly for a long moment, glanced at Llowell, then blew out a breath. "All right. Against my better judgment, you can both come. I have a feeling I'll need all the help I can get." He then turned to her. "Zimmie, can you spare Jaeger to coordinate field communications? There's no radio and cell phone contact with a submarine when it's submerged. We'll have to bring in surface support."

He was asking her because she was in charge of home base operations. But last-minute adjustments were par for the course. It was why there were always six on a team. It gave them wiggle room.

She nodded tightly. "Jaeger's clear to go."

She wasn't going to repeat her objections about Zane, but she was not happy with Quinn's decision to take him into the field. In her mind, that was a recipe for disaster.

Turning to Walker and Edwards, she asked, "With Jaeger gone, can you two handle the com for your part of this shindig?"

They both nodded. "No worries."

"Let me go with you," DeAnne said to Quinn.

Seven sets of eyes cut to her. A day for surprises, for sure.

"I can help," she said. "I speak the language. I—"

"No," Quinn responded.

At the same time, Llowell said, "*Hell*, no."

"But—"

"Out of the question," said Quinn emphatically.

"Over my dead body," Llowell added, making DeAnne scowl fiercely at him. But she clamped her mouth and didn't argue.

Darcy was glad. There was no point in arguing with a brick wall. Make that *two* brick walls.

She gave the woman a sympathetic ghost of a smile.

And hoped to hell Llowell's words weren't prophetic.

"I can't believe you would do this!"

An hour later, DeAnne was pacing in the corridor while Kip bent over his belongings, spread out over their bunk, repacking his rucksack. She was furious with him for volunteering, but more than that, she was afraid. Deathly afraid.

Deep-seated memories of her father going off to his various wars, sometimes coming back in pieces, clawed at her insides. Memories she hadn't thought about in decades. From back when she was a girl and still thought the moon and stars rose in his cocky smile. Before the protective wall her mother had constructed around her crumbled, and unvarnished reality set in.

"They're going to find you and put you in prison," she muttered, pacing back in the other direction. "You know that, right?"

"Nobody's going to find us. Quinn and Alex are clearly pros. I trust this team almost as much as I trust my own unit."

Speaking of which . . .

"And where *is* your unit, by the way?" she demanded. "I

would've thought they'd pick you up by now." If they had, he wouldn't be running off on this harebrained scheme. "You did contact them, didn't you?"

Of course, if they came for him, he'd be gone from her life for good.

He peered over his shoulder at her. "How did you know that?"

She snorted. "Please. I told you my father was a Marine. I know exactly how you people operate."

On second thought, his unit of macho Marines probably wouldn't be able to resist joining in the dangerous mission, thereby escalating the risk even more. And maybe starting World War Three.

He turned around and regarded her as she paced. "So we're back to the Marine thing, are we?"

She halted, folding her arms across her twisting stomach. "Kip, we never really got past it."

She felt ill. How had she gotten here? How had she let him get under her skin like this? How had she allowed herself to fall so fast and hard for the man? A man who hit all her wrong buttons.

And all the right ones . . .

They stared at one another for a long moment, her heart aching so painfully she thought she might die right there.

He turned back to his packing. "Then it shouldn't really matter to you if they do catch me."

She wanted to kick him. "Don't be a jerk. We just spent the night making love. Of course it would matter to me. A lot."

For a nanosecond, his shoulders tightened. "But not enough to get over your ridiculous childhood issues, it seems."

Her jaw dropped in outrage. "*My* issues? This coming from a man who hasn't spoken to his own family in over ten years?"

He paused in tying up the rucksack and drew in a deep

breath. "Touché." He finished up and turned to face her, slinging the pack's strap over his shoulder. "I guess we both have things to work through before we could ever make a go of a relationship. It's probably just as well I'm leaving. If I stayed, I'd never be able to keep my hands off you, and that would just make everything harder in the long run."

Tears prickled behind her eyes. "Just because we're not right for each other doesn't mean I don't care about you, Kip. Because I do."

His eyes softened. "I know, princess. And I care about you, too. Far too much to do either of us any good." He gave her a sad smile. "Come here."

He opened his arms and she went into them, feeling the moisture spill over her lashes, wishing her feelings could spill out as easily. How she wished she could tell him how she truly felt. But he was right—neither of them was ready for this. Telling him would only complicate matters even more.

So instead, when he gave her a long, intense, parting kiss, she opened herself, wrapping her arms around him, and kissed him back. She poured into it all the passion and emotions she held inside, telling him with her kiss how much she'd grown to love him.

"Please, promise me you'll be careful," she whispered.

"I promise." He kissed her forehead. "And we'll be back with Captain Romanov before you know it."

She prayed he was right.

But she had an ominous feeling about this mission. She couldn't even begin to guess how they would carry out the rescue, but it was going to be insanely dangerous. Her arms slid down his torso a bit, colliding with the gun and holster tucked against his ribs, which only drove home the bad feeling with deadly certainty.

With a final kiss, he pulled away, and guided her toward the ladder to the upper deck. The sub-speak chatter on the overhead com punctuated the silence between them as the crew brought the submarine to the roof. She could feel the pressure in her bones when the angle of their ascent rose acutely, the sub's nose slashing through the water toward the air above. Kip gathered her and held her in his arms while they broke the surface and leveled off, so she wouldn't stumble and fall. Then they climbed up the ladder to the main deck.

Bobby Lee Quinn, Rand Jaeger, and Alex Zane were waiting for Kip at the foot of the barrel ladder leading up to the conning tower, gear bags at their feet. Darcy stood nearby, along with a couple of men from the submarine crew.

"We're just waiting on word from the helo," one of them said as Kip approached.

"You sure you ladies are up for this?" the other submariner teased the men with a grin.

DeAnne sidled in next to Darcy and murmured, "Up for what?"

Darcy pulled a face. "Harness lift up to the helo. Quinn didn't want to wait for a boat pickup."

Harness lift . . . ? DeAnne's eyes widened. "Yikes."

Darcy waved it off. "All in a day's work for my guys. Yours, too, I'm guessing."

DeAnne would be totally freaked out if she had to be airlifted into a helicopter that way. But Darcy was probably on target about Kip, judging by the singularly unconcerned look on his face at the prospect.

"Want to go topside and watch?" Darcy asked, her eyes alight.

Heck, no. "Um. We can do that?" DeAnne managed.

"You know, in case one of them falls in and we need to toss him a life preserver or something." At her horrified look, Darcy laughed and bumped shoulders with her. "Just kidding."

An announcement came over the com that the helo was

approaching, and to proceed with the disembarkation. After going through a safety checklist, one of the crewmen scampered up the barrel ladder and cracked open the outside hatch. A waft of fresh air swept over DeAnne, and she realized how hot it had gotten inside the sub. Outside, the temperature must be at least eighty degrees, but the breeze felt cool on her skin.

At the crewman's signal, Jaeger started up the ladder.

Quinn gave Darcy a quick, hard kiss. "Catch you on the flip side, baby," he murmured, and then he was climbing, too.

Kip turned to DeAnne, hesitated, then gave her a tight hug. "I'll see you soon."

She nodded, hugged him back, and watched him disappear through the hatch, her heart lodged painfully in her throat.

And fought down the terrible, inexorable feeling that this would be the last time she would ever hold him in her arms.

27

"So how the hell are we going to get him out?" Kip called over the noise of the helo's rotors.

The small, private craft was flying low over the water to avoid detection, bringing them to a large yacht anchored just inside international waters. The vessel's owner was a Hong Kong businessman who apparently had business dealings with STORM and Commander Bridger.

Everyone but Jaeger—who'd be staying on the yacht running com—had changed into black, full-body rash suits and put their equipment into dry bags. After sunset, the yacht's speedboat would ferry them close to shore, but they'd be swimming the final half mile or so.

Once on the island, Julie Severin was supposed to meet them and provide transportation. After that—

"Fuck if I know," Quinn returned with an irreverent grin. "I'm open for suggestions."

Kip had been afraid of that. He was all about being

flexible, but there should be at least a glimmer of a plan to start out with.

Making a face at the noise, Jaeger handed out high-tech earpieces, and they all put them in.

"Waterproof," Jaeger said.

Kip could barely tell he was wearing the small, sleek set. He was definitely impressed with the technology STORM issued to its operators.

Quinn tapped his earpiece and said, "STORM lima, STORM zulu, STORM romeo, this is STORM alpha six testing com. Do you read me, over?"

Despite the noise of the helo, Kip had no trouble hearing. "Loud and clear, alpha six, over," he responded. He'd been designated lima for Llowell. Zulu was Zane. Rand Jaeger was romeo. Alpha meant the away team, and six was the standard designation for team leader—in this case Quinn.

"That's an affirmative, over," said Zane.

"Yep," said Jaeger.

Quinn had explained that STORM generally used a relaxed military com protocol, strict enough to keep things orderly when the situation heated up, but loose enough to be casual when the bullets weren't flying.

"So, any ideas how the fuck we're going to pull this off?" Zane asked no one in particular, picking up the discussion again now they didn't have to shout.

"Do we even know where Romanov is being held?" Kip asked.

"According to our sources, they've still got him locked up at the navy base," Quinn said. "But word is they plan to move him to the new high-security prison in Tiandu."

The prison had been marked on the map Kip memorized before jumping in. He'd paid special attention to the area around it in case he ended up there himself.

"When's the transfer?" he asked.

Quinn shook his head. "Don't know."

"Swell," Alex Zane muttered. "I love stakeouts."

Quinn looked at Jaeger. "Do we have eyes in the sky yet?"

The South African pursed his lips. "There's a NOAA satellite I could redirect—optics aren't ideal. An army Predator—at least thirty-four hours out. *Impeccable*'s got a ScanEagle—only a twenty-two-hour flight window and bound to show up on radar." He shrugged. "Shit for choice."

Kip wasn't about to ask if they actually had permission to change the focus of NOAA's satellite, or to use either of those unmanned aerial vehicles. He had the distinct feeling these guys lived as close to the edge as he did and wouldn't really care about such technicalities.

"What about the Russians?" Zane asked. "They got anything flying around?

Jaeger just snorted and muttered, "Sputnik, maybe."

Kip chuckled. He was also coming to appreciate how skilled these STORM operators were, so he suggested, "How about spoofing a Chinese UAV? Surely, they've got something up there." When the other three just stared at him, he said, "Hell, you're already planning to hijack a damn Chinese AUV prototype. Water, air, what's the difference?"

For a second no one reacted. Then Jaeger grinned. "I knew I liked you." Then he pulled out his tablet and was instantly immersed.

The helo banked a few minutes later, and approached for a landing. They'd reached the yacht.

After setting down, they piled out with their gear and were greeted by the yacht's captain. If the man thought it strange three of them were dressed as frogmen, he didn't comment.

Jaeger picked up his stuff and went below without a backward glance. From the looks of the antenna array poking up from the bridge, he'd have no trouble coordinating communications between the away team, STORM Command, the Russians if necessary, and the submarine when it was at radio depth.

"Sure you want to join this war party?" Quinn asked Kip as they hopped down onto the speedboat. The sun was just setting, and they were oscar mike. "Still time to bail. No one would blame you."

"Hell, no." Kip tossed his dry bag into the hold and grabbed a seat next to Zane. Already adrenaline was hitting his bloodstream. "I live for counting coup."

Quinn tilted his head and studied him. "Damn, I may just have to offer you a job, Major," he said in that molasses accent of his. "Ever think about leaving the Marines?"

Kip didn't quite know what to say to that. "Not really. I like what I do."

"I can see that."

The speedboat took off immediately, heading for the darkening mass of the big island. It was a narrow black cigar boat, incredibly fast and surprisingly quiet. The kind drug dealers used.

Half an hour later, they pulled on their snorkel gear, dropped silently into the water, and started swimming toward the shore, aiming for a deserted enough spot that they could make landfall unobserved.

Tired as Kip was, it felt good to stretch his muscles and push himself a little physically. The water was warm, the stars above twinkling brightly, and his companions easily kept pace. He was totally in his comfort zone.

Well, except for the conflicting thoughts zinging through his head. The adrenaline had kick-started his mind as well as his body.

What should he do about DeAnne? Anything? Or should he just let it be . . . ? He felt like a ping-pong ball, his inclination bouncing first in one direction, then the other, then back again.

On the plus side, they had chemistry together out the wazoo. And they liked and respected each other. A lot. They seemed to have similar values and ethics. And, despite the danger and uncertainty of the past few days, they'd also had fun together. He could well imagine that a life with DeAnne would be everything he'd ever wanted—if he'd ever wanted to settle down.

Which brought him to the minus side.

He didn't want to settle down. He liked his exciting life just the way it was. Yeah, he could easily see her in it, sharing time when he was home, relaxing and having phenomenal sex.

Hell, he could even imagine sharing his adventures with her. She'd been amazing on this trip. Always keeping up with him. Never complaining about the hardships or the danger. Even when she was terrified, she'd kept her cool. If she were a Marine, he'd want her in his unit, absolutely.

And right there was the other downside in a nutshell.

She wanted nothing to do with a Marine like him. She wanted a domesticated, non-adrenaline-junkie kind of guy she could marry and have a family with. Someone she could rely on. Someone who'd be there day in and day out.

But Kip wanted nothing to do with marriage or family.

At least . . . he hadn't.

Not until he'd met DeAnne Lovejoy.

Now? He wasn't so sure. To accept being in a relationship, she needed a commitment from him. More than he'd been willing to give, up until now. But he was having a really hard time picturing his life without DeAnne in it.

How could he make himself walk away from her, from something this good, just because he didn't want to deal with his snobby, controlling family, and the trust fund that would change his life inexorably, and forever?

Jesus. *Talk about shit for choices.*

He'd come no closer to making a firm decision one way

or the other when they reached the island, hitting a necklace of waves that crashed along the beach. Beyond the narrow band of glistening sand lay a dark void of dense jungle, which they'd have to traverse to reach the rendezvous point where Julie Severin waited with their transpo.

Hopefully.

Pulling off their masks and fins, they ran as silent as wraiths across the sand to the cover of the trees. At the edge of the jungle they tugged on their boots, slid on their night-vision goggles, and slung the dry bags over their shoulders. They would change clothes once they got to the car, so they wouldn't soil or rip their civvies on the nighttime trek through the thick vegetation.

Quinn tapped his headset, and said quietly into it, "STORM alpha six to romeo, over."

"Alpha six, romeo. How's the weather out there, over?"

"Storm is brewing. Going to find shelter. Over and out."

The exchange was short and sweet, using prearranged phrases to let the home team know they'd made it safely to the island.

Quinn got out his lighted compass, Kip pulled out his Ka-Bar, and Zane drew his weapon, all at the same time.

Their gazes met. As one, they flipped down the eyescopes of their NVGs.

Zane grinned. "Time to rock and roll, baby."

"Hoo-ya."

"Let's go get us a Ruskie."

28

When Darcy's phone rang it startled DeAnne. It was so peaceful and calm up here where they were standing on top of the sail that the mechanical melody was totally out of place.

"Damn. I forgot to put on my headset," Darcy muttered, pulling a satellite phone from her windbreaker pocket. "Zimmerman," she answered, then listened for a brief moment and winced. "Yeah, sorry about that. I'm doing it right now. So, did the package arrive safely?"

She listened again, fishing in her other pocket, and a measured smile broke over her lips. "Great. Let me know how she likes it." She rolled her eyes, sliding on a thin headset. "Yeah, yeah. Love you, too, sweetie."

"The guys?" DeAnne asked anxiously.

"Jaeger. The guys're good. They made it onto the island and are hoofing it to the rendezvous with Julie Severin."

DeAnne blew out a breath of relief. Albeit short-lived.

The real danger was just beginning for the men. "I can't believe they're even attempting this. It's insane to think they could succeed."

Darcy made an I-wouldn't-be-so-sure face. "I don't know, Quinn's a pretty enterprising operative. It's why they put him on the STORM Board of Command. And Zane is as brave as they come." She slanted her a look. "Your man seems like he's cut from the same cloth."

"Not my man, Darcy," she said automatically, turning her gaze west, to the vast expanse of black sky and indigo water that lay between them and China. The moon spilled a streak of liquid silver over the undulating surface. They were too far out to see the island even if there had been daylight, but she sent good vibes in that direction.

"Uh-huh. Because you didn't just spend three hours in bed with him. Or maybe you were"—she made air quotes—"just sleeping."

DeAnne couldn't help but laugh at Darcy's amused skepticism. Mainly because she was right, and they both knew it.

She let out a long sigh. "Yeah, that'll be the day it snows in Hades. Honestly, Darce. I can't control myself around the man. I turn into some insatiable sex maniac or something."

Darcy's eyes danced. "You dream about him, too, I'll bet."

DeAnne slapped her hands over her eyes and groaned. "I am in so much trouble."

"Why? Great sex is a rare thing. When you find it with someone, you should hang on to that guy."

"Only if it's the right guy."

She could feel Darcy's curious gaze on her. "Why isn't he right? He seems amazing."

DeAnne glanced up at the spangle of stars overhead, and the dark clouds scudding across them. "Oh, he's amazing, all right," she said resignedly. "It's just . . . Well, our lifestyles don't exactly mesh. He's a Marine. And I'm . . ." She nibbled her lip. "I need a man I can rely on to be there for me. With me."

Darcy's eyebrows lifted. "And you don't think a Marine can be that?"

She knew she was on shaky ground, considering the other woman's occupation and circle of friends. "Not in my experience." She gave her a bleak look. "My father was a Marine. I didn't have the best childhood."

"Issues, huh." It wasn't a question. More like a commiseration.

"You could say that."

"Join the freakin' club." Darcy's words were ironic but serious. "And the funny thing is, Quinn's been the only person on the planet I've ever really been able to rely on to be there for me." Her eyebrows flickered. "Once we got past the other women, of course." She sighed and looked up. "He was a Marine, too, you know."

"I didn't. But I'm not surprised. About the Marine thing, anyway." She winced. "Sorry about the other women."

Darcy shrugged. "My own fault. We had . . . an arrangement . . . so I didn't tell him about my feelings for a long time. He was just being a guy."

"Trust me, I know all about men's dislike of commitment from my dad. Which is exactly what I'm afraid of with Kip."

"That he'll use you and then abandon you?"

DeAnne hadn't thought of it in precisely those terms, but now that she mentioned it . . . "Pretty much."

"I get it," Darcy said, folded her arms, and leaned over the rail of the crow's nest, concentrating on the sub's wake as it cut through the waves, the white foam illuminated by the moonlight. "It's tough to put your trust in someone so completely when you haven't had a lot of luck doing that in the past."

It sounded as if Darcy was speaking from experience. All at once DeAnne felt an unexpected kinship with her. "Yeah," she agreed. "Really tough."

They watched the inky waves for a few minutes, enjoying the warm night breeze and the feeling of being high above everything.

"I'm having a hard time setting our wedding date," Darcy confessed. "Not because I don't love Bobby Lee," she hurried to say, "because I do. Deeply and madly. It's just . . ." She squeezed her eyes shut and shook her head. "Hell, I don't know why."

"You're afraid." DeAnne could totally relate.

"I'm terrified he'll change his mind and leave me standing at the altar like a fool. Terrified I won't know how to keep him happy. Terrified he'll grow tired of me after a year or two and trade me in for a newer model." She gave a little laugh. "Dumb, huh?"

"No. Not dumb," DeAnne assured her. "It's every woman's worst fear."

"Sounds like you and I have a bigger dose of that fear than most."

DeAnne smiled wanly. "Lucky us."

Just then, one of the crew stuck his head up through the barrel hatch. "Ma'am? Lieutenant Commander Walker and Master Chief Edwards are asking for you."

They both turned. DeAnne shivered against a sudden chill. She'd been so wrapped up in the girl talk she'd totally forgotten about the mission that was the reason they were there on this submarine.

"We'll be right down," Darcy told him.

"What do you think they need?" DeAnne asked her after the rating disappeared back down the ladder.

"Lord knows."

She knew Clint and Rufus were in charge of executing the daring plan to pull a switch on the new, cutting-edge

Chinese AUV, so the U.S. Navy could design countermeasures to prevent a fleet of them spying and possibly wreaking havoc on our shores in the future.

"Think something has gone wrong with the plan?" she asked.

Darcy looked worried. "God, I hope not." She headed for the ladder. "Come on. Let's go find out."

Kip was getting that feeling again. The one on the back of his neck that was telling him something was not right.

He, Quinn, and Alex Zane had been traversing the jungle for a couple of hours now, making good time. The two STORM operators really knew how to move silently and swiftly, their trail of disturbance nearly imperceptible. They would easily fit in with his own crack Intelligence unit. So he felt more than comfortable with their level of competence on this op.

And yet, something was bugging him. Something he couldn't quite put his finger on.

Probably the whole DeAnne issue worming its way into his mission mentality. He hadn't quite been able to banish his conflicting thoughts about her to the back of his mind, where they belonged during a dangerous mission. No doubt that's what was niggling at him.

So far, everything had gone according to plan. The landing had been textbook, they'd made contact with Jaeger, and hopefully Julie Severin would be waiting with a car in the appointed spot, which they were fast approaching, along with unavoidable civilization.

Quinn signaled a halt a quarter mile from the perimeter of the jungle, and they stopped to powwow while they pulled off their NVGs and rehydrated.

"We should make the rendezvous right on time," Quinn said quietly, consulting his watch after taking a long drink.

"But we still need a plan of action. Anyone come up with a brilliant idea?"

"I say we do it old-school," Zane said, gesturing with his water bottle. "A stickup on the transport vehicle, guns blazing. Grab him and run."

Old-school was right. But the idea had merit—since they didn't have time or equipment to set up anything more elaborate. In fact, it was probably about the only option.

"We'll need intel on when they're making the transfer," Kip pointed out. "If we're not already too late."

"That would totally suck," Zane muttered.

Kip smiled. The kid was a man of many contrasts. He had a colorful vocabulary, but his speech patterns reflected a good education. Which matched the air of well-kept affluence about him, even dressed in BDUs. But those guarded eyes were windows into an uneasy depth that lurked well below all that surface stuff. Definitely not anything you'd want to meet in a dark alley.

Quinn got out his cell phone, set it to speaker so they could all hear, and punched in a number. A few seconds later, Jaeger answered.

"Yep."

"How are those party invitations coming along?" Quinn asked.

"They've been delayed. Tanya's got a sample for you."

Which, decoded, meant Romanov was still being held at the naval base, the transfer was set for tomorrow, and Julie had the details.

"You seen them yet?"

"Just the basic design. Should have more tomorrow."

Which meant he'd managed to find eyes in the sky somehow and was focused in on the naval base, but hadn't spotted Romanov yet. Hardly surprising since he was being held indoors.

"Tanya still coming over tonight?"

"That's the plan."

"Sounds good. Talk to you later." He hit the "off" button.

"I don't like it," Kip said with a frown.

The others looked over at him. "What's bothering you?" Quinn asked.

"If the decision has already been made to transfer Romanov to Tiandu Prison, why wait until tomorrow afternoon? It's only fifteen klicks between the two places. Not like the transfer needs a lot of preparation."

They regarded each other somberly in the darkness. None of the possible reasons for the delay were pleasant to consider.

"If they're torturing him, we're screwed," said Zane, voicing what they were all thinking. "We need him mobile."

Quinn rubbed a hand over his chin, and the scratch of stubble broke the silence of the jungle. "Yeah." He blew out a breath. "Well, we'll ford that stream when we get to it. And carry him if we have to."

Kip noticed that the water bottle in Zane's hand was shaking slightly. Not a good sign. "You doing all right?" he casually asked.

"I'm good," Zane answered, a little too fast.

Kip nodded, and stuck his own empty bottle back in his dry bag. "Of course, the other possibility is that they're expecting a rescue attempt, and they're busy setting up a trap for us."

The two operators looked grim as they stowed their empties.

"Fuck that," Zane said, and took off toward the road where they were supposed to meet Julie Severin.

"We'll just have to be ready for them," Quinn said, and moved off after him.

Right.

Kip thought briefly of the two PLA jeepfuls of soldiers he and DeAnne had barely managed to elude—how determined they'd been, and how gun-happy. And how badly they were going to want revenge on the man who'd played them for fools.

And then he wondered how damn many soldiers they'd send out to man their trap, if the Chinese had the slightest whiff of a plan to rescue their prisoner. A dozen? A hundred? A whole fucking battalion?

Oh, yeah. Five hundred to one. The three of them could definitely take on those odds and win, no problem.

Fucking piece of cake.

29

Fifteen minutes later, Kip and the others came to a halt inside the tree line next to the road at the rendezvous spot. It was just after midnight, and there wasn't a sign of life in either direction. Good. They were a little early, so there would be no surprises.

Finally, the hum of a car motor sounded in the distance. Kip cocked an ear and listened. It was getting closer.

Julie Severin? Or a PLA patrol . . . ?

"Incoming," he murmured, and they all held their weapons at the ready.

Bright headlights swept around the bend, and the car slowed as it approached their position. It looked as though there were no passengers, just the driver. A woman. She pulled to the side of the road a few yards away, and peered around, looking for them. The headlights blinked off and on.

They held back under cover of the trees for a moment, to see if any other vehicles would appear. None did. So they all sprinted for the car.

"Ms. Severin," said Quinn as they jumped in and she took off again. "Good to see you again. I just wish these were different circumstances."

"Me, too," she said, casting a quick glance at them through the shadowy car. Quinn was in front, and Kip and Alex were in the cramped back seat. "I think you're crazy for trying this, but I'm so grateful you are. I don't know what I'll do if you can't get Nikolai out." Her voice cracked and she took a deep breath. "The idea of what they could be doing to him . . ."

"Don't even go there," Kip interrupted. "We'll do everything we can to get him back for you."

She swiped at a cheek. "This is payback, you know. For the embarrassment he caused the Chinese navy a while back."

"Oh?" Quinn asked. "What did he do to them?"

She grimaced. "It was back when this whole operation started. When I, um, covertly *acquired* the navigational software for the new Chinese AUV. The small storage disk was hidden on Nikolai's submarine, and the Chinese knew it. So they sent one of their nuclear subs after us, to get it back. Nikolai's sub at the time was a kilo class. Hardly a fair fight."

"Wait," Kip said. "*You* were on a Russian submarine?"

She gave a watery smile. "Nikolai was transporting a scientific expedition that I was with, undercover. Anyway. He and Walker came up with some pretty creative ways to harass the enemy sub, and ultimately to shake them off. We kept the disk, and the Chinese were not pleased."

"They also have very long memories," Zane remarked. "Hell, no wonder they arrested his ass."

"Do you think maybe that was their plan all along, and the diplomatic tour was just a way to get him within reach?" Kip asked.

"It's possible. Finding the thumb drive he'd planted was

exactly the excuse they needed to arrest him with impunity," Quinn said.

"It's almost like they were watching him, expecting something like that."

"It could well be," Julie agreed uneasily.

They drove in silence for a few minutes, each contemplating the implications of that supposition.

"Where are we heading now?" Quinn asked at length.

Julie glanced up and gathered herself. "Jaeger said to get you a room somewhere safe, so I went online and rented a small place close to the beach, where foreigners won't stick out too much. It's kind of a dump. I hope—"

"It'll be fine," Quinn assured her.

She passed him some papers that had been sitting on the dashboard. "This is a printout of the house information, along with a map showing how to get there."

"Good. Where can we drop you? I don't want you seen with us."

She named one of the big hotels. "But I'll take a taxi so you don't have to deal with the checkpoints."

Quinn nodded. "All right. Tomorrow, be sure to stay in plain sight, so they don't suspect you of being part of the rescue. Don't want to have to pull off another one."

She shot him a quick, anxious look. "Oh, God. You don't think—"

"Don't go there, either," Kip said, cutting off her burgeoning panic. "No sense buying stress."

She jetted out a breath. "No. You're right. I just have to believe that you'll succeed, with no hiccoughs, and I'll get him back safe and sound."

"Amen to that," Zane said soberly.

Quinn steered the conversation off the emotion and back on point. "Jaeger said you have the details of Nikolai's transfer?"

Her fingers tightened on the steering wheel. "Yes. It's supposed to be tomorrow at 8:20 a.m."

"Kind of a random time," Kip ventured. Seemed odd.

"Maybe," Julie said. "But one thing I've learned about the Chinese authorities, they never do anything random. Unless it's on purpose."

They all digested that.

"Dissimulation," she went on, "is their strategic cornerstone."

Deceit and misinformation. Yeah. That fit.

" 'To take the enemy,' " she recited, " 'you must begin by making an artful appointment, and cajole him into going there.' "

Kip raised his brows at the quotation from *The Art of War.* Every Marine's favorite book. But this feminine, sophisticated redhead didn't seem the type to study warcraft. "Sun Tsu?"

She smiled weakly. "I'm on the China Desk at Langley."

"Ah." A spook. That explained a lot. "So you think the Chinese authorities are lying about Nikolai's transfer time?" he asked.

She shook her head. "No. Not subtle enough."

Okay.

"Eight-twenty does seem very specific for a lie," Quinn said. "Why not eight? Or eight-thirty?"

"Exactly," she agreed. "And they allowed that information to leak out. It all adds up to a very calculated plan. There must be a reason for it. A reason that will help them achieve their true purpose."

"Which is?" Kip asked.

She eased out a breath. "The AUV test is at nine a.m., right?"

Quinn nodded.

"They're making you choose. Sabotage the launch or rescue Nikolai."

Kip frowned, not following her reasoning. "That makes no sense."

"Sure it does. They believe they're dealing with one man—the American spy they've been chasing. And he can't be in two places at once." She met Kip's gaze in the rearview mirror. "The Russian spy is bait. To lure you out and capture you, too."

His brows shot up. "You think this is about *me*?"

"You made them lose face in the eyes of the entire world, Major Llowell. They don't like that."

Okay, on a theoretical level it made sense. Sort of. But . . .

He shook his head. "How could they possibly have connected me, or any American spy, with Nikolai? He's a Russian submarine captain! What would make them think I'd come to help him?"

She shifted gears as they drove around a curve. "The law of averages. Two anomalies occurring in the same place just days apart, both involving spying, and probably the AUV launch. They wouldn't necessarily try to understand the connection. They'd just accept there is one and act on it."

He leaned his head back on the seat and pondered that. It was subtle, all right. And a real stretch by Western, evidence-based standards.

But textbook Sun Tsu. " 'Begin by seizing something which your opponent holds dear; then he will bend to your will,' " Kip murmured, also quoting *The Art of War.*

She darted him a glance and gave a wobbly smile. "They probably know he's engaged to an American CIA officer, too."

Duh. Okay, maybe not such a stretch, after all.

"So they pretty much know I'm coming for him."

"Yeah," she said. "And if not you, then someone else. They'd prefer if it's you, but capturing anyone at all will allow them to save face."

Now it all made an awful kind of sense.

"Okay," he conceded. "So this whole transfer thing is a trap. For me." *Great.* "What do we do instead?"

"The last thing they'd expect from you," she answered.

"Which is?"

Her lips curved downward. "Hell if I know. I'm just an analyst. You're the behind-the-lines intelligence operator."

"Well, that's a fucking shitload of help," Zane muttered.

Thankfully, that got Julie to laugh—if a bit bleakly. At least she didn't burst into tears.

Jesus. If she was right, it was probably a good thing they didn't have a set plan and were just winging it.

And he had a sinking feeling she was exactly on target. That itch on the back of his neck? It was bugging him now more than ever.

"Thanks for your insight," Kip told her when they dropped her at a taxi stand in the busy nightclub district. "And have faith." He wasn't about to tell her not to worry. That would be just plain bad advice. "Sometimes having no plan is the best plan of all. Keeps you flexible and alert for possibilities."

She didn't look convinced. In fact, she looked worried as hell as she closed the car door and headed for the taxi line. More like she was barely keeping it together.

Her expression had reminded him all too much of the look on DeAnne's face as he was lifted off the submarine and onto the helo. That face still haunted him. He'd really hated leaving his woman behind and on her own.

Except . . . she wasn't on her own. She was there with Darcy Zimmerman and Master Chief Edwards.

And Clint Walker.

That thought had him scowling, even as he lectured

himself all the way to the fleabag hotel not to be a goddamn idiot. The man was *married*, he reminded himself as they dodged the pimps and hookers surrounding the roach motel's entrance and checked in. She wasn't *interested* in Walker, he told himself sternly as he showered and changed.

"Hey. What's got your knickers all in a twist?" Alex asked as they settled down for a few hours sleep in their luxury suite. *Not.* Aside from the highly questionable clientele sashaying down the dingy halls, the beds were atrocious, the rug threadbare, and the bathroom less than sanitary. But the shower actually had hot water, and it beat sleeping out in the jungle. Just.

Kip scrubbed the glower off his face with his hands, and raked back his wet hair. "Nothing. Just tired."

"Uh-huh. Don't even try."

He peered over at the other man. They'd already flipped off the light, but he could see Zane's tall form stretched out on the rollaway, leaving the second twin bed for Quinn who was last in the shower. "Don't try what?"

"You're thinking about the woman. I can tell."

"Who, Julie Severin?"

Alex snorted. "Hardly. DeAnne *Love*joy." He drew out the syllable suggestively. "You're wondering if she's back there getting busy with the handsome and infinitely sexy Lieutenant Commander Walker."

Kip stared at him incredulously. How the *hell* did he know that? "You find Walker sexy?" he retorted. "Your wife know about this?"

Alex's white teeth glinted in the moonlight streaming through the curtainless window. "She's the one who told me. She says most of his eight thousand Twitter followers are female. His numbers skyrocketed after all that hoopla about saving that cargo ship from terrorists last year. He's a gen-u-ine hero in a spiffy white uniform. Women love that stuff."

Twitter? Was he kidding? "You mean his *wife's* cargo ship?" He emphasized "wife" as much to remind himself—*again*—as Alex.

"Former cargo ship," Zane corrected. "She quit that job, and now they're sailing around the world together."

Yeah, yeah. Kip knew all about the damn sailing trip around the world with the wife. An extended honeymoon, Walker had said. They were madly in love, blah blah blah.

"I take it you're one of the eight thousand," Kip said dryly, flopped back onto the lumpy bed and punched the rock-hard pillow, ignoring the annoying twinkle of Alex's grin. Eight fucking *thousand*? Kip had . . . twenty-two. If you counted the guys in his unit.

"Nah. The wife is. Speaking of which. You going to propose, or what?"

Kip blinked at the abrupt left turn in the conversation. "To Walker?" he asked, being deliberately obtuse. And trying to figure out what the freaking fuck the man was driving at. "Hadn't planned on it. Bigamy's illegal, you know . . ."

Alex actually snickered. "You're hysterical, Llowell. A regular Seinfeld. Anyway, want my advice?"

"No."

"Just admit you're in love with DeAnne, get down on one knee, and marry the woman. Save yourself a whole lot of irrelevant shit going down that you don't want or need. Believe me, been there, done that. It ain't pretty. Better just to accept the inevitable and get on with it."

Kip didn't even know where to begin to respond to that.

But Alex was not going to shut up. "That kind of love . . . it can save your miserable life. Trust me. Been there, done that, too."

The tone of Zane's voice had shifted, growing faraway and darkly serious, causing Kip to swallow his sarcastic comeback. "Yeah?" he said softly instead.

"Yeah," Alex returned quietly. "Don't throw it away,

man. You'll regret it. And a guy seldom gets a second chance."

Just then Quinn came out of the bathroom, toweling his hair dry. "Second chance at what?"

"Doing things right," Alex murmured solemnly, then rallied. "So I guess we'd better think about what Julie said, and figure this damn situation out."

So they lay on their beds and talked for a while, hashing out a strategy for the morning, then fell silent as they started to doze off.

But Kip couldn't shake Alex's words.

Just admit you love DeAnne, get down on one knee, and marry the woman. Don't throw it away, man. You'll regret it.

It was too early in Kip's relationship with DeAnne for that kind of serious commitment, even if he hadn't had a valid reason for avoiding marriage altogether.

But for the first time, he started to think maybe, just maybe, he should consider taking Alex's advice. Not the getting-down-on-one-knee part, but the accepting-the-inevitable-and-getting-on-with-it part.

Kip dragged in a breath. Did he honestly, deep down, think he could avoid dealing with his family and his inheritance for the entire rest of his life?

No. Not really.

Whether or not he ever got married, sooner or later he'd have to face them. To accept the existence of the trust fund. And decide what to do with the damned money.

To be even more honest, he'd begun to seriously wonder if he could actually stay single for the rest of his life. Being with DeAnne . . . it felt good. As absurdly unusual as their circumstances had been so far, they'd managed to achieve a deep sense of connection and optimism together that he'd never have expected in an everyday life, let alone while being chased all over the map by enemy soldiers. They felt . . . right . . . together. Like they belonged together, and could face anything together, come what may.

Wasn't that what marriage and family were supposed to be all about, ultimately?

Now that he'd found that kind of connection, he was hard-pressed to imagine a life without it. Or without the person who made him feel this way.

Which really made him wonder . . . had he been selfish all these years? If family was about having a solid connection, come what may, should he have stayed at home and fought for what he wanted, stood his ground against his father—but kept that family connection, as rocky as it was, instead of running away and severing it completely . . . ?

That was a hard truth to face head-on.

During the past couple of days, he'd been thinking a lot about his mother and father, about how he'd feel if one or both of them died before he saw them again. Or if Kip, himself, died tomorrow . . . or next week . . . or next year?

Would his father regret not making amends before it was too late?

Would *he*?

How would his family feel if things went terribly wrong on this op and he was killed? How would he feel if he was captured and disappeared into a Chinese prison for the rest of his life, and they never found out what had happened to him?

No doubt he could rely on DeAnne to track them down and let them know. Strangely enough, that was a far bigger comfort than he ever would have thought.

And maybe . . . just maybe, letting her assume that burden was taking the coward's way out.

Kip knew himself to be many things, but he was not a coward.

If he survived this mission, he'd have to do some serious thinking about his future.

About confronting his family.

About dealing with the damn trust fund instead of spending every minute of his life avoiding that huge responsibility.

About seeking a real relationship with DeAnne, and finding out if it could work between them.

Yeah. He'd definitely have to think about all that.

If he survived the day tomorrow.

30

Darcy jarred awake to the booming screech of a Klaxon. It scared her so badly she vaulted from her bunk onto her feet, weapon drawn from under the pillow, in less than a second.

After three blasts, the Klaxon cut off and the loudspeaker blared out a warning, "Report to battle stations! Prepare to dive!"

She obeyed orders and dove for her clothes. *What the hell was going on?* She pulled on her shirt to the static of several more orders from the overhead speaker.

Then, "Dive! Dive! Dive!"

Yanking on her cargo pants, she felt the acute shift of the deck under her feet as the submarine slipped downward into the ocean depths. She grabbed the door frame to steady herself and struggled to jam her feet into her boots.

Her ears popped at the increasing heaviness of the atmospheric pressure—or maybe it was just nerves. Was it her imagination, or was it getting harder to breathe in here?

For the past day, the submarine had been playing

possum, lingering amongst the valleys and seamounts that surrounded the Paracel Islands, well away from Hainan. Even if patrolling PLAN planes or coastal cutters had spotted the sub before today, the Chinese wouldn't worry about the sub later this morning when the AUV test was launched. In fact, the enemy navy might even try to use them as a target for testing their new toy.

Which Darcy knew was exactly what Walker hoped.

Was it already morning? Had she overslept and something gone wrong?

Something with Bobby Lee?

Oh, sweet Lord.

She careened out of officer's country and up the ladder to the main deck, swinging to an abrupt halt at the top when she found the control room crammed with submariners laser-focused on their tasks. The captain snapped orders, which were echoed by two or three other officers before being executed, reports were shouted, and the overhead intercom crackled with a chaos of information being relayed back and forth.

She'd seen it all before at various times in the past when her STORM teams had been transported via submarine, but it never ceased to amaze her that anyone on the crew actually knew what the heck was going on. It was a pure miracle the damn thing didn't sink. But it never did. And it wouldn't. These Silent Service guys were the bomb.

She sidled past the bedlam to the sonar room, praying she'd find Rufus Edwards there. Sonar techs never wandered too far from their beloved shack.

Sure enough, the master chief was parked in a swivel chair at one of the consoles, big black earphones on, peering intently at a trio of monitor screens that were cobbled up in front of him—obviously not part of the standard equipment, but something he'd brought with him. Between him and the real sonar guy, and the packed jumble of instruments, there was hardly room to breathe.

She stuck her head into the tiny space, and when no one paid the slightest bit of attention to her, she slid inside next to Edwards.

"Chief," she said, and when he didn't hear her, she tapped his shoulder.

He glanced up questioningly, and she pointed to her ears.

He lifted off the headphones, but kept one eye on the monitors. "What's cooking, sugar?"

At the endearment, she did a double take, but he was definitely not being disrespectful, and certainly not flirting. He was all about the monitors.

"That's my question," she said. "What's going on? Is it the away team?"

"What? No. They're fine. Talked to them an hour ago." He peeled his gaze from the colorful snow falling across his monitors. To her, it looked like close-ups of the aurora borealis in a blizzard. Well. Except for the three solid silhouettes of torpedoes swimming in it.

"Holy crap," she exclaimed, her eyes bugging out. "They're firing torpedoes at us already? We haven't even done anything yet." She blinked at him. "Have we?"

He hooked his headphones around his neck and smiled, his eyes crinkling. "First, not torpedoes. Those are submarines. Vietnamese submarines, from what we can make of the signatures and the language being spoken onboard. Damn new shielding's a bitch to hear through. Second, no. We haven't done anything to prompt being attacked. As you say—yet."

"Vietnamese?" she asked, her anxiety notching down. "So this has nothing to do with the Chinese AUV test? Or our away team?"

"Extremely doubtful on both counts," he assured her. "However, this harassment could seriously interfere with our ability to carry out our plans later this morning."

She peered closer. "They're harassing us?"

He lifted a shoulder. "Part of the general anti-access, area-denial cold war being waged between China and its neighbors in the South China Seas."

She'd have to ask about that mouthful later. Right now she was more concerned about how this Asian power struggle would affect their mission. "But why harass us? We're American. And not their neighbors."

"True. But they just acquired these new subs from Russia in the past couple of years. They probably intend using us to test their stalking skills, hiding in our baffles, practicing their angles and dangles."

She had no idea what any of that meant, but whatever it was, it meant trouble. *Unbelievable.* She checked her wristwatch. It was already after six a.m. The AUV test was slated to start at nine o'clock. *Shit.*

"So cut to the chase," she said. "What are we doing about it?"

His grin turned evil. "Why, giving them what they want. A little practice."

As if on cue, the sub made a steep turn to the left, still diving, heading into the network of faults and troughs that formed the bottom of the South China Sea between the Paracel Islands and Hainan. She'd checked the charts last night and knew that the seabed varied quite a bit, from the water depth to the geology—some places shallow and sandy, some deep and rocky. The perfect place for a submarine to play hide and seek.

But they didn't have time for this nonsense.

"Will we be able to shake them in time?" she asked worriedly. "How close do we have to be to Yulin to do the intercept?"

He pushed out a considering breath. "Good question. I honestly have no idea. Clint was working all night on setting up our two UUVs with the necessary software for the bait and switch. He'd be in a better position to tell you."

"In that case—" She turned to go find Walker.

"He's catching an hour of sleep," Edwards said, bringing her up short. "He was pretty much a zombie."

Damn.

The sub made another steep turn, and she grabbed onto the back of his seat to keep from falling on her butt.

"Jeez Louise. Good luck sleeping through these loop-the-loops."

Edwards chuckled. "Hell, girl, this is nothing. He'll be sleeping like a baby."

"Who'll be a baby?" came a voice from the door.

Darcy turned to see Walker standing there, rubbing a hand through his hair, making it stick up every which way.

"*Sleeping* like a baby," she corrected.

"Which you should still be doing," Edwards said. "You've still got fifteen minutes. Why are you up?"

"Figured something was happening, what with all the commotion. We were supposed to be running quiet."

Again the sub made a deep turn and Darcy hung on for dear life, her stomach lurching, while the men simply leaned their bodies with the motion, not even seeming to notice.

Edwards gave Walker a quick rundown of the situation, and she repeated her question. "How close do we have to be to the launch site for you to make the switch undetected?"

Walker shook his head. "We could launch our UUVs now, except"—he frowned at the screens—"those other subs out there would pick them up on sonar. That would kind of blow the whole 'undetected' thing."

She gritted her teeth against another circus maneuver, swallowing her stomach back down where it belonged. "So I guess this roller-coaster ride is for good reason."

The two men nodded, lopsided grins creeping across their faces. "Why? Feeling a little queasy, sugar?"

She scoffed. "Who, me?" She would *not* get sick in front of them. Not if it killed her. Which it just might.

Walker swiped a hand through his hair again, making it stick up in the other direction. "I suppose I could reprogram the mission sequence so the UUVs would launch and then wait until all other vessels are out of acoustical range before proceeding to the target."

"Would that be hard?" she asked.

His head wobbled back and forth. "No. Just a pain. But what's new?"

She looked at Edwards. "What do you think?"

"Might be a good idea," he said. "Who knows how long we'll spend ditching these bozos." He tilted his head. "Of course, we could always use the sound library. My guess is their sonar guys are rank amateurs. Shouldn't be too hard to fool."

Walker nodded. "And it'll give *us* some practice." He yawned. "All right. Let me grab some coffee and we can get to work."

DeAnne dreamed she was riding Space Mountain at Disneyland.

Space Mountain had always been her favorite ride. Well, other than Alice in Wonderland, which was the all-time best.

Kip was strapped in next to her, his arm wrapped tightly around her shoulders. But instead of a brilliant light show of laser beams shooting past them in the dark, it was bullets whizzing past. Real bullets. She twisted and turned to escape, but their seat belts were welded shut, so they couldn't get away.

The ride whipped back and forth, this way and that, the car hurtling down the mountain at breakneck speed. Which was the only thing that saved them from the bullets.

Suddenly, the ride swerved violently. DeAnne was torn from Kip's arms and thrown from her seat. Flying into the black void of space, she screamed and screamed, grabbing for Kip, but he was carried away at the speed of light, the ride disappearing into the blackness.

She came awake with a desperate scream, her heart pounding, and a feeling in her gut that tore her apart from the inside out.

Oh, God. Had something happened to Kip?

She blinked open her eyes and attempted to sit up.

And realized with a start that she was sprawled on the floor of her stateroom, tangled in the blanket. She'd fallen out of bed.

How the—

Suddenly, the room around her tilted and dipped wildly to one side. Which explained how she'd tumbled from the bunk. She squeaked, and grabbed for purchase on the mattress frame, managing to follow the boat's movement with her body.

Good night. She didn't think she could ever ride Space Mountain again.

She thought of Kip again, wondered where he was, what he was doing. And if he was all right. She'd never been psychic before this, and she prayed that hadn't changed. Those dream bullets had felt all too real.

She shivered, and knew she'd never get back to sleep again. So she gingerly rose from the floor and got dressed.

The feeling that Kip was in trouble wouldn't leave her alone. It had lodged in the pit of her stomach and sat there gnawing at her, like the monster from *Alien* waiting to burst out.

She squeezed her eyes shut and took a deep, steadying breath. *God*, she hated this. Hated being useless. Hated being the extra wheel, waiting on the sidelines for something bad to happen. Or even something good.

That was Kip's fault—the impatience.

Before meeting him, before being dragged all over

kingdom come and back again, eluding men with guns, making love under the stars, outwitting tracking dogs, being kidnapped at gunpoint, before all that she never would have believed herself capable of any of it.

She was a diplomat. She waited patiently. She was practical and sensible. She used her words.

She didn't shoot at foreign army jeeps, didn't sleep on the ground and ride motorcycles, didn't climb rope ladders onto submarines.

She didn't even *like* people who did that stuff, people who were like her father. People like Kiptyn Llowell.

God. People like *she'd* become.

Except she did.

She'd loved doing all those things! Even when she'd been frightened to the roots of her hair, she'd felt a thrill in her soul that she'd never before experienced.

She'd loved every minute of the past two days.

And most of all, she loved Kip.

The man who'd taught her it was okay to take a risk. That sometimes jumping off a cliff was the only way to get rid of all that baggage you'd carried all the way up there, for all of your life.

She opened her eyes and slowly let out her breath. And knew that it was high time to do something about it.

Time to admit she'd been wrong.

Time to jump off that cliff.

And tell Kip how she felt.

31

They knew they were walking into a trap.

So they'd come prepared.

Kip and the others had decided on a plan, and after grabbing a couple hours sleep they'd risen, made a few calls, hired more than a few players, and put it into motion.

They'd just parked Julie's rental car in a grungy alley off the main road in Tiandu village, half a klick from the prison entrance. They were all wearing peasant jackets and black wigs. Not that they'd fool anyone in those disguises for more than a few seconds. But a few seconds were all they needed.

What they hadn't counted on was Jaeger calling to tell them he couldn't get hold of Darcy.

The submarine had gone dark.

Which meant something unforeseen had happened out there in the South China Sea.

Possibly something bad.

"Sonofabitch." Quinn cursed as he hung up the throw-away cell phone Julie had given them along with a car boot full of other equipment that Bridger had somehow scrounged through his mysterious channels. The man was seriously connected.

Alarm clawed through Kip at the idea that the submarine had suddenly disappeared. *DeAnne was on that sub.*

"What the hell? They were supposed to wait for our okay to submerge," Kip said unnecessarily. They all knew the plan. The sub was to do its thing *after* everything was in place here.

Quinn cursed again. "Think I don't know that?" he snapped.

Okay. His fiancée, Darcy, was also onboard, Kip reminded himself. But still.

Before this, nothing else had remotely rattled the commander. Not even when Julie Severin's astute analysis had convinced them all they were about to embark on a suicide mission.

"Don't worry," Alex assured him. "Nothing's happened to the sub or the team. They're fine."

"That your Spidey sense talking?" Quinn muttered.

Alex didn't seem to take offense. "Bridger would have called us." He pointed to the cell phone. "He knows our number."

At that astute observation, Quinn's worried expression became a grimace of chagrin. "Hell. You're right." His shoulders notched down visibly. "Jesus on a goddamn stick. That woman has me tied in fucking knots."

Alex's lip curled. "Welcome to my world, buddy."

Kip wasn't about to say it out loud, but he could definitely relate. He had to take a breath and count to ten, forcing his heartbeat back to normal. The kid *was* right. There would be a perfectly good explanation for the sub submerging. It's what submarines did. No need for concern. DeAnne was fine. Darcy, too.

God almighty. What a sorry bunch of tough guys.

He eased out a breath.

"Shit," Quinn ground out. "I just wish she'd pick a god-damn wedding date. It's bugging me that she won't, and I don't need that kind of distraction."

Kip's jaw nearly dropped. *Can you say displacement?*

"Don't even try to figure it out," Alex returned. "Women are a mystery we'll never understand. Get used to it."

Quinn slashed out a hand in disgust. "What's the god-damn problem, anyway? Women are supposed to *want* to get married. *I'm* the one who should be stalling."

Kip blinked. He was ass-deep in a category-five op, and they were bitching about women and *wedding dates*? He was pretty sure he'd been transported to an alternate universe.

His new watch vibrated against his wrist.

He cleared his throat and looked down at the gadget he'd been given from Bridger's bag of tricks: a watch that could send and receive texts. The screen was tiny, but enough for a word or two. Amazing the difference in sophistication between the equipment STORM supplied and what he had access to in the Marines. Light years. He could get used to this stuff.

But this vibration was just the alarm going off.

"We should get in position," Alex informed them. His had gone off, too.

They still had an hour, but they didn't want to take a chance on missing Romanov's transport, should his transfer happen early despite predictions to the contrary.

The good news was that during the night, Jaeger had somehow managed to get eyes in the sky. He was now watching the vehicles and exits at Yulin for any sign of Nikolai Romanov being escorted out of the brig.

"All right," said Quinn, putting his com earpiece back on. "Let's do it."

Kip and Alex followed suit and they went through a

quick sound check, then Quinn dialed in Jaeger and Julie Severin. "STORM alpha six to romeo and juliet. Y'all set, over?"

Julie answered immediately. "Looking forward to a stormy breakfast."

"I hear ya. Romeo? Howzit with the rich and famous?" Their prearranged code for his setup on the yacht.

"Hundreds, six," Jaeger came back. "Chow's *lekker*."

At Kip's baffled expression, Quinn rolled his eyes, tapped his earpiece, and said, "Afrikaans slang. In three words he managed to convey everything's fine, the food is great, and he probably got laid last night."

"*Befok* you, romeo, over," Alex retorted, and Jaeger snickered.

Kip didn't really need a translation.

Alrighty, then.

Kip liked how easy they were with each other. He and the men of his MOC unit were a solid, tight-knit group, and had the utmost respect for each other, but his rank was ever-present, coloring all their personal interactions. He would trust his life to each and every one of his men without hesitation, and vice versa. But would they invite him over for a backyard barbecue? He honestly didn't know.

But these guys would, he had no doubt.

Quinn tapped his earpiece again. "Anything on our lost dog?" he asked Jaeger, clearly still worried about the status of the submarine.

"Unexpected company, I hear."

Quinn frowned. "Who?"

"Unknown."

A muscle worked in his jaw. "Keep me in the loop, over."

"Yep. Out."

Quinn hit his com with a curse. "I do not fucking need this right now," he muttered, scooping up an MP7 from the car boot along with several ammo magazines.

"Bobby Lee," Alex began, but Quinn held up a hand.

"I'm good."

Kip hoped so. This was no time to go off the rails. He was concerned about DeAnne, too. But not about the submarine. He'd met the crew, and they were top notch. She was in a lot less danger with them than she'd been on the run with him . . .

"Any word on the bus?" he asked, steering the conversation back on point as he slid his rucksack over the Chinese peasant jacket he was wearing, and checked his Beretta. They'd met the tourist bus driver in front of the roach motel chatting up the hookers, and had instantly recruited the cheerful but wily man with a pile of cash, altering their plan slightly. A bus was even better than a truck.

"Standing by for our signal," Quinn confirmed, stuck the ammo in his peasant jacket pocket, and tucked the machine gun under the front flap. He grabbed three stun guns from the trunk and passed them around.

"I hope to God this works," Kip murmured, sliding his into the back of his waistband.

"Amen, brother," Alex agreed.

They all bumped fists, grunted, "Oo-ra," and turned to head for their assigned positions. But before Kip could take two steps, Quinn touched his shoulder and shook his head. Curious, Kip held back while Alex trotted away and around a corner.

"Problem?" he asked.

"No. It's just—" Quinn slashed a hand through his hair. He was a study in contrasts, this tall, blond Viking in Chinese peasant garb and combat boots. He glanced after Alex, looking torn.

Kip figured it was something to do with his hesitation to bring the younger man in the first place. "Worried about him?"

"Yeah. No." Quinn jetted out a breath. "He seems fine.

But if something goes wrong, or if he has one of his—" He gave his head a quick shake. "If anything happens, anything at all, grab Romanov and get him the hell off the island. Find Julie. Call your men. Steal a boat. Do whatever you have to do."

Kip studied him. "What about you and Alex?"

Quinn met his gaze soberly. "I won't leave him."

Seeing the unshakable resolve in the commander's expression, Kip's respect for the man went way up. "Understood," he said.

With that, Quinn nodded, turned, and loped off.

Kip headed in the opposite direction.

Not good, he thought. The leader of this little sortie had too many things on his mind other than the mission. That was a recipe for disaster.

Which meant Kip must stay extra vigilant.

He arrived at his position at a crumbling stone wall that overlooked the road that the PLA transport had to take to reach the prison, and looked around for a good place to hide.

In choosing this spot, they'd taken a page from Sun Tsu and avoided the expected. The transport's route went through several miles of dense jungle, past wide tracts of fields, as well as skirting the shore of a large reservoir. All prime places to stage an ambush. Which was why they'd avoided picking any of them. Another possible route would have taken Romanov's transport smack through the middle of the National Tourism Area, which was a real temptation, but it was unlikely the PLA would choose that way.

In the end, the team had decided to go with a far more exposed place, and a riskier plan that they hoped would truly take Romanov's guards by surprise. They were making their move just blocks from the entrance to the prison, at a main highway interchange on the outskirts of the village.

With any luck, there wouldn't be a single shot fired. That was the idea, anyway.

Supreme excellence in battle consists of breaking the enemy's resistance without fighting.

The plan was dicey, but doable. Definitely old-school.

Very old-school.

The big question was, would Romanov's military guards be young enough to fall for their little surprise?

If not, Kip, Quinn, and Alex would be stepping into a goddamn shit storm, and landing in a world of hurt.

32

They didn't call the Kilo class 636 "the black hole" for nothing.

That's what DeAnne was learning as the crew took the submarine through a set of maneuvers that would rival a chase scene in a Tom Clancy novel.

The submariners were bent with laser-like concentration to their individual tasks. The atmosphere was tense and on edge, but rife with quiet excitement. This was what these men lived for.

More adrenaline junkies.

Oddly, that no longer bothered DeAnne.

There wasn't an inch to spare anywhere on the vessel, every space was packed to the gills with instruments and crew—and nowhere she could easily tuck herself. No way was she hiding in her stateroom, not knowing what was going on. But every other square inch seemed to be occupied.

The control room was off limits, the radio room too

crowded, and the engineering space too hot, dangerous, and chaotic.

She'd finally found an empty swivel chair in the forward torpedo room next to Walker. She was steadily quizzing him as to what the sub was doing, why, and what she was watching on the indecipherable console monitors. It all looked like static to her. And the ride still felt like Space Mountain.

But she was getting used to it. And the crew's excitement was catching.

"I still don't understand why a submarine with a clunky diesel engine could possibly be quieter than a nuclear-powered sub," she said.

"Because you can shut the engines off," he explained as he typed on three different keyboards and watched the monitors like a bird of prey. "You can't shut down a nuke. It's the engine noise that gives you away. Ever driven in a Prius?"

She had. She owned one, in fact. The hybrid was completely silent when it switched over to electric power.

"Ah." Sometimes the simplest explanation was the least obvious. "I get it."

"There's a bit more to it than that—the way things are built and put together—but basically that's the reason."

"That makes sense. So why doesn't our navy have diesel-electrics anymore?" She knew that officially, the U.S. Navy had been using nuclear subs exclusively for a couple of decades now.

"Yeah." Walker shot her a sardonic look. "Don't get me started."

She swiveled toward him in her chair. "Not a fan of nukes?"

"Oh, hell, yeah. Gotta have our boomers. But in my opinion we need both types. They've got much different strengths." He shrugged. "Unfortunately, I'm not in charge."

She looked around at the space. "Well, maybe this super-secret navy Kilo is a sign they're changing their minds."

"I'm not holding my breath." He peered closer at a screen. "Hello. What have we here?"

A second later, the overhead speaker blared, "Tube door opening on tango three! Stand by!"

DeAnne straightened instantly. "Tube doors?" Her voice went an octave higher all by itself. "As in *torpedo* tube?"

Walker reached over and put a hand on her arm, though his eyes stayed on the monitor. "Don't panic yet. I doubt they're launching a torpedo."

"Tube flooding!" the speaker boomed, followed by a flurry of orders.

Panic filled her veins despite his assurance. "What else are torpedo tubes used for, other than launching torpedoes?"

"Oh. Getting rid of garbage. Burial at sea. Scientific instruments." He winked. "Launching UUVs."

She cut her gaze back to the monitor. "You think that's what they're doing?"

"A torpedo attack would be a political nightmare for their government. And we haven't killed anyone. Yet."

Her eyes widened.

"Kidding."

She punched his arm.

She doubted the other submarine was expelling galley scraps—or scientific instruments—in the middle of a high-speed chase, either, so it must be either a UUV or a torpedo. She prayed Walker was right.

He pursed his lips. "Hmm." He suddenly jumped to his feet, said, "Wait here," and ducked through the watertight door to the control room.

She snapped her mouth closed, and listened intently to the overhead speaker for any hint of an impending torpedo attack from the harassing submarines. Thankfully none came.

Instead, she heard the captain order their own tube

doors to be opened in succession, and then flooded. Her jaw dropped again. What the heck was going on?

Meanwhile, Walker had sprinted back to his chair and was now typing furiously on the keyboards.

"What's happening?" she asked, her pulse speeding.

"We're creating a diversion. So I can launch our UUVs."

She listened as the captain ordered the tubes to be randomly blown and the doors closed. Then he started the sequence all over again. In the middle of it all, Walker sent the UUVs out and dropped them to the seabed, putting them into sleep mode.

"Wow," she said, realizing what he'd done. "That was pretty smart."

He grinned over at her. "It was getting down to the wire and I didn't want to lose our window on the Chinese AUV. Our fish will wake up after we're all out of range, then proceed with the mission sequence."

She checked the time on the computer screen. The Yulin test would begin in just over an hour. "How long will it take our UUVs to intercept it?"

"Hard to say. Depends on what the Chinese are having it do." He frowned. "We'd planned to steam around making a handy target for it to latch onto. But with all this hullabaloo going on with the Vietnamese subs, I'm not sure what'll happen. We'll have to play it by ear."

"You mean this could fail?"

"Always a possibility. But don't give up so easily. We've still got a few tricks up our sleeves."

God, she hoped so. She'd hate for all this to have been for nothing.

Speaking of sleeves and tricks . . .

She thought about Kip and the away team, and wondered how they were faring. She really hoped they'd been able to figure out a way to rescue Nikolai Romanov without getting themselves killed in the process.

She hated that Darcy hadn't been able to communicate with the guys since the sub was forced to crash dive. She had no idea how they were doing. Or if their mission was going well. Or even if they were still alive.

Darcy didn't seem too worried. She said Bobby Lee always scraped through, no matter what was thrown at him. He was a genius at strategy and getting out of tight places.

"I do wish I was there, though," Darcy had admitted. "I feel better when I'm there to watch his back. And then there's Alex . . ." She let the thought trail off. "Hell, they'll be fine. No worries."

Unfortunately, DeAnne had gotten the distinct impression she'd been about to say something like, "And then there's Alex, who may go off the deep end into crazyville at any moment," rather than, "And then there's Alex, who's a crack sharpshooter and a black belt in six karate styles."

Ho boy.

Darcy may not be worried, but DeAnne certainly was.

She sent up a little prayer for them.

Suddenly, the torpedo room tilted precariously, yanking her back to the present. She grabbed onto her seat. Around them, the hull shuddered, and she felt the sub slow down dramatically.

"What the—"

Walker lifted a hand. "Wait. Listen." The shudder melted away into a smooth glide.

The chatter from the overhead speakers cut off abruptly, as though a switch had been flipped. The entire sub went quiet as a tomb.

After two days of listening to the hot, noisy diesel engines, the utter silence was unnerving. It was like going from the streets of New Delhi to the absolute stillness of the Antarctic.

She looked at Walker questioningly, and he mouthed, "Electric power. We're hiding," putting a finger to his lips.

She'd seen submarines do this same thing in World War Two movies. *Silent running.* Good grief. Talk about old tricks . . .

Turning back to the monitors, Walker studied the solid blips suspended in snow, then another screen undulating with mysterious squiggles and lines. After a minute, he indicated the first one to her, and she realized the blips for the three other submarines were slowly moving off the screen.

Walker smiled and gave a thumbs-up.

Apparently the ruse was working.

Her blood pressure slowly eased back to normal.

Right up until a ridiculously loud *ping* blasted through the submarine, exploding the silence and reverberating against every metal surface around them.

Walker swore, his voice joining a collective curse that rose from the entire crew.

"Active sonar," he said disgustedly. "They've found us."

Instantly, the mechanical noise and human chatter was back. The engines rumbled, and DeAnne gripped the console as the propellers bit into the water, sending the vessel forward with a groaning lurch.

"Hang on to your hat," Walker said, listening intently to the overhead commands. "This could get hairy."

33

"STORM romeo, alpha team. Stand by."

The com had been mute for so long the sound of Jaeger's voice almost startled Kip. He'd been sitting on his heels leaning his back against the flip side of a stone wall that overlooked the interchange on the main road where they'd planned their action.

Finally. It was the prearranged signal letting the team know Jaeger had spotted Romanov and the transport, and it was on its way.

"STORM alpha six. Standing by," came Quinn's acknowledgement.

Kip checked his watch. *Oh-eight-twenty.* Right on time. He didn't know whether to be relieved or worried about that.

Moments later, Jaeger said, "STORM romeo. I've got one charlie and four fat juliets."

Jesus. The car was to be expected. That's where Romanov was sure to be, along with his guards. But four jeeps filled with soldiers . . .

Kip did not like those odds.

He spent the next fifteen minutes going over in his head every possible scenario that might come about, and how to handle each. The more he thought about it, the crazier he thought they were for ever believing this insane plan could work.

But he wasn't about to back down now.

His earpiece crackled, and Jaeger said, "Two minutes."

"Sending in the pastry," said Quinn.

They all acknowledged, and Kip took a deep breath, letting it out slowly.

This was it.

Lifting up so he could see over the stone wall, he focused his binoculars on the spot below where two roads intersected in an elongated traffic circle. The roads weren't too busy, but there was a steady stream of morning traffic going in both directions.

A tourist bus approached the interchange, then bumped off onto the dirt shoulder just before it got to the roundabout. There was movement inside. The bus was full of people.

So far, so good.

He swung the binoculars and checked out the opposite side of the traffic circle. There, an ancient tractor was putt-putt-putting up the road toward the interchange, pulling a rickety trailer piled high with a huge, towering load of hay.

If the situation weren't so damn serious, Kip would have laughed. Clearly, Quinn had been watching too many Three Stooges movies. This idea was so fucking preposterous . . . hell, it just might work.

He could hear the commander speaking on the cell phone to the driver. "Almost, just a little—"

Jaeger interrupted. "Fifteen seconds."

"Okay, go," Quinn told the bus driver.

Its engine revved, and the bus lurched, barreling onto

the road, scattering cars right and left as they swerved to avoid a collision. Horns beeped, and motorists shouted insults through open car windows.

The hay tractor was already in the roundabout, nearly to the crossroad.

Behind the bus, the convoy came into view through the trees. *Perfect timing*. The lead jeep was just a few cars away.

The bus sped into the traffic circle.

Too fast.

It saw the tractor too late, and couldn't stop.

It swerved violently and clipped the back of the overloaded trailer. Hay flew up into the wind, scattering in every direction, obscuring windshields, covering the road in great drifts of straw.

Good God. That bus driver had to be kidding.

An accident was not part of the—

Shit.

Blinded, the bus skidded to a halt across both lanes. More horns blared. The hay farmer leaped off the tractor, shouting at the bus driver, waving his fist. Traffic ground to a halt.

The convoy was trapped, penned in by cars piling up behind it.

Good. *That* was the plan.

Aggravated drivers jumped out of their cars yelling, adding to the noise and the chaos.

Now would be the time to—

"Go!" Quinn barked.

Kip slipped over the stone wall and darted toward the road, sidling in behind a tree. He hung back, waiting for an opening.

The soldiers in the jeeps hopped out uncertainly, alert and brandishing weapons, gazes darting all around, seeking the source of an attack they were clearly expecting.

Even more drivers popped from their vehicles, wondering what was going on.

Just then, passengers began pouring off the bus. Ten, fifteen, twenty of them. Drawing even more attention than the accident.

They giggled and waved, beckoning to the startled soldiers.

Who lowered their weapons in surprise and delight. And strolled toward them, chests puffed, momentarily forgetting their guard duties.

After all, what red-blooded young soldier could resist? Especially in a country with a thirty-five million surplus of men.

The passengers from the bus . . . were all hookers.

It didn't take long for all four jeeps to completely empty of men. Most of the soldiers were distracted by the women, but Kip saw that a few were staying alert at their posts, guarding the car with the prisoner, weapons up and at the ready.

However, they all stood facing forward, warily watching the confusion of the accident—and the tempting sight of the women.

Which made it an easy task for Alex to scramble underneath the last three jeeps and pull out some essential part to disable them. The lead jeep was impossible for him to get to, but it was penned in by cars on every side and wasn't going anywhere until this mess got cleaned up.

Kip noticed one of the soldiers on his radio, undoubtedly speaking to either the prison personnel or his superiors at Yulin. Either way, any minute now they'd simply walk Romanov to the other side of the traffic circle where a prison vehicle would soon be there to complete the transfer.

He hit his com. "Ticking clock," he reported, slipping from the cover of the tree trunk and moving casually over to a car that had been abandoned by its looky-lou owner. He made himself small leaning casually against the front fender. He saw Alex do the same a couple of cars over.

Kip estimated they had maybe four minutes, tops, to get the Russian out of there, or he'd disappear into the Chinese prison system and be nearly impossible to extract.

Time for stage two.

Right on schedule, Quinn said over the com, "Lighting the candles in three, two, one—"

Suddenly, there was a ka-*boom*, and a burst of fireworks lit up the orchard next to the roundabout. Seconds later, the rapid *pop-pop-po*p of firecrackers crackled through the air on the opposite side of the road.

Everyone froze. Then, almost to a man, the soldiers snapped up their guns and ran in every direction, searching for the source of the explosions. All except for two of the men guarding the car with Romanov in it. They stayed firmly put.

Another round of fireworks went off in a third location. More chaos ensued.

Kip pulled the stun gun from his waistband and hit the "charge" button.

"Lima and me," Quinn said a moment later. "On three, two, one." They fired simultaneously.

Both guards sank to the ground.

Kip ejected the cartridge, stowed the gun, and pulled a dirt brown sheet from his rucksack.

He held his breath.

But no one reacted.

"Go," said Quinn.

The team moved in swiftly. Kip was to grab Romanov and run. Quinn would plant a blow-up doll in the back seat in his place, and Alex was to cover them.

As another volley of fireworks went off, Kip kicked the guard's gun away, then swiftly searched his pockets and took his keys. He reached in the transport vehicle, popped the back door locks, and swung open the door.

Romanov was right there, ready to jump out. He was

wearing a red jumpsuit and his hands were cuffed behind him.

Unfortunately, his legs were also shackled.

"Fuck," Kip swore, wrapping him in the sheet to cover the red prison suit.

"Sorry," Romanov said, looking grim. And bloodied. *Jesus*, they'd beaten the crap out of him.

"Don't be," Kip said, and picked him up, threw him over his shoulder, and headed for the alley. *Jesus*. The man weighed a ton.

Quinn was right behind him.

That's when they both noticed Alex wasn't.

Quinn halted and turned to see what was keeping him, and at the corner of the alley, Kip couldn't stop but glanced over his free shoulder.

His blood froze. The kid was crouched down, hanging on to the back bumper of the transport vehicle, hyperventilating.

Ah, hell.

34

Skidding around the mouth of the alley, Kip dumped Romanov onto his feet and scooped the driver's keys from his pocket, leafing quickly through the ring to find the handcuff key.

There were three possibles. He spun Romanov, tossing the sheet aside, and stabbed the first key into the lock. It didn't turn.

Crap.

He put his head around the corner and saw Quinn sprinting back to Alex.

"*Shit.*" He tried the second key. "The car's down this alley. The blue one. Guns, phone, and clothes in the trunk. Keys sitting on the back left tire. Julie's number is programmed in the phone. She'll guide you out of here."

"You're not coming?" Romanov asked in surprise.

Kip jetted out a breath. "I've gotta go back. Alex is in trouble."

"Then I'm coming, too," Romanov said, pulling his

wrists in front and rubbing them when the cuff lock sprang free on the third try.

"*Hell*, no," Kip said. "Not happening." He shoved the keys into Romanov's hands so he could open the leg shackles.

"You risked your lives to free me—"

"Exactly. So don't squander that. Get out of here. Now."

With that, Kip started after Quinn—he didn't run, because he didn't want to attract undue attention, but walked as fast as he dared, keeping his face down. He slid the Beretta into his hand, keeping it covered by the flap of his peasant jacket.

Quinn had already reached Alex, and was kneeling down beside him, glancing around, speaking quietly while urging him to his feet.

Alex had his arms crossed over his chest, eyes squeezed tightly shut, rocking slightly back and forth on his heels. He was trying to catch his breath and not paying any attention to Quinn.

Pulse pounding, Kip halted at the tree he'd hidden behind before, and did a thorough scan of the entire scene, looking for any sign of danger. Chaos still reigned everywhere. But it wouldn't last much longer. Any second now the soldiers would find the fireworks and realize this was all a diversion. They had to be already starting to suspect.

God*damn* it. What had Quinn been thinking, bringing Alex along?

Quinn caught Kip's gaze and shook his head, motioning forcefully for him to go back to Romanov. Kip gave his own head a shake and continued to scan the area. He could see Quinn's lips press into a thin line, all the way from here.

Quinn grasped Alex's arms and tried to pull him to his feet. Alex struggled against him.

Kip cursed under his breath. He was *really* starting to get nervous. The fireworks and firecrackers had gone silent. The prison vehicle would be here momentarily. The hookers' novelty would soon wear off and the soldiers would remember what they were here for. The blow-up doll in the back seat was not going to pass any kind of closer inspection.

This had clusterfuck written all over it.

Come on, come on, come on.

Abruptly, Alex looked up at Quinn, then around. It took him two seconds to realize what had happened. The next second he practically flew to his feet. Quinn grabbed his arm and they took off.

All right.

They hustled quickly toward Kip.

They almost made it.

Suddenly, a strangled shout rose above the noise and chatter. One of the stunned guards had woken up.

Angry as hell.

Kip wanted to kick himself. He should have watched them more carefully!

The guard was still lying prone on the ground. But he'd managed to get to his pistol.

Kip whipped up his Beretta.

Too late.

A shot exploded through the air.

Quinn faltered in mid-motion, then stumbled and started to fall. Blood blossomed on his upper thigh. A grimace ripped across his face.

Alex caught him before he went down, but struggled under his weight.

Kip catapulted out from his hiding place, rushing to their aid.

Another shot rang out.

Alex staggered and his shoulder bloomed crimson. Quinn slumped and started to slip from his grasp.

Kip reached them in three long strides, and slung an arm around Quinn, taking the burden from Alex.

"No. Leave me," rasped Quinn. "Take Zane and—"

"Shut the fuck up, Commander," Kip growled, all but dragging them toward the shelter of the alley. "We all make it, or no one does."

"Then we're all in deep shit . . ."

That was the last thing he heard before the next shot split the air, and the bullet found its mark dead center.

And everything in his world went black.

35

DeAnne was growing antsy.

It had taken another whole hour of playing hide-and-seek before the Vietnamese subs finally gave up and left them alone. The captain hadn't wanted to show them any of his A-game—no sense educating the enemy about your best strategies—so he had basically given them a pretend chase, all the while deliberately moving closer and closer to Hainan Island.

Which was where they wanted to be anyway, in order to make the AUV switch. So in a way, it had worked out well.

Unless you counted the several Chinese naval vessels up top, monitoring the AUV from above as it went through its test paces. The sub crew had been warned to keep their voices low so listening ears wouldn't pick up any sensitive information. Such as the impending plan to spoof their top secret AUV.

At some point, the radio room had plugged someone's iPod into the overhead speaker, and heavy metal rock was playing throughout the main deck, helping to mask the sounds.

Naturally, the sub still hadn't gone anywhere near the surface, and therefore couldn't receive any radio or satellite signals.

So DeAnne was getting more and more nervous about what was happening with Kip and the away team.

She had a really bad feeling in the pit of her stomach.

And it wasn't from the late breakfast she and Darcy were enjoying in the wardroom. Well. Sort of enjoying. The pancakes were delicious, but DeAnne was just not hungry.

"I hate this," she complained. "I wish we could just pop our noses up for a minute."

Darcy didn't look exactly worried, but she wasn't as relaxed as she'd been earlier. She didn't like being in the dark, either. She was used to running things.

"You know the captain's top priority," Darcy said, stirring her black coffee. "He's not going to do anything to jeopardize that."

"No, of course not. I just . . ." DeAnne bit her lip.

Darcy nodded. "I know. I'm anxious about the guys, too." She put down the spoon and made a face at it.

The wardroom door opened and a rating poked his head in. "Lieutenant Commander Walker wanted to let you know it's showtime," he said quietly.

DeAnne perked up. "Really?" She started to rise. "Can we come watch?" she whispered.

"It'll be standing room only, but you're welcome."

It turned out that Clint and Rufus Edwards were at the consoles manning the controls. The captain was standing behind them observing along with a few of the officers, and many of the crew followed along via the repeater monitors scattered around the sub.

Everyone else seemed to understand what was going on. But to DeAnne and Darcy, it looked like just another snowstorm. DeAnne knew the plan was to spoof the enemy AUV, hijack it, take it apart and document every inch of it inside and out, download copies of all of its software, then return it to the water, switch it back from its spoofed state, and pray the PLAN never figured out what had happened.

It was going to take ridiculous navigational skills from Clint, mad sonar signature spoofing by Chief Edwards, techs who could take things apart and put them back together in their sleep, split second timing all around, and an insane amount of pure luck.

It would be a miracle if they could pull it off.

Especially with all the enemy vessels above pointing the most sophisticated sonar equipment that country possessed at them and analyzing every nuance of every sound on board.

The excitement in the torpedo room was contagious. When the three unmanned, torpedo-like vehicles came close enough for the sub's array to pick up their signals, the monitor lit up with squiggles and lines. Everyone leaned in for a better view.

Clint and Edwards exchanged a tense look and a curt nod, and everyone held their collective breath.

Clint hit a short sequence on the keyboard, and they all watched the squiggly lines without moving a single muscle.

DeAnne peered at them, too.

This was the critical moment.

Suddenly the lines on the screen blipped. If she'd blinked she would have missed it.

The crew erupted in mute cheers.

Wait.

That was *it*?

The men punched the air with their fists, grinning widely. It was weird. No one made a sound.

She glanced at Darcy and they exchanged a silent *okay-then* look.

The celebration stopped as quickly as it started, but everyone's expression remained jubilant.

Clint grabbed a joystick off the console. "Okay. Let's bring this baby in," he murmured softly.

Chief Edwards slapped on his headphones and monitored the spoof UUV, making sure it acted the way it should.

Ten minutes later, the Chinese AUV had been coaxed into the torpedo tube and the crew hoisted it gingerly off the rack.

Ten minutes after that, all the sections that could be taken apart were in pieces, spread out on the deck. Cables had been attached, portable drives plugged into ports. Two crewmen were photographing everything meticulously.

Darcy looked over at her. "Kip was supposed to do this part."

"Yeah." DeAnne nodded.

"He's a great photographer. Have you seen his work?"

DeAnne shook her head. "No. Never had a chance. Though he was always taking pictures when we were . . ." Running. Hiding. Catching their breath. Admiring the view. *Making love* . . . "Together."

"Some of his photos are posted on the internet," Darcy said.

"I'll have to check them out." Though DeAnne would much rather he showed them to her. She hoped he would, someday.

If they were still together.

"I read he has a few in galleries, too."

"Yeah?"

"He's really good."

She felt her eyes well up. "Yeah. He is." In more ways than one. Everything about him was good. She'd be a fool to let him go. Regardless of what kind of relationship he wanted.

Every minute she'd had with him had been happier than any she'd ever spent before.

If he wanted no strings, she'd give him no strings.

Just please let him come back to me now.

In less than half an hour, the AUV had been put back together again and loaded into the torpedo rack. And then it was gone, back in the sea and swimming away.

Clint steered it close to the imposter and typed a few keystrokes. Once again, everyone held their breath.

Nothing happened.

Clint cursed, and typed some more.

No one moved an eyelash.

Overhead, the heavy metal guitars wailed. They waited. And waited.

And suddenly the monitor blipped.

Another silent cheer erupted.

Clint and Chief Edwards sagged in their seats, exhausted but grinning like coyotes.

Success!

DeAnne met Darcy's gaze and smiled. Now, finally, maybe they'd be able to go to the surface and get some news.

The captain seemed to read their minds.

"Guess we're due for a surface run," he said, and strode off to the control room.

DeAnne had to restrain herself from tagging along and urging him to hurry. Instead, she and Darcy returned to the wardroom, where the STORM equipment was still set up. As soon as they got within range, Darcy's computer would connect with the STORM servers and download all communications within seconds.

They waited on pins and needles. Until at last the com page appeared and several messages scrolled onto the screen.

The top one read: URGENT.

Darcy clicked on it and scanned the message.

Her whole body froze. A sound DeAnne had never heard before came from deep in her throat. “Oh, God,” Darcy said, and turned to her with horror etched on her face.

“What?” she demanded, suddenly terrified. “What’s happened?”

“They’ve all—” Darcy gave a choked cry. “They’ve all been shot!”

36

DeAnne could not believe she was doing this.

But she had no choice.

There wasn't a chance in hell she'd let Clint and Darcy leave her behind on the submarine and ride off to rescue the guys without her.

Oh, they'd tried to talk her out of it. Till they were blue in the face. But they'd been wasting their time. Time the men might not have.

"I'm going," she'd told them, more determined than she'd ever been in her life. "And that's final."

So they'd given in.

And now she was actually going.

Ho-boy.

She could do it. She *could*.

DeAnne swallowed heavily and held out her arms while the rating fitted her up in a harness for the lift into the same small, private helicopter that had taken Kip away last night.

Had it only been twenty-four hours since she'd seen him?

It seemed like an entire lifetime.

And it may well have been. If he was dead . . . she'd want to die, too.

She loved him that much.

But she was not going to cry. *She was not.*

Tears would not help the man she loved. Only action would.

Rand Jaeger had sent the urgent message. After reading it and nearly breaking down, Darcy had collected herself and e-mailed him right back demanding details. But an unsecure satellite connection was not the place to share that kind of information, so Jaeger only supplied the bare bones, and had sent the helo instead.

Apparently, all three men had been shot—Quinn in the thigh, Alex in the shoulder, and Kip square in the chest. Thankfully they'd all been wearing Kevlar, so Kip was battered and bruised, with two broken ribs, but blessedly alive.

But the plan had worked. They'd been able to spring Nikolai. *Thank God.* Because it had been Nikolai who'd gotten to the car and managed to scoop them up amid a hail of bullets just before the soldiers reached them. It had been a very close thing. They'd barely escaped with their lives.

Now they were holed up in a scuzzbag hotel somewhere near the harbor, in desperate need of real medical attention. Quinn had lost a lot of blood. Julie knew where they were, but she was being watched and didn't dare go to them.

Even so, it was only a matter of time before the PLA found them.

And that wasn't an option.

With her harness secured, DeAnne climbed up the barrel ladder to the sub's aft upper deck. Clint had gone up the rope to the helicopter first, so he could help her and Darcy. Darcy was just now climbing in through the open cargo hatch.

DeAnne looked up, her heart pounding out of control.

The wind whipped through her hair, the rope on its descent dancing and jumping in the gusts like a devil round a fire. The rotor blades above her whooshed, fighting the updraft.

Oh, lord, what was she doing?

This was *not* who she was! She wasn't some kind of kick-ass female commando! She was a *diplomat*, for heaven's sake. She used her words, not—

Oh, fuck it.

She grabbed the rope and hung on for dear life.

Stop whining, girl, and go get your man!

37

Leave it to Bobby Lee to get himself into a fix she needed to bail him out of.

Darcy kept telling herself that over and over. Keeping her façade of female chauvinism front and center. Just so she wouldn't go nuts with worry about the damn man.

Outwardly, she stayed calm and confident.

But inside . . .

Oh, sweet lord. He *couldn't* die. Couldn't be captured. *What would she do without him?*

Her heart trembled at the thought.

No, she told herself firmly. That was *not* going to happen.

He'd be fine.

All three of their men would be fine, she amended, spotting the borderline panic in the face of her traveling companion. DeAnne Lovejoy's hands were shaking so badly they put her own wobbly knees in the category of rock solid.

"So, what's the plan?" Clint Walker asked. He looked

marginally relaxed, if a little haggard after being up all night with the difficult programming, then focusing like a brain surgeon on the UUV switch earlier.

She regarded him through narrowed eyes. "If I recall correctly, aren't you pretty high on the PLA most-wanted list? As in, shoot-him-on-sight high?"

He gave a bored wave. "And your point is?"

"My *point* is," she said pointedly, "do not think for a single minute that *you'll* be setting foot on that island."

His brow hiked.

"What?" she said with a snort, "three guys shot up all to hell aren't enough for you? Gotta make it four?"

He didn't comment, but glanced from her to DeAnne and back again, looking vaguely amused. Which irritated her to no end.

This was good. *Feed the anger.*

Banish the despair.

She leaned over and got in his face. "Something you want to say, Lieutenant Commander?"

"I keep telling you people. I'm retired. Call me Clint. Or Walker. Or Wolf Walker, if you're going to go all *wendigo* on me."

She frowned, momentarily caught off guard. "What's that?" Then she whipped up her hand. "Never mind! I know what you're trying to do, Walker, and it won't work."

"And what would that be?"

She had to give it to him. He was probably an ace interrogator. Didn't his file say he used to be in naval intelligence?"

"Say," she said. "I don't suppose you'd be interested in a job?"

He looked at her blankly, then his face broke and he gave a bark of laughter. He poked his finger at her. "You, Ms. Zimmerman, are very good."

The corner of her lip curled. She could really get to like

this guy. They spoke the same language. "Yes. I know that. But don't think buttering me up will change my mind. You're *still* not setting foot on that island."

He exhaled through his nose. "Okay. I know when I'm beaten. I'll stay on the yacht with Jaeger and let the two little girls go rescue the big, bad spec operators."

Her lip-curl turned into a grin. "Who're you calling little?" She was five-seven if she was an inch.

"I swear," Walker said at the same time, "if you ask for red capes with hoods, I'm jumping overboard."

She winked. "Only if they've got a big *S* emblazoned on them."

DeAnne was staring at her and Walker as though they'd grown horns. "Our men are wounded and may be dying even as we speak," she managed, her voice fraught with pent-up emotion. "How can you two *joke* at a time like this?"

Darcy softened her gaze and let her smile slip away. And told her the damn truth. "Oh, sweetie, it's either laugh or cry. And there's no crying in special ops."

Naturally, that made DeAnne's eyes well up. But she battled the tears, and Darcy's admiration for her went way high when DeAnne actually succeeded in keeping them at bay. The woman was a fighter, that was for damn sure.

Forget Walker. She should offer *DeAnne* a job.

She reached down into her duffel bag of goodies, drew out a Mossberg 500 Persuader, and held it up. "Ever shoot one of these?"

DeAnne blanched. For a second, Darcy thought she might pass out. Then she took a deep breath, cleared her throat, and said, "No, I don't . . . um . . . No, I never have."

"Here."

Hesitantly, the other woman reached out and gingerly took it. "I thought . . . Shouldn't I be carrying a pistol?"

"Shotgun's better. You don't have to aim as accurately." Darcy gestured a cone shape. "Broader kill zone."

DeAnne winced at that last part. But to her credit, she didn't protest. "Whatever we have to do to get our men out," she said, her voice rough as gravel.

Yeah, thought Darcy, the chick definitely had guts. She was starting to feel a whole lot better about this little unplanned sortie.

Together, she and DeAnne were going to do just fine. They'd get the guys out, come hell or high water.

And she pitied the poor slob who tried to get in their way.

So much for using her words.

DeAnne regarded the big, black shotgun in her hands and knew without a doubt she'd use it on anyone who tried to hurt Kip.

It was kind of a shocking realization.

No, she didn't want to do this. Yes, she was scared to death. This was the furthest away from "comfort zone" she'd ever been in her life.

But she was not about to let down the man she loved.

He'd do it for her. Hell, he *had* done it for her—and also done it *her* way . . . and that had made her respect him even more than if he'd killed a dozen men for her. Because that's what she'd have expected from a Marine.

But Kip Llowell had surprised her at every turn.

The least she could do was return the favor. And show him that she respected his way, and could—and *would*—do whatever she had to, in order to keep him safe and with her.

Well. Safe, anyway.

She, Clint, and Darcy landed on an incredible private yacht where they found Rand Jaeger working furiously on his computers, talking on his satellite radio with STORM Command, trying to figure out some kind of angle or plan to get the operators out.

Jaeger wordlessly handed the sat phone to Darcy before she'd opened her mouth.

"Hey, baby," she said after a few seconds. Her voice was heartbreakingly tender. "How are you doing?"

DeAnne couldn't listen. It was like listening to someone making love.

She took the shotgun and walked over to the other side of the salon. The room was nearly as big as the entire submarine had been. Which was good, because if she had to listen to Darcy and Bobby Lee, she'd probably break down and cry and wouldn't be able to stop.

There's no crying in special ops.

Or in life. Not in DeAnne's experience, anyway. Crying about life's unfairness never did a bit of good. It just made you feel like shit and ruined your mascara.

It wasn't Kip's fault she'd fallen head over heels in love with him. Or couldn't imagine a life without him in it. She desperately wanted to try a relationship with him. A *real* relationship.

Too bad that's not what he wanted from her.

Whatever.

She'd get over it.

None of that self-pity stuff mattered now.

What mattered was getting him off that island in one piece, along with the others.

She lifted the shotgun and attempted to lay her cheek against it to sight down the barrel.

"Here. Let me show you," Clint said from behind her, grasping the shotgun and adjusting it in her hands. "Set it here against your shoulder. Your cheek here. Finger here, never on the trigger. Not until you pull it."

"Okay. That's much better." It felt almost natural in her grip.

How weird was that?

Her father would be so proud . . .

Clint showed her how to load it, and tucked a box of cartridges in her pocket. "Sure you want to do this?"

"Do I have a choice?"

"Sure, you do. You could let me go instead."

She smiled dryly. "And have your blood on my hands? No thanks."

He made a face. "Gee, thanks for the vote of confidence."

She shook her head, her smile wobbling. "No. This is something I have to do myself."

"Don't be ridiculous. No one is expecting you to—"

"*I* am. It's too easy to condemn a man's life without walking a mile in his shoes. I need to take that walk, so I can make my judgments from a place of knowledge. Not from fear or prejudice. I've been doing that for too long."

She wasn't sure if she was talking about her father or Kip. She supposed it didn't really matter. It was all about the same things.

Clint studied her for a long moment, then he slowly nodded. "Llowell's a lucky guy, DeAnne. And if he doesn't take care of you, I want to know about it. I'll give him a little reminder."

Okay, so maybe Kip.

Her smile dipped a little. "Thanks, Clint. But I doubt that's going to happen. However, the same goes for you. I hope Samantha knows what an amazing guy she's got in you."

He smiled back, his eyes filled with love for his new wife. "Oh, she knows. I remind her every day."

DeAnne managed a chuckle before she had to turn away or lose it, pretending to aim the shotgun at a porthole.

Why was everyone around her so darn much in love?

It made her feel as though there was something fundamentally wrong with her. Was she not worthy of a love like that?

Yes, she was.

And that's what she was going to tell Kip as soon as it was her turn to talk on the sat phone.

"Ready?" Darcy asked, striding over, all business. The phone was back on Jaeger's worktable.

Oh. Okay . . .

The minute Kip was off that damn island, then.

"Ready as I'll ever be," DeAnne said, determined not to be hurt that Kip hadn't asked to speak with her. My God. He was wounded and trapped behind enemy lines. Clearly, he had more important things on his mind.

"Oh," Darcy said as an afterthought. "Sorry. Kip wanted to talk with you, but the connection got cut off. I figured it was better to get going and see him in person."

Her heart swelled. That was all she needed to hear.

"Come on," said Darcy, heading up on deck to the small speedboat they were going to travel in to the island. "It'll take us a good hour to get to the harbor. We'll talk on the way."

She nodded, and exchanged a glance with Clint. He sent her an encouraging smile. "Good luck, ladies. I'll be here, just a call away if you need me."

"Thanks," Darcy said, threw him a mock salute, then slid down the ladder to the cigar boat.

"You'll do great," he told DeAnne when she hesitated at the rail. "Go bring them home safe."

Yeah.

"We'll do our best," she said, and took a cleansing breath. She tossed the Mossberg down to Darcy, and followed her into the speedboat.

Good lord. It was official.

She had completely lost her mind.

38

DeAnne could tell the cigar boat had been specially outfitted for smuggling. It was full of secret compartments and hollow spaces. Not that she was noticing . . .

She and Darcy hid in a shallow hold while the driver steered the small craft into the crowded Sanya harbor. Customs officials weren't looking for people being smuggled *in* to China, and because the small boat had a Hong Kong registry, it slid through with just a casual wave.

Even so, DeAnne was shaking in her sandals. How did these STORM operators do this dangerous stuff all the time? She'd be a nervous wreck. Heck, she *was* a nervous wreck.

And this was the easy part. The hard part would be getting the guys back to the boat. She didn't even want to think about what would happen if the customs agents wanted to inspect the speed boat on the outbound trip.

Approaching the forest of docks, she and Darcy crept from their hiding place and straightened their clothing—just plain jeans and T-shirts, along with black wigs. They didn't want to attract any kind of attention. Definitely saving the bikinis and light hair for the return trip.

The boat driver pulled into the marina where Julie had arranged for a car to be left for them in the parking lot.

"Wait for us here," Darcy told him. "Be ready to rock and roll when we get back."

They found the car, and Darcy got behind the wheel. "Now comes the fun part," she said with an irreverent grin.

"You are utterly insane," DeAnne muttered, but without a bit of heat. Truth be told, she was terrified and nervous as hell . . . but she was also excited. This was way better than composing dry, ineffective, diplomatic memos.

She was actually *rescuing* four people. Talk about an adrenaline rush.

As much as she hated to admit it, she was starting to understand the appeal, and how it could so easily become addictive to a man . . .

Although there was never a good reason for abandoning your wife and child. For that, she would never forgive her father.

Darcy stuck the GPS onto the windshield and took off, following a circuitous route to the back-alley hotel, just to be sure they weren't being followed. Along the way they spotted several PLA jeeps roaming the streets like sharks. They smiled pleasantly at every one of them.

"Jeez Louise," Darcy said. "They are really out in force."

DeAnne clung to the strap of the duffel bag in her lap holding the guns, making sure the zipper was down. "What do we do if they stop us?" she asked nervously.

Darcy cut her a look. "I'm relying on your diplomatic skills. But when in doubt, shoot first and ask questions later." DeAnne opened her mouth to protest, and Darcy added, "With the stun guns, of course."

DeAnne let out a breath. "Of course." Thank God for

those. The whole international-incident-leading-to-World-War-Three thing weighed heavily on her mind, to be honest. She did not want to go down in history as the new Archduke Ferdinand.

Especially since he'd died.

"Then why did we bring the shotguns?" she asked.

"It's always good to have options. If it comes down to us or them, we definitely want it to be us."

DeAnne still struggled with the idea of pulling an actual trigger on a fellow human being . . . but if they were shooting at her, she could probably get past her aversion.

Following the GPS arrow, Darcy crept the car past the rundown hotel, and DeAnne peered up through the window to the second floor where one of the guys was supposed to be watching for them.

She spotted a tall, dark man standing at a flyspecked window, mostly obscured by a dingy curtain. When he saw their car slowly passing by, he flicked the curtain back for a moment. She'd only seen Nikolai Romanov from a distance that one time just after she and Kip were "kidnapped," but the man looked like him. She lifted her hand in greeting . . .

Just as another large figure filled the window. He leaned his forearm on the glass pane, his other hand gripping a white band across his midsection.

Her heart stopped, then took off and soared like a dove in flight.

Kip!

Her hand reached for him, her fingers splayed against the car window.

His face was grim, but when he spotted her in the car he straightened and his expression went rigid, first with dismay, then with pain.

"You didn't tell him I was coming," she said.

"Not exactly," Darcy admitted. "No sense worrying him."

They drove past the hotel and were about to turn into the

alley behind it when they saw another PLA jeep coming in the opposite direction. Darcy kept driving.

"Crap," she muttered. "They are freaking everywhere."

This time, the soldiers in the jeep turned in their seats to watch their progress. *Uh-oh.* Despite the black wigs, she and Darcy were obviously Westerners. And this was not exactly a tourist district.

"We may have trouble," she said.

Darcy kept checking the rearview mirror. "Spread out the map over that duffel," she instructed as she whipped the GPS off the windshield and stuck it in the bag.

DeAnne snapped open the thin roadmap on her lap, as if she were studying it, sliding the duffel onto the floor, but still within reach.

To her horror, in the side mirror she saw the jeep do a tight U-turn and speed after them. DeAnne's pulse skyrocketed.

"God *damn* it," Darcy swore. "Okay, just be cool and follow my lead."

The jeep zoomed after them, catching up, and drawing even. Brandishing their weapons, the soldiers indicated they should stop the vehicle.

Darcy stopped.

None of the men spoke English, and DeAnne wasn't about to let them know she spoke Mandarin. They were speaking some kind of dialect she wasn't familiar with, but she caught enough of it to understand they were very suspicious of two Western women in this section of town.

Darcy was amazing. Using sign language and a lot of smiles and deprecating laughter, she pointed at the map and showed them where they wanted to go—an ethnic tourist zone somewhat nearby—and said they'd gotten hopelessly lost. She was so convincing even DeAnne believed her story. She just sat there and nodded and kept a big smile plastered on her face . . . and her trembling fingers gripped in her lap.

As the lead guy showed them the way to the tourist zone, the other soldiers looked into the backseat and asked Darcy to pop the trunk, which she did.

Apparently they passed muster, and the head guy finally indicated they could go. Which they quickly did, waving and calling their thank-yous. Darcy carefully followed their directions. At least for a few blocks.

DeAnne let out a shuddering sigh of relief. "Oh, my God. I thought I was going to have a heart attack."

Darcy laughed. "That was nothing. You need to toughen up if you're going to be in this business, girl."

DeAnne looked at her aghast. "If that's what you think, you're delusional."

The other woman shrugged. "Well, if you're going to be with Kip . . ."

DeAnne folded the map to give her hands something to do. "I could never do this for a living," she said. "And even if I wanted to, Kip isn't interested in a 'be with' kind of relationship. He's more of a no strings guy."

"So you say. But I've seen the way he looks at you. He wants to be with you. *Be with* be with. He may just not have admitted it to himself yet."

DeAnne refused to let Darcy's words give her hope. She had decided to tell him how she felt and accept whatever part of himself he would give her. She desperately longed for more than no strings. But she didn't dare hope.

"Anyway," she said, swallowing down the twisting knot of emotion stuck in her throat, "I'm not cut out for this kind of life."

"If you say so." Darcy took a quick right turn, and doubled back toward the hotel. "Keep your eyes peeled. We don't want to run into those soldiers again. I got the distinct feeling they didn't believe a word I said."

They made it back, and turned into the narrow, garbage-laden alley behind the hotel, driving slowly up it.

"Do you see them?" DeAnne asked, searching for any sign of the men. They were supposed to meet them back here. It would be too risky for a woman alone to enter the hotel. That would be an instant red flag to anyone manning the desk.

"There. Behind that Dumpster."

DeAnne spotted Nikolai Romanov hailing them. Wow. His face looked awful—full of cuts and bruises. One eye was nearly swollen shut. She tried not to think about what he'd gone through to get that way.

Darcy sped up and pulled in next to the overflowing garbage container they were hiding behind, then leapt from the car, rushing straight for Bobby Lee Quinn. She didn't quite throw herself into his arms, but almost—just mindful of his wounded thigh. She gave him a quick but passionate kiss. "Hey, baby. Ready to go home?"

He gave her a smile that DeAnne could feel the heat of all the way to where she was standing. She'd gotten out of the car, too.

"Hell, yeah, baby. Get us out of this dump, would you?"

Darcy kissed him again. "By the way. How about a May wedding?"

Bobby Lee looked momentarily nonplussed. "But it's May now."

Darcy beamed back at him. "Yeah. I know."

Alex cut into the happy scene with a groan. "Okay, you lovebirds. Enough of this shit. Can we get the fuck out of here, please?"

The pair broke apart and DeAnne came to with a start. She'd been watching them with such a powerful mixture of happiness for them and pure, unadulterated envy that she had to take a cleansing breath to shake it off.

That's when she realized Kip was watching her, not them, with an indecipherable look on his face—and it didn't look like happiness or envy.

Flustered, she opened her mouth to say something, but her mind went completely blank. Which was fine because everyone started to move at once.

"One of you, get in the trunk," ordered Darcy.

Alex headed for the back of the car, but Kip spun him around again by his good shoulder. "Not you." He grabbed DeAnne's arm and hauled her along. "You're coming with me."

"Hey!" she protested. She did not want to get in the trunk, with him or anyone else.

"What the *hell* are you doing here?" he growled, practically shoving her into the car boot.

"Rescuing you," she said testily, landing on her butt with an *oof* in the cramped space. "You could be a little grateful."

He snorted. "Scoot in more."

"Is this really necessary?" she demanded.

"Yes!" When she didn't move, he pushed her down and climbed in gingerly after. He lay down on his back, grunting in pain at his ribs as he squished in next to her.

She canted onto her side and pressed herself as far into the recess as she could get, to give his huge frame more room. Her arms ended up around him, her body half over his, and her face pressed against the crook of his neck.

Nikolai Romanov appeared and shut the trunk on them. It went pitch black inside, and the smell of gasoline and old tires almost made her gag.

"You really know how to show a girl a good time," she muttered.

"DeAnne," he said, his voice rife with warning. "You should not be here."

"That makes two of us," she returned heatedly.

The car started with a lurch.

He took a deep breath. "It's my job, DeAnne."

"No," she said. "It's not. Your job is being a U.S. Marine."

"Maybe not for much longer," he said darkly.

She stilled, her irritation temporarily on hold. "Why not?"

The car sped around a corner, throwing them closer together.

"Julie left us a cell phone, so I called my commanding officer to let him know where I was. He said he was quite aware of where I am. He said we needed to talk. And that I should start rethinking my career." He eased out a breath.

She tightened her arm around his shoulders. "I'm so sorry, Kip. I know your career is everything to you."

Boy, didn't she.

"I used to think so," he murmured.

The tires jolted over a series of bumps and potholes, jostling her into him again. He grunted in pain and she felt him press a hand to his ribs.

"Sorry!" She tried to ease away, but he held her fast.

"DeAnne, there's something I need to tell you."

A terrible sense of foreboding flooded through her. Her heart went cold with dread.

"Oh?"

"Yeah. I haven't been completely honest with you about . . . well, about myself."

The dread turned to a tight, hard lump in her stomach.

Oh, God. Here it comes.

"Oh?" she managed again.

Please, please, don't tell me you're married.

"No. I'm . . ." He hesitated. "I have a—"

Suddenly, the car accelerated fast, swerving hard to the left, then right. They were thrown together and it was all she could do to help keep him from smacking into the sides and cracking his ribs all over again.

"What's happening?" Panic swept through her as she felt him reach over and pull his pistol from its holster.

"They've spotted us," he gritted out, racking the gun. "And now they're hunting us down."

39

Darcy jammed her foot on the gas, pedal to the metal.

Of all the damn luck!

They *would* run into that same jeep full of soldiers, and naturally the bastards had recognized her. Except now, instead of two innocent women, her car was filled with brawny, broad-shouldered, bruised-and-bloodied men.

They were so screwed.

They'd never make it to the boat.

"Faster, baby," Bobby Lee calmly urged her. He was sitting in the front now, in DeAnne's place. He reached down for the weapons in the duffel and passed them around.

"You want to drive?" she asked, taking the turn to the marina at full tilt.

"Not really," he said, glancing down at the bloody wrapping around the gunshot wound on his thigh. "Working the clutch would be a bitch."

She careened into the marina lot and sped down the narrow aisle to the dock where they'd left the speedboat, scattering gulls and a half-dozen fishermen. Pulling up, she screeched to a halt, threw open the door, popping the trunk as she leapt out of the car, desperately scanning the water for the boat. There were a dozen or more crafts cruising the bay.

But theirs was gone.

"Crap!" she swore in desperation. "Where the hell is it?"

Kip and DeAnne had tumbled from the trunk, and DeAnne called out, "There!" pointing to the speedboat, tied up a couple of docks back the way they'd come.

Darcy hesitated. All of them piling back into the car would take just as long as covering the short distance on foot. "Run!" she told everyone, waving frantically to the boat driver. But he was turned the other way and didn't see her.

"Incoming," Romanov warned, jerking his chin at the marina entrance. The jeep was speeding around the corner toward it. Make that *two* jeeps.

Alex swore, and they all started running.

All except Bobby Lee, who couldn't run because of his wounded leg. Darcy slowed to help him, but he waved her off.

"Go! Get the damn boat and come back for me."

She hesitated, but saw he was right as usual. They had to come back this way anyway to get out to sea. "Be ready to jump in," she told him and started to turn. At the last second she turned back. "I love you, Bobby Lee Quinn."

He grinned, loping along in a lopsided gait. "I know, baby."

She grinned back. He was such a jerk, but she loved him so much it hurt. She turned and started sprinting.

And heard him call after her, "Love you, too, Zimmie."

By the time they reached the speedboat, the driver had realized what was happening, and had the lines off and the motor running. He threaded the boat through the other moving vessels, coming as close to the dock as he could, and they all leapt onboard, making it rock wildly.

"We need to pick up Quinn," she called to him over the

noise of the revving engine, pointing at Bobby Lee as he limped quickly toward them. He was about fifty feet away.

The jeeps were closing in fast.

Quinn saw them, too, and limped faster.

"Hurry!" she shouted. To both him and the driver.

This was going to be close. *Too damn close.*

A crowd had gathered along the pier, gaping at the chase. *Thank God.* The soldiers surely wouldn't shoot with so many innocent people in the line of fire.

She prayed like crazy. And her heart pounded like a fusillade.

Come on, baby, come on!

Alex and Romanov braced themselves to catch him when he jumped on board. She stretched out her arms, ready to pull him into them.

The jeeps were nearly on him, the soldiers shouting and waving their guns.

Bobby Lee reached the edge of the dock. The boat fishtailed in toward him, the back end nearly touching the cement.

He backed up a step to make a running leap.

Darcy held out her arms wider. "Hurry!"

The jeeps screeched to a halt yards away.

Bobby Lee bent to jump.

And caught his foot on a cleat.

He stumbled. And in slow motion, fell to the ground.

She screamed. *"Bobby Lee!"*

The other men swore.

She started to jump out of the boat to help him.

Romanov and Kip grabbed her arms. "Darcy, stop."

"Let me go!" She struggled vainly against their iron grip, desperate to get to the man she loved.

"Get her out of here!" Bobby Lee roared.

"No!" she screamed.

And then the soldiers were on him.

40

DeAnne watched the rapidly receding dock in horror as the PLA soldiers dragged Bobby Lee Quinn away. She couldn't believe this was happening. She felt literally sick to her stomach.

Darcy was stone-faced, her jaw clenched, her eyes following her lover. Kip and Romanov had made her sit, since the cigar boat was now speeding out toward open water.

DeAnne's gaze was reluctantly drawn to Nikolai Romanov, whose expression was grimly somber beneath his cuts, bruises, and swollen eye. She knew with a sinking heart that Quinn was in for the same treatment. If not worse.

She was already mentally composing her entreaty to Roger Achity to help get him out of prison as soon as possible. But she didn't have much hope. Bobby Lee would be accused of espionage, and found guilty. Of that there was little doubt. He would be lucky if he wasn't summarily executed.

DeAnne closed her eyes and pressed her face to Kip's chest. She wanted to cling to him and cry her eyes out.

Just minutes ago Darcy and Quinn had been so happy.

And now, total devastation.

She let Kip go and took a steadying breath, and slid over to Darcy. She put her arms gently around the other woman, tears filling her eyes. "Oh, Darce. I am so very sorry."

Darcy didn't return her hug, but she didn't push her away, either. "Thanks," she said, her voice thick. "I'll be okay."

"You know the State Department will do everything we can to get him out. STORM, too, I'm sure."

Darcy swallowed. "It's not the first time he's been locked up. He knows we'll come for him."

All at once, a chorus of sirens began to wail. DeAnne sat up with a start, along with the others. Even Darcy whipped her head around.

"Harbor police." Kip gestured to a small patrol boat scudding toward them, giving chase with loudspeakers blaring warnings in Chinese. "It'll never catch up," he said. But it was soon joined by a bigger gunboat. "Okay, that one might."

Alex let out a string of curses as he dove for the stash of weapons the driver revealed in one of the holds. Alex tossed them each a deadly-looking rifle, but DeAnne passed hers to Kip and went for the shotgun in the duffel, remembering what Darcy had told her about not having to aim it as accurately.

She checked the magazine and racked the gun one-handed as she stashed another magazine in her pocket.

Kip was watching her again. This time the look on his face was pure admiration. After a moment he shook his head and turned away to check his own weapon, an odd smile curving the very corners of his lips. Despite the dire situation and ridiculous odds, that little smile made her feel invincible.

And gave her the courage to believe that anything was possible.

Even a life with him.

As soon as they were clear of the crowded marina, the harbor police started shooting at them. Thankfully, they were still out of range.

Even so, the driver steered the speedboat into a series of high-speed zigzags. DeAnne swayed with the rhythm of the turns and the waves, getting her sea legs.

"Get down," Kip commanded, putting his hand on her shoulder to urge her into one of the smuggling holds.

She shrugged him off. "Not a chance." She took a knee on the deck with the others, one elbow propped on the bench, aiming her shotgun over the aft rail. "We need all the firepower we can get."

The gunboat was catching up fast. They started shooting at them, too. The bullets were hitting precariously close. Then she saw the police crew swing their big, deck-mounted machine gun so it pointed right at the speedboat.

She sucked in a breath.

The driver zigged, and everyone leaned.

"This could get ugly," Kip muttered.

"They wouldn't actually shoot that thing at us?" she asked, horrified.

"Depends on if we stop or not," Alex murmured, the boat zagging.

She was even more horrified. Was he *kidding*?

One look at his face told her he was deadly serious.

Stray bullets started to hit the aft hull.

"We're not stopping," said Darcy evenly.

Everyone looked at her, then back at the gunboat. Bullets whizzed past and they all ducked. A whole zigzag went by.

No one contradicted her.

DeAnne swallowed. *Okay, then.* Maybe not so invincible.

More like Butch and Sundance.

"Aim for the petrol tank," said Nikolai, lifting his rifle to his shoulder. In his melodic Russian accent, he described exactly where the tank was located.

"Will it explode?" she asked worriedly. They were back to the Archduke Ferdinand thing.

Was there no happy medium?

He shook his head. "That only happens in the cinema. But if we're lucky, it leaks and they run out of gas."

Better.

The speedboat completed another pattern. Kip was giving her that strange look again.

"What?" she asked, pressing herself close to the wall of the bench.

"Nothing. Later," he said.

Suddenly, she remembered when they were in the trunk he'd been about to confess some terrible thing about himself.

No doubt what he was referring to now.

Yeah. And she was really looking forward to *that* conversation.

Not.

Invincible, she reminded herself.

What was the worst that could happen?

Oh, God. She didn't even want to think about it.

Besides, right now there were more urgent things to think about. The shots plinking into the side of the boat were getting deadly.

"Ready?" Nikolai said.

They all raised their weapons.

"Aim," he said.

She did her best, positioning the shotgun as Clint had taught her.

"Fire!"

The roar of the guns made her ears ring.

They may have hit the target. She couldn't tell from this distance.

The big deck-mounted gun lowered its sight on them.

She ducked down. *Holy crap.*

Suddenly, an even larger boat, big, shiny, and white, swooped down on them. *Where had that come from?*

Two dozen men lined the rail, weapons aimed.

But not at them. They were pointing at the Chinese gunboat.

In English, a bullhorn roared out at their pursuers, "This is the U.S. Marine Corps. Lower your weapons and stand down!"

DeAnne's jaw dropped.

Saved by the Marines?

How the heck—

She darted a look at Kip. He appeared even more astonished than she was. His lips parted and a deep furrow sank between his brows.

The bullhorn swung toward the speedboat. "That goes for you, too, Marine."

Startled, Kip's arms jerked down, lowering his weapon abruptly. He peered up intently at the man holding the bullhorn.

She looked, too. Because there was something vaguely familiar about the man dressed in battle fatigues. It had been a long time, but—Oh, my God. Wasn't that—

"Colonel Jackson?" Kip called up in surprise.

At the exact same moment as she said, *"Dad?"*

41

“So, let me get this straight,” Colonel Jackson—*DeAnne’s father*—said with an ominous scowl. “You hijacked my daughter, got her hunted by every branch of military and police in China, faked her death, dragged her through a hundred miles of jungle on foot, had her kidnapped by some crazy private military outfit and taken out on a submarine, which was then chased by enemy vessels, only to involve her in a goddamn prison break in a foreign country, and then get shot at and practically blown to smithereens?”

Kip cringed inwardly. *Well, technically* . . . “Yes, sir. That about covers it. Though I didn’t know she was your daughter at the time. Sir.”

The colonel’s scowl deepened. “Would that have made a difference?”

“Probably not, sir.”

Next to him, DeAnne’s toe tapped slightly. “Don’t forget the part where he locked me in a woodshed and ravaged me all night.”

"What?"

Kip could actually feel his ears turn red. "She's kidding, sir." *Not really.*

The colonel was not amused. "Give me one good reason I shouldn't kick your worthless ass right out of the Corps and straight into the brig, Major!"

Kip's throat suddenly felt as though a steel band had tightened around it. He swallowed and cleared it. "Well. Because I plan to marry her, sir."

DeAnne gave a soft gasp.

The colonel was momentarily taken aback. "What was that?"

"I haven't exactly asked her yet," Kip admitted. "But I'm hopeful she'll say yes when I do."

He could feel DeAnne staring at him, eyes wide.

"I see." The colonel's voice became marginally less aggressive. "And what do you have to say to that, young lady?"

Kip didn't think she even heard the question. She was still staring at him all agog. "So you're *not* already married?" she blurted out.

"What?" the colonel roared.

Kip blanched. "No! What gave you— How— *No!*"

Her gaze lasered in on him. "Then what were you going to tell me in the trunk?"

"What trunk?" Colonel Jackson demanded.

DeAnne said impatiently, "We were locked in the trunk of a car for a while." She turned back to Kip. "Well?"

Would somebody please just shoot me now? Maybe he could get that Chinese gunboat to finish the job it started.

"DeAnne," he pleaded. "Can we please discuss this in *private*?"

"A private's just what you're going to be if you don't explain yourself pronto, Major!"

Kip drew in a breath. *Jesus.* Was he really going to say this? Yeah. He was.

"A court-martial won't be necessary, sir, because as soon as I'm back in the States I'll be resigning my commission."

Jackson seemed even more taken aback by that news, which was odd because he'd just threatened Kip with demotion. "Why the hell would you do that?"

"Well, sir. The woman I want to marry would prefer I'm not a Marine."

The colonel's back went even straighter than it had been. He cut DeAnne a look of scorn. "You get that bullshit from your mother?"

DeAnne returned his look in full measure. "No. I got that bullshit from you, Father."

"Father? What happened to Dad?"

"Yeah. What *did* happen to you, Dad? Like for the past, oh, twenty-five years?"

He huffed. "I had a job to do. I was busy keeping our country safe for you and your mother! And everyone else who takes their freedom for granted," he grumbled. It was a familiar tune for Kip.

But he had never seen DeAnne so quietly furious.

He took a step back. This was a private, family conversation, and although the complaints were totally different, the vibe was hitting just a little too close to home for comfort.

"You keep telling yourself that, *Dad*," she fumed, fists balled at her sides. Then she made an inarticulate noise in her throat, spun around, and stalked toward the door.

"Where do you think you're going, young lady?"

"Like you give a good goddamn," she muttered.

"I'll have you know I knew exactly where you've been every day of your life!" he called after her. Her steps faltered when he continued, "I knew where your Little League team played, and where your math competitions were held, and that year you were in band I even attended your concert. I stood in the back through the whole thing because I'd just gotten back from Afghanistan and couldn't get a ticket. But they let me in because of my uniform." He marched a few steps after her. "And I attended your graduation from Georgetown University, too. I've never been so proud in all my life as seeing my daughter walk across the stage with that summa cum laude diploma. I've watched your career at the State Department, and though that place is a hotbed of worthless geeks, I was proud of the way you outshined every one of them. Deputy director at your age? Unheard of."

Kip glanced over at DeAnne and saw tears glistening on her lashes. His heart swelled to bursting, knowing firsthand the kind of agony she must have gone through growing up, believing her father didn't love her, yet needing that love so desperately, wanting his support but never getting it for a single minute.

As he said, way too close to home.

She banded her arms across her abdomen. "For someone who disappeared off the face of the planet for twenty-five years, you know an awful lot about me. I'm guessing you had one of your information officers keep track of me for you."

Puzzlement flashed across the colonel's face, as though he couldn't figure out why that might not be a good thing. "You're my daughter. Of course I keep track of you."

Clearly, he missed her point.

"Too little, too late," she said, the tears cresting, and walked out.

Kip started to go after her, then stopped and turned to the colonel. "You are a real bastard, sir. *You're* the one who cheated on her mother and abandoned your daughter. The least you could have fucking done is say you're sorry."

With that, he hurried after the woman he loved.

Ah, well. So much for that honorable discharge.

They'd been talking in a conference room on *Impeccable*, the navy ship the STORM team had been briefed on before the operation, having been escorted out to it from Hainan by the Coast Guard cutter that had come to their rescue. Impeccable was a big ship, so Kip wasn't sure where DeAnne might have gone.

But she was really upset, so he guessed she'd be heading to her quarters to cry it out.

In the passageway leading to their staterooms, he ran into Clint, Darcy, Alex, and another man. They were carrying their duffel bags over their shoulders, each looking somber and downcast, like they'd lost their best friend. Especially Darcy. Every time he'd seen her before this, she'd walked tall and straight and confident. Now, she appeared . . . almost fragile. As though she'd break at any moment.

"Hey, Darce," he said softly, and gave her a quick hug. "Any word?" He skimmed his gaze to the others, who subtly shook their heads.

Her lips compressed as they trembled a little. "Nothing yet. But thank DeAnne for me again for making that phone call. Her boss has already started petitioning for Bobby Lee's release."

Kip nodded. "That's good. They'll get him out if anyone can."

She gave a little smile but there wasn't an ounce of humor in it. "Either that, or I will," she murmured.

Alex looked grim. "And I'll be right there with you, girl."

The other man at her side squeezed her shoulder. "There'll be no heroics by either of you. Leave this to the diplomats, and to me. You know I'll take care of Quinn." He looked at Kip and stuck out his hand. "I'm STORM Commander Kurt Bridger. I understand you've had quite a week, Major."

Kip shook it, introduced himself, and said, "You could say that, sir."

"We're about to head back to D.C. You and Miss Lovejoy are welcome to join us. Plenty of room on the jet."

He hesitated, then politely declined. "DeAnne and I both have a bit of unfinished business to clear up here before we can take off."

"Understood." Bridger handed him an embossed business card. "When you get back, give me a call. We'll talk."

Kip glanced at the card, and tucked it into his pocket. "All right."

Clint Walker stuck out his hand. "Good working with you, Major. You've got yourself a good woman. You take care of DeAnne, you hear?"

"Oh, yeah," Kip said, "I intend to," surprised when he didn't feel even a twinge of jealousy. He knew DeAnne loved him, not Walker, or anyone else on the planet. Just him.

It was a great feeling.

He exchanged a shoulder slap with Alex, and gave Darcy another hug. "Hang in there. Let me know if I can help."

"Thanks. I will." She nodded bravely, and then the STORM team was off, striding down the passageway shoulder to shoulder, the care and solidarity between them clear as day.

Kip's thoughts zoomed back to DeAnne, determined to show her just as much care. And show her that she could depend on him. That at least one person would always be on her side, come what may. Against her father. Against the whole world, if need be.

He prayed she felt the same about him.

He knocked on her stateroom door when he got there. "DeAnne? Sweetheart, it's me. Let me in, honey."

A moment later the door opened. She was standing there, her cheeks wet with tears, and his heart just broke. He wanted to flatten the colonel for doing this to her.

"Come here," he murmured, kicking the door closed and scooping her into his arms. "Forget the bastard. He doesn't deserve a daughter like you."

Her body heaved in a sob. "But he's my father. He should love me. That's his job."

He hugged her tight, ignoring the pain in his ribs. "Oh, honey. He does love you. That's so obvious to me. He just doesn't know how to show it like a normal human being." And who did *that* remind him of? God, was he talking to himself, or to her? "I guess I really get the Marine thing now," he admitted.

"Yeah." She shuddered out a breath. "Even so, I know I have to go back there and talk to him. In my head, I understand you're right and he's doing the best he knows how. I just need to accept what he can give me and realize in my heart that his issues are not my fault."

He didn't think he could admire this woman any more than he did already, but that pushed his respect up to a whole new level. "You're a pretty amazing woman, you know that?"

She sniffled, and gazed up at him with such love in her eyes he felt about ten feet tall. "You're pretty amazing yourself, Major." A shadow touched her expression. "Oh, Kip, I don't want you to quit the Corps. I know you love being a Marine, and honestly, I realize now that my father's choices had nothing to do with his career. It was all about him as a person. You are nothing like him. I know you'd never—" Suddenly, her eyes went wide. "Oh, my God. Did you really mean it? I mean about—"

He quickly put a hand over her mouth to keep her from completing the thought. "Wait. Don't say it. Let me do this properly, okay?"

Her eyes filled all over again. "Okay."

He let her go, running his hands down her arms and grasping her hands in his, lifting them to his lips. He kissed her fingers. "DeAnne, I know we only met a few days ago, but I feel like we've known each other all our lives. The thought of not having you right there, next to me, for the next seventy years makes me realize how empty my life was without you in it."

She let out a tiny sob, but this time he knew it was from joy. "Oh, Kip, I—"

"Wait. Not finished." He smiled down at her when she laughed out another sob. Then he got serious. "There are still a few things I need to tell you about myself before I do the official down-on-one-knee thing. Plus, there's the whole broken ribs situation . . ." He cleared his throat. "So I thought I'd wait until I could do it good and proper. You know, champagne, nice dinner, beautiful ring, the works."

She glowed through her shimmering tears. "Okay. I guess I can wait. But it won't make a difference. I'm still going to say yes."

He smiled at that, relief pouring through him. "I was hoping you'd feel that way." He kissed her fingers again. "But I still need to tell you."

She nodded, a ghost of worry flitting through her eyes. "Do I really want to know?"

"Yeah. You really do. It'll affect our lives in a big way."

Now she looked really nervous. So he took a deep breath and began. "I told you a little about my background. How I left home after a disagreement with my father over my choice of profession, and that I haven't spoken to my family since then . . ."

Although he knew that she, of all people, understood his choice, it still filled him with shame that he'd been so selfish for all these years. That he'd never even tried to reach out to them. To his mother, at least, even though he knew she'd never go against his father's edicts or stand up to him. Kip knew how much it must have cost DeAnne's mother to do exactly that, and admired her for it already.

"Anyway. You may have gathered from what I said that my family is somewhat wealthy and influential. That's true, and it's been that way for many generations. Which naturally comes with a lot of baggage for the heir. Which is me."

Shock made her jaw drop. "Really?" she managed.

"Yeah. And one of the biggest pieces of baggage comes in the form of a fairly large trust fund which entails upon my marriage." He blew out a breath. "It'll be my responsibility to choose something to do with that money, and to manage and increase it for the next generation. Because of the situation with my father, up until I met you I avoided even the idea of marriage, so I wouldn't have to deal with any of it."

A million emotions cascaded through her eyes, ending with uncertainty. "I, um . . . Wow."

"Yeah." He took a cleansing breath. "DeAnne, you have taught me so much about what courage really is, and about myself, and what I truly want out of life. And . . . well, about taking responsibility instead of avoiding it." He squeezed her hands. "I need to go back to my family and accept my rightful place with them. And there's nothing I want more than for you to come with me and share the burdens and the joys of that position with me, as my wife."

Her lips parted.

He winced. "Shit. I just blew it and proposed, didn't I?"

She pulled a hand from his and covered her mouth, both crying and laughing at the same time. "Yeah, I think you did. Want to take it back?"

"Hell, no. Not in a million years."

She slid into his arms and put hers around him, holding him in an embrace that he felt through his whole body, clear to his very soul.

"In that case, yes. I'll go with you and help you through it all, and be your emotional rock, the same way you've been mine since the moment I met you." She smiled up at him through her happy tears. "And when your ribs have healed and we're back home, remember you still owe me that date."

"Oh, I'll remember," he assured her, and leaned in to give her a long, tender kiss. A wonderful kiss to seal their love and their future together.

Then he brushed the tears from her cheeks with a thumb. "I love you, DeAnne. More than I ever thought was possible."

"I love you, too, Kiptyn Llowell. I trust you with my life and my heart, and I know you'll always be there for me. Believe me when I say I'll always be there for you, too. No matter what you decide to do with your life, and your family, and your career, I'll always be by your side, your biggest fan and supporter."

His prayers had been answered.

Kip felt the sting behind his eyes, and thought for a moment he'd lose it right there. The big, tough Marine was on the verge of tears because this incredible woman was willing to trust him with her heart and her hand. He felt humbled and blessed, and knew without a doubt, he was the luckiest man in the world.

"Love me like that forever," he whispered.

She reached up and kissed him. "Forever and always."

FROM

NINA BRUHNS

A KISS TO KILL

"Suspense just got a whole lot hotter!"

—Allison Brennan, *New York Times* bestselling author

Eight months ago, Dr. Gina Cappozi and CIA black-ops commando Captain Gregg van Halen were lovers . . . until he committed the ultimate betrayal. She knows that Gregg lives in a shadowy world of violence and darkness—and that he is watching her every move.

But Gregg is not the only one following her . . .

With the threat of enemies at every turn, the passionate pair will be forced to realize that the power of betrayal and revenge is nothing compared to the power of love.